MANIFESTING DESTINY

CHANGERS
BOOK ONE

AMANDA INNES

For my three little dragons

PROLOGUE

Upon first transformation, the Placement Officer will be immediately notified to contact the Clan of Origin and arrange for Relinquishing.

—Transformation Handbook

ONLY FAMILY COULD STAND in the circle during the Relinquishing. Old family on one side of the circle, new on the other. Witnesses at the fringe, which is where Cee and her family stood, along with the rest of Morrowville.

Cee stood as close behind Marcus as she dared and didn't realize she'd moved forward until her father grabbed her arm and pulled her back.

The Relinquishing Green on the west side of town sparked with dew as the sun ventured behind the distant hills and the ground gave up its heat. The day had been unseasonably warm for the last of March, and humidity

1

hung heavy in the air making the townspeople dewy as well.

In the center of the circle stood Marcus's older brother Arlon. He wore gray-blue robes and a white surplice that Mrs. Doyle had worked like mad to embroider in time for the ceremony. Three days was all one had from the time they first morphed to the time they were Relinquished to their Clan.

Across the circle, a silhouette against the bright sky, the Aerie leader began to speak in a language Cee did not and might never know. Arlon did not know it either, but he would.

The words, understood or not, held power. Arlon's long, straight nose grew a sharp curve; his dark hair drew up into a snowy white cap. The sleeves of Arlon's robe shrank as the cloth transmuted into feathers and Arlon, now an eagle, took flight.

Cee's breath stopped as she watched Arlon wheel above them. The Aerie leader extended a hand gloved in heavy leather, and Arlon swooped in to land on this living branch. The leader lowered Arlon gently to the ground and screeched a command. Around Arlon, the other Aerie transformed until a flock of eagles stood in their stead.

The largest eagle gave a piercing call, and the Aerie took to the sky, Arlon lost among them.

Wordlessly, the townspeople broke into clusters and drifted apart. Mr. and Mrs. Doyle turned to go, and Cee wondered if that meant she was free to speak to Marcus. But Marcus hadn't moved. He stood looking up and away toward the west, in the direction of the Aerie, one small tear glinting on his cheek like wayward glitter.

ONE

N o *Pre-Morph shall participate in any familiar physical contact with another Pre-Morph, nor with any Unaltered Permanent Resident of their Town of Placement.*

—Code of Conduct, XV.6a

"Vulpes." Marcus rested against the quilted pink headboard of Cee's narrow bed, his feet nearly touching the white iron vines at the end. "Cee, you're not listening. What are the defining characteristics of Clan Vulpes?"

There wasn't room for them both on the bed, so Cee sat on the moss green shag that covered her floor. "Can't be trusted," she sighed, leaning her head against the bed and looking up at Marcus.

"You'll never get a full essay out of that," Marcus told her. "And anyway, I hardly think it's fair to boil a whole Clan down to one generalization."

"Stereotypes exist for a reason," said Cee. "They're born from a kernel of truth."

"And then spread like... What's that plant?"

Cee cocked her head in her best don't-be-stupid look. "There are a lot of plants in the world, Marcus."

"The one that takes over everything. Like, a vine..." He had that cute little frown he always made when he wasn't sure about something, or was trying to remember; it made parentheses around his mouth. Just for a moment Cee could picture Marcus, much older, sitting behind a desk and frowning down at... Something. That little frown would never change. At least, she hoped it wouldn't.

"Ivy?" Cee suggested.

"No... I'll think of it later. What about Ophidan?"

"I'm thinking about changing my room," Cee told him.

Marcus's gaze darted right then left, taking in the white paneling and frilly pink accents. "I'm not sure what that has to do with Ophidans, but okay. Why?"

Cee jumped to her feet. "I'm sixteen. It's time for a change."

"You're not going to sing, are you?" Marcus asked.

"What?"

"I don't know. The way you jumped up had me worried you might burst into song."

Cee reached down for one of the pillows Marcus had tossed off the bed to make room for his lanky self and went in for a hit that he batted aside easily. "I suppose we're not going to get any more studying done then," Marcus said, swinging his legs off the bed.

"At the very least I need a bigger bed," said Cee.

Marcus barked a laugh. "Your dad would never."

"Why not?"

"Because so long as only one person fits in it..." He lifted his eyebrows.

Cee snatched up the pillow again, but Marcus bounded to the door, grabbing his backpack along the way. "Tomorrow," he said and was gone.

Collapsing onto her bed, Cee let out a long breath and stared up at the ceiling. It was a cozy room, and sweet, tucked under an eave like something from a fairy tale. Cee remembered her parents taking her to pick out the bed and other furniture, the pale pink paint, and the carpet. She had chosen the long, green shag because it had reminded her of grass and she'd liked the idea of having a meadow in her room.

But she had been five at the time. She had outgrown pink, felt ready for something deeper and darker. "I'll keep the green, though," she said to herself. "His eyes are green."

"Kudzu."

Cee gasped and bolted upright. Marcus was leaning around the doorjamb.

"What?" Cee demanded.

"The plant I was thinking of. Kudzu. Which is also green."

Marcus disappeared before the pillow Cee launched could find its target.

CEE FLOPPED BACK onto her bed and blindly pulled a frilly pink-and-white corner of her bedspread around her. The room felt colder without Marcus, and dimmer, as if he took light and heat with him when he left.

And soon he would go forever.

Cee hoped she morphed first. It was selfish, and she felt guilty about that, but she couldn't bear to watch Marcus fly away like Arlon had. Or walk or whatever he would end up doing when the time came. It would be bad enough to have to part at all, but Cee couldn't stand the thought of Marcus literally leaving her behind.

What if he, like Arlon, never looked back?

Cee's heart crumpled like a rejected essay assignment at the thought. She pulled more of the covers around her, cocooning. They had a little more time. She resolved to make the most of it. She was still trying to figure out exactly how to do that when the intercom beeped.

"Dinner's ready!" her mother said, though through the speaker it sounded like a screech.

Cee pressed the button and attempted to infuse her tone with matching enthusiasm. "Coming!"

Reluctantly, she threw off the warmth of her bedspread, the pink ruffles of childhood falling away with an almost inaudible rustle.

THE FIRST WORDS out of her mother's mouth as Cee entered the kitchen for dinner were, "How's Marcus?"

It was asked in the too-bright tone of a perpetual optimist, which Lynne Klinger definitely was. Her work as a Placement Counselor demanded a sunny disposition and an unflagging belief that everything worked out for the best.

Cee often wondered what prompted the Klingers to choose her as their first foster, but she'd never had the courage to ask, and as kind as her parents were, they had not volunteered any retrospection. Lynne's job was to place Clan children with foster parents until they morphed and were Relinquished, and many things could not be discussed.

For one thing, no child knew from which Clan he or she was taken. Cee wasn't even sure the Klingers knew. Based on the Doyles' reaction when Arlon had morphed—and the Doyles were, in Cee's opinion, somewhat jaded after having gone through many fosters—they had been just as surprised as Arlon himself when he turned into an eagle.

Still, someone had to know, didn't they? There had to be records somewhere, right?

Cee also wanted to know who'd named her and why, but she'd never found the courage to ask that either. None of her classmates knew whether they had come with their names or if their parents—they called them parents out of respect, and because the title accurately described their roles if not their biological connections—had named them.

"Cee?" The sound of her name just as she'd been thinking about its origin pulled Cee back to the immediate world, and she saw her mother's grey eyes clouded with concern.

"Sorry." Cee tried to smile, but it felt lopsided, like maybe part of it was broken. She went to the table and stood behind her seat. Erwin Klinger didn't sit at the head of the table, exactly; the table itself was square, so anyone might be the head. But he did sit ensconced between the two women in his life, and though fair, his rule was absolute. Cee and her mother waited behind their chairs for him to sit before taking their seats as well.

"Is everything okay?" Cee's mother pressed.

"Yeah, it's fine," said Cee. She waited for her father and mother to serve themselves, and finally her mother pushed the pork medallions in gravy across to her.

Cee did not miss the glance her mother threw her father, but if he saw it, he did not respond.

"How is Marcus doing now that his brother is gone?" her mother asked.

Cee shrugged. "Okay, I guess. We haven't really talked about it." A hunk of fresh-baked bread. Potatoes. More gravy. Her plate was turning into a puddle, islands of food floating around its edges.

"Cee..." her mother began.

"You know—" her father started.

"I know," said Cee, cutting them both off before the litany of warnings could begin. "But, like you always say, the alliances we form now may be important to the futures of the Clans."

"True," her father said. "It's unlikely you and Marcus will be part of the same Clan. Not impossible, but the odds aren't in your favor." Cee sighed; her father was an engineer and liked facts and numbers. "But your friendship may be key to any negotiations your Clans might enter into. In 2311, an entire war between the Ursans and Aerie was prevented because—"

Her father's hobby was history. Cee tuned him out, nodding periodically and shoveling dinner into her mouth. All the while she felt her mother's eyes on her, though Cee carefully avoided looking back, afraid of what her own eyes might give away.

CHAPTER

TWO

M embers of different Clans may not meet outside regulated assemblies such as the Convention of Clans. At such conclaves, no two members of differing Clans shall be alone together without a chaperone provided by a third Clan.

—Code of Clans

EVERY MORNING the students whiled the time before class guessing at Clans, so Cee mostly ignored the conversation floating around her as she entered homeroom as things like, "Kind of webbed, so maybe Anatidae?" and, "Too short to be Giraffa," flew through the air like spitballs. Until through the hubbub came the words, "Well, but Arlon Doyle ended up being Aerie anyway and—"

Cee's head swiveled in the direction of the conversation. In the corner Rand Corbin slouched lazily in his seat while Guin Dacre perched on his desktop. They were an odd juxtaposition, the muscular and dark Rand and the pale and slender Guin, yet they were seldom seen one without the other. Rand so serious, Guin so light-spirited. Cee wondered whether people thought the same thing when they saw her and Marcus together. But what would be the verdict? That they didn't belong together? Or that some-how, despite it all, they did?

Rand's bistre brown eyes flew up to meet Cee's when he realized she was staring at him. "What about Arlon Doyle?" Cee demanded so sharply the last two words came out squeaky, like sneakers on a gym floor.

Rand shrugged and shifted in his seat, the chair threat-ening to give way beneath his muscular mass. On the desk-top, Guin's thin body bounced visibly with his movement. "Nothing. We were just saying he ended up being Aerie."

"So?"

Another shrug, another shift, another creaking protest from the desk. Guin wrapped her fingers around the edges of the desktop as if holding on for a ride. Her big, brown eyes turned to Cee, but Rand was the one to answer. "Everyone thought for sure he'd be Vulpes is all."

"Who's everyone?" Cee asked, but then Mr. Jacobs entered and told the class to take their seats, and Cee spent homeroom urging the clock toward break. When the bell finally released them, she made a beeline for her locker, only two down from Marcus's. He was there, shoving in one textbook while simultaneously trying to pull another free. Cee paused to watch. Light and warmth emanated from him, though she appeared to be the only one able to see it.

Cee joined him at his locker and, unable to resist, touched his arm. He nearly dropped the books he was juggling.

"Did Arlon think he would be a Vulpes?" Cee asked.

Marcus took a tiny step away from her, forcing air between his arm and Cee's hand. "What?"

"It's just, I heard Rand saying everyone thought he'd, I mean Arlon, would turn out to be Vulpes." Cee caught her breath after the rush of words and took her time with the next bit. "And I just wondered whether you and he ever talked about it."

"Not particularly." Marcus examined the books he still held and returned one to his locker. "We'll be late for Al-Cal if you don't hurry."

Cee grimaced and opened her own locker to retrieve her book. In a world populated with uninteresting subjects, Alchemical Calculations was her least favorite. At least Marcus was in class with her and understood it all so he'd be able to walk her through the homework.

She spent the period sending sidelong glances in Marcus's direction, which wasn't unusual. Less typical was his lack of return glances or encouraging smiles. Never once did Marcus look her way; his attention volleyed between Ms. Boyd and his notebook. Cee tried to look studious, too, but ended up with a page filled with sketches of birds and foxes and lighting bolts setting fire to trees. When class was dismissed, Marcus's eyes fell to Cee's still-open notebook, and she would have sworn for a second his expression turned grim. But all he said was, "You'll never turn straw into gold that way." Then he swept up his things and was gone.

MARCUS WAS TWITCHY AT LUNCH, so Cee avoided asking any more questions about Arlon, and by the time school let out, Marcus seemed his usual self. "Trees?" he asked. "Or home?"

It was spring, not yet really warm, but sunny enough. "Trees," Cee decided, and they directed their steps toward one of the stands of trees that flanked the road to Morrowville Prep.

They were oaks, or so Marcus said, and given the carpet of acorns each fall, Cee was inclined to believe him. Though widely spaced near the road, the trees grew in denser clumps the farther back one traveled from the school. Cee and Marcus wended their way without thinking; habit made them sure, even when the road and school became lost to view.

Marcus stopped at the place where two oaks stretched strong, low branches toward one another as if they meant to clasp hands. The "friend oaks" Cee and Marcus had once called them, though the name seemed too childish to speak aloud now. But they continued to choose it when they opted to stay outside rather than going directly home.

It was shady, making it cooler, and Cee shivered as the upper branches nodded in a slight breeze. Marcus noticed and slipped off his teal Morrowville Prep blazer. "Here." He dropped the jacket over Cee's shoulders. "You should have worn yours. Or your sweater."

"Yes, Mother," said Cee, but she gratefully threaded her arms through the jacket sleeves and relished the warmth and lingering smell of whatever it was Marcus wore. Aftershave?

"Do you shave?" Cee asked.

Marcus looked briefly startled but answered with cheer. "I can't give away all my secrets, you know."

"I just wondered if it's aftershave," said Cee. She turned her head and gave her shoulder a sniff. "Or cologne?"

"You're full of questions today." Marcus folded his long limbs and settled under the tree; Cee thought he looked like a guru from an old painting. If she dared scoot closer, she could get warmer still, but she didn't want to risk making Marcus uncomfortable. Now that he was acting normal again, more or less, Cee wanted to keep it that way. "Maybe you should save your enthusiasm for Al-Cal," he went on.

Cee flopped down beside him and tilted her head back against the rough bark, looking up into the spots of blue amidst the green. "It won't be long now."

She felt Marcus move beside her but didn't bother to turn her head; all at once she felt tired, her body heavy, and it was too much effort to move. "Until what?"

"You know what," Cee said softly. They hadn't talked about it. Giving voice to it made it real and true. But her fears were too strong now to hold it in any longer.

"Not necessarily," Marcus said. He didn't mean he didn't know; he was saying time wasn't as short as Cee was suggesting. "The oldest known morph was twenty-three years and seven months old."

"But that's not normal," Cee countered. "Eighteen is the average."

"And three months. To be precise."

"Why do you even know these things?"

"I could ask why you *don't* know them."

Cee rolled the back of her head against the bark and felt it pull at her hair. She eyed Marcus's straight, sharp profile and wondered if he would end up an Aerie like Arlon. "What's the youngest then?"

"Fifteen years four months," Marcus answered promptly. "David James of Oronto."

"If you wonder why I ask you questions, it's because you always seem to have answers." Marcus had no answer for that, so Cee added, "But I guess that means we're in..." She tried to recall the term they'd learned for it.

13

"Within orb," Marcus supplied. "Yes, technically it could happen any time now, and is getting more likely every day the closer we get to eighteen. Assuming it happens at all."

Cee didn't need to ask what he meant; she'd thought about it often enough herself. Would it be worse never to morph? To be left in Morrowville while her classmates were Relinquished? She felt a strange tugging in her stomach whenever she imagined what it might be like to watch them leave, one at a time, her life slowly emptying of those she'd known since elementary school. But only one of them mattered.

"And what are the odds of that?" Cee asked.

"One in thirteen never morph," said Marcus. And as Cee screwed up her face in an attempt at math, "A little less than eight percent. Though," he added, "the number of Unaltereds has risen over the past three decades."

"Speaking of math," said Cee. She couldn't talk about it anymore; it was too much like probing an open wound. If Marcus had admitted he didn't want to leave her... But he was all facts and logic.

Cee reached into her backpack and extracted her Al-Cal text and notebook, and she suspected Marcus looked relieved, even eager, to retreat to the safety of schoolwork. They did homework until the spots of sky in the canopy of oaks began to turn dusty violet. Then, as they packed away their things, Cee made a final attempt. "I guess I wouldn't mind, so long as you stayed too."

Marcus's brow quirked.

"Not morphing, I mean. It can't be all that fun to be an animal anyway."

Marcus stood and offered Cee his hand to help her up. "Maybe you'll get lucky and turn out to be a Magus."

And that was that. No, "I'd rather stay with you, too," or even a simple, "I'll miss you." Cee swung her backpack over one shoulder. "Magi are rare, though, aren't they?"

"It's all relative. But on the whole, other Clans produce more offspring," said Marcus. "Just as some animals have litters of several young at a time versus humans not often having multiple births."

"Then how can the Magi keep running things if they're so outnumbered?" Cee followed Marcus's lead as he navigated them through the near dark of the trees.

"They hardly ever die, either."

"And they have all that magic," Cee pointed out. "That probably helps."

Marcus looked back and treated her to a genuine smile this time. "Yes, it probably does."

They reached the road, vacant now as the purple sky bent toward black and the first stars winked on. The smell of grass and earth became stronger as the ground yielded its heat and, in the quiet, even the hum of crickets was loud. A light fired briefly directly in front of Cee's face and she stopped walking with a gasp. "A firefly!"

Marcus stopped, too, and together they watched as first a few, then dozens, then seemingly hundreds of the incandescent bugs appeared in the night air around them. "It's early for them," Marcus said, his voice low, as if to avoid frightening the fireflies away. "Usually they don't come until late May."

"Don't tell them that," said Cee. She looked over at Marcus and yelped.

"What?" he asked.

Cee laughed and brought a fingertip to Marcus's cheek. "This one likes you." The wayward insect refused to move.

"Quit poking me." Marcus drew away and brought

15

tentative fingertips to the side of his face. This time the firefly climbed aboard his index finger. He brought it carefully around for a closer inspection.

"You look cross-eyed," said Cee as Marcus held the finger near the tip of his nose.

"It's getting too dark to see." Marcus waggled his finger. The firefly didn't budge.

"Someone you know?" Cee asked.

Marcus appeared momentarily disconcerted. "I don't think I know any Insecta." He frowned at the bug on his finger. "Do I?"

Suddenly, Cee found the fireflies a little less delightful. She scanned the illuminated air. "It's weird to think they could be here and we'd never know the difference."

The firefly abandoned Marcus's finger, and he and Cee set off for home, walking faster this time. In fact, they were in such a hurry that it wasn't until Cee was inside and Marcus had gone on that she realized she was still wearing his blazer.

And if she slept with it folded under her pillow that night, the smell of him infecting her dreams, who was to know?

CHAPTER
THREE

*S*undays are declared Days of Gathering for the strength
and unity of the Towns and Communities.

—Magistrates' Guidelines

"YOUR HAIR!"

It was Sunday, and the residents of Morrowville gathered at the Central Commons for the weekly picnic. Cee had brought Marcus's school jacket with the intent of returning it, but she almost hadn't recognized him.

"You cut it!" she went on stupidly.

Marcus shrugged and gently pulled his blazer from her clinched fingers. "What did you do, sleep on it?" he asked as he smoothed the wrinkles and plucked some of Cee's blonde hairs from the teal cotton.

"No!" Seeking to change the subject, Cee pressed, "Why did you cut your hair?"

"Because the school code requires it to be above my collar. Where are you sitting?"

Cee gestured in the general direction of the Klingers' picnic blanket. "Want to get in line?"

A dozen or more long tables crowded the park green, each filled with carefully organized food. Every family brought a dish to share, and the tables were arranged by meat, dairy, vegetables, and again by what might be an appetizer, a side, a main dish, a dessert. Cee and her mother always made a massive bowl of potato salad; their Saturdays—Family Days—ended in the kitchen, peeling potatoes and boiling them with eggs while her father ensconced himself at the table with the newspaper and occasionally volunteered a bit of recent news or an opinion on how much more mustard they needed.

Cee and Marcus joined the line for side dishes, and Marcus put some of the potato salad on his plate. Cee did, too, along with one of Mrs. Doyle's fresh-baked rolls. "Did you help your mother make these?" she asked Marcus as they moved on to fruit.

Marcus had picked up a wedge of watermelon and already taken a bite, so Cee was forced to wait for him to swallow. "You know how Mum is," he said.

"Then what did you do for Family Day?" They strolled toward the patchwork of picnic blankets that surrounded the bandstand. Cee didn't think it was quite fair that Marcus's natural grace allowed him to move between with hardly a thought while she ended up having to apologize to every other person they passed, nearly crushing food and fingers with each step.

"Got my hair cut," Marcus said, oblivious to Cee's personal minefield. "Then stayed in. Read. Hello, Mr. and Mrs. Klinger."

Cee's parents looked up and Lynne Klinger smiled. "Marcus! Join us."

"Thank you." As was his custom, Marcus made sure Cee was settled before seating himself.

"What's new this week?" Cee's father asked.

"Besides your hair," her mother added. "It looks very nice."

"Thank you, Mrs. Klinger. It was overdue."

"I liked it long," grumbled Cee.

"School going well?" her father went on. It was the same conversation they had every week. Not for the first time, Cee wondered whether the Doyles felt slighted because Marcus always picnicked with them. And now, with Arlon gone, the Doyles would be eating alone.

"Why don't we eat with your parents next week?" Cee suddenly asked, disrupting Marcus and her father's discussion of some alchemical principle as applied to the recent fire in the Far Eastern Wilderness.

"Cee, it's rude to interrupt," her mother said.

But Cee was watching Marcus. He turned to look at her, a small frown marring his features. "Why?"

"Arlon's gone, so..."

Marcus blinked, and Cee felt sure there was much he was not saying. But his only answer was, "But then your parents would be alone."

"We could take turns," suggested Cee. She was aware now of looks passing between her parents, but she did not take her eyes off Marcus, desperate to read any little line of his face. She almost never went to his house; he came to hers. He ate with them on Community Day. Cee had always assumed it was because Marcus needed a break from Arlon, but Arlon was gone now.

The sound of a microphone being tested at the bandstand drew the gathering's attention. All the noise and chatter of the crowd drained away as Commissioner Beaulieu cleared his throat and welcomed everyone. He read the names of new fosters (there were two), and deaths (old Mrs. Easton), and he read Arlon's name as having been Relinquished to the Aerie. *As if no one knew*, Cee thought, but she supposed it was meant as an honor.

The Commissioner went on to announce Morrowville's Volunteer Corp would be leaving Tuesday morning to aid the Clans displaced by the wildfire. "The Corp hasn't been activated in more than forty years," Beaulieu declared. Then he grinned, though it was oddly lopsided. "But I trust all our training will hold up against whatever we may confront." Cee glanced reflexively at her father, but his face was impassive. She breathed a tiny sigh of relief that Marcus was not yet eighteen and wouldn't be going.

The Commissioner finished and around them talk began to bubble up like small founts once more, but their little island remained dry and silent. Finally, Cee's mother said, "Well! We'll have some girl time then, won't we, Cee?" She turned to Marcus. "And you're welcome any time, Marcus."

"I'm sure my Mum will..." Marcus's voice trailed. Cee was sure he'd been about to say his mother would need him, or want him home, but the grimace that passed over his face suggested it might not be true. And Cee knew Marcus couldn't bear to lie. He was terrible at it.

"Of course she will," Cee's father said, and Cee blinked at him in surprise; it wasn't like Erwin Klinger to go out of his way to make anyone feel better. "But I would feel more assured if I knew you were checking up on Lynne and Cee now and then. If you think you'll have the time."

Marcus swallowed hard, and his next words came out somewhat choked. "Yes, sir. I'd be happy to."

"We shouldn't be gone long," Cee's father went on. "Every town will be sending its Corps. Many hands make little work."

Cee's shoulders relaxed. Adages. That was more like her father's usual self.

Marcus gathered his empty plate, plastic utensils, and barely touched napkin—how he ate so neatly was an ongoing mystery to Cee—and said, "I should probably find my parents."

Marcus stood and Cee handed up the school jacket, which he draped over his arm. There were murmurings of goodbyes as he departed. Cee watched Marcus wade his way through the sea of blankets, stop at the recycling and compost bins, until he rounded the bandstand and disappeared from sight.

So much of her life lately seemed to consist of Marcus walking away.

ON TUESDAY MORNING, every man in Morrowville between the ages of eighteen and fifty except the Administrators and Safety Brigade gathered at the park, and the rest of the town came to see them off. It was early, the sky a flat gray and overcast so that the gathering appeared washed out and monochromatic, like the black-and-white photographs Cee had seen in the Morrowville History Museum.

The Morrowville Caravan was parked along Main Street, and Cee couldn't help but ogle. Cars were only for emergencies, and Cee had seen the occasional ambulance, but never so many large vans at once. "Do you know how to drive one?" she asked her father.

"Yes," he said absently.

"How did you learn?" Cee asked.

"What?" Her father was distracted as he checked his duffel bag against the official checklist for the third time. Once satisfied, Cee's question sunk in. "We learn as part of the Corps training." He gave her blonde bob an affectionate ruffle. "Be good. Hopefully we'll be back in a week, two at the outside."

Cee thought she'd be lucky to learn to ride a bicycle and get her license, never mind ever riding in—or driving—a car. She half-mindedly scanned the crowd, ignoring the way her parents were squeezing each other's hands, and caught Marcus's eye. He and his parents clustered together three yards away. Cee started to smile and wave, but Marcus grimaced as his mother said something and turned his attention back to his family. Cee watched him punctuate his parents' serious expressions with occasional nods of his own to show he understood, and would comply with, whatever they were saying.

"Be good now, Cee." The sound of her name drew her back to her own family; her father put an arm around her shoulders and she allowed him to pull her into a sideways squeeze, her shoulder bumping his ribcage. His lips grazed her hair and then, as the Corps leaders shouted names from their rosters, he disappeared into one of the vans.

Cee looked to her mother. "Will you miss him?"

Her mother's eyes went wide for a fraction of a second as if the question scared her. But then the bright smile was back. "Of course! And you will, too."

The cars' engines roared to life, and those left standing along Main Street cheered and waved as the Caravan rolled out. But Cee had turned away long before the vehicles were lost to sight. And when she looked to where Marcus had been, he and his mother were already gone.

FOUR

N o one shall receive monetary gain for games of chance, nor shall such games be played for anything more than entertainment. Gambling, betting, and wagering is strictly prohibited.

—Code of Conduct, X.5b

THE SCHOOL FELT WEIRDLY EMPTY. Many of the young men were gone, and the majority of the ones who remained were visibly restless. A number of them had wanted to go with the Volunteer Corps and resented being left behind. Others took it as their duty to shoulder the load while the men of Morrowville were away. Either way, it meant the teachers struggled to get anyone to focus on schoolwork.

News drifted in from the Far Eastern Wilderness. The fire was out. Volunteers were salvaging as much as they could and distributing aid to impacted Clans.

"Why don't the Magi do it?" Cee overheard Annice Bradshaw grumble one afternoon during History. "They could just..." She waved a hand.

Cee turned to where Marcus sat on her right. "Could they?" she whispered.

But Marcus didn't hear.

It wasn't until lunchtime that she got the chance to ask him. "Could the Magi fix the Wilderness without help from the Volunteers?"

Marcus dragged his brilliant eyes up from contemplation of his carefully stacked mound of carrot sticks. "How should I know?"

Cee felt the words as if he'd struck her across the cheek with them. "You always know."

Marcus sighed. "You'd know just as much if you paid attention in class. Anyway, no one knows much about the Magi."

"They have magic," said Cee.

"Yes."

"They're in charge."

"Yes."

"They live a really long time."

"Even Unaltereds can live to be two hundred if they follow the exercise and nutrition guidelines."

"Why are you behaving this way?" Cee slapped the table with her palms, and Marcus started in his seat. "You're supposed to find this interesting! You're supposed to help me figure things out! *You're supposed to care that these might be the last days we have together!* But she couldn't very well shout that at him. He would probably never speak to her again if she did.

Marcus's shoulders fell a couple inches in surrender. "I

don't know, Cee," he said, his voice flat and toneless. "Could they fix the Wilderness? Maybe. But that's not the point."

"What do you mean?"

"Do your parents fix everything for you?" Marcus asked.

"No." When things went wrong, she always went to Marcus first. Surely he knew that.

"The Magi are like parents," said Marcus. "They want us to work together as a society rather than just depend on them to make everything better."

"That's stupid," Cee said through mouthful of turkey sandwich. "If they have the power to do it, they should just... *do* it!"

Marcus didn't answer, merely went back to stacking his carrots, only to have them collapse when Rand walked by and slapped him on the back. Cee narrowed her eyes, expecting Rand to move on, then opened them wide when Rand took a seat next to Marcus. The table rocked under his heft.

"Hey."

Marcus only blinked, so Cee asked, "What do you want, Rand?"

"No need to get snippy," said Rand. He turned back to Marcus. "We're meeting this afternoon, right? For the Lit project?"

"What Lit project?" Cee asked, but this time Rand completely ignored her. Marcus nodded, and Rand snatched one of the carrot sticks from his tray. "Cool."

Cee stared at Rand, waiting for him to leave, but he didn't move. So she asked, "Why did you think Arlon would be a Vulpes?"

Rand's skin was too dark for Cee to tell if he blushed, or blanched, or had any other reaction to the question. He munched the carrot a minute longer and didn't look at Marcus, nor did Marcus look at him. For a second Cee wondered if she'd become miraculously invisible and impossible to hear, but then Rand swallowed and said, "You know how it is. We're always trying to guess." Then, with a look at Marcus, "No hard feelings, though, right?"

"Did you lose any money on it?" Marcus asked, and Rand laughed.

"You know that's not allowed! But... yeah. A little."

"So long as *you* have no hard feelings, then," said Marcus.

Cee felt like there was a volcanic eruption building inside her. How could Marcus take it so easily? They'd been betting on his brother to be a sneaky, untrustworthy Vulpes of all things!

"He did have a fox-shaped face," said Rand.

"Yes, but his nose was too beaky," Marcus pointed out.

Rand cocked an eye at Marcus. "You knew?"

"No one knows," said Marcus. "Not until it happens."

Rand set his elbows on the table, and Marcus winced at the breach of etiquette. Rand leaned in. "How *did* it happen?"

Cee's eyes darted between the two young men seated across from her. Though she suspected Marcus wanted to move away from Rand, maybe even leave, she noticed with a smidgen of pride that he stayed put. In fact, Marcus had grown almost unnaturally still.

"How did what happen?" Marcus formed the words slowly, carefully, as if having to shape them the way they did in Incantations class.

"The morphing," said Rand. "Did you see it when it first happened? Was it weird?"

Cee held her breath and silently urged Marcus to get angry, to say something that would drive Rand away.

Marcus turned his head just slightly as if to get a better look at Rand. His green eyes met Rand's almost-black ones. Cee found herself leaning forward as if to read what was passing between them, but suddenly Rand mewled—a ridiculous sound in such a big guy—and sat back as if physically repelled, like invisible hands were pushing him back. He exhaled through his nose the way a horse would after a hard ride, and Cee saw spots of sweat breaking out along Rand's brow, noticed the way his massive hand shook before he set it flat on the table to steady himself.

"Right," Rand said. "I should... I have..." He started to stand but his legs failed to support him the first time; it took two tries before he was able to get up and walk away.

"What just happened?" Cee asked.

But Marcus was busy fixing his carrots.

"HE'S NOT the person you want him to be, you know."

Guin folded her legs under her, faun-like, and settled onto the grass beside Cee. Her long, blonde hair nearly touched the ground, and Cee wondered if Guin purposefully kept it cut just short enough to keep it from getting dirty.

"They'll never be the people we want them to be," Guin went on. "You need to eliminate the extra argentum, by the way, else the whole compound will oxidize."

Cee pulled her Al-Cal notebook closer to her chest.

"I can help you with it, if you want," Guin offered.

"Thanks, but..." Cee shook her head.

"They're going to be working on the Lit project all week," said Guin.

Cee frowned. She'd known Guin since grade school, but they weren't particular friends. Marcus was Cee's only true friend, and Cee supposed Rand was Guin's. Now they were each without their other half, and though she understood why Guin would devolve to her, Cee wasn't sure she wanted the company.

"It's painful, isn't it?" Guin asked, and Cee stole a quick glance at her. The question felt like a trick.

"Being with them hurts because we know the more we come to love them the harder it will be to part," Guin went on. "But being without them hurts more."

Cee's gaze traveled down the hill to the school where somewhere inside Rand and Marcus were working. She wondered if Guin saw in Rand what she saw in Marcus— that aura. Did Rand feel warm to Guin like Marcus did to her? But she didn't know Guin well enough to ask.

"What will you regret?" Guin asked, "When it's over? Not the time you spent with him. Only the time you didn't."

Cee felt as if something had broken just over her head; a numbness was drizzling from her crown down her back. She eyed Guin speculatively, but Guin only smiled in a half-sad way and dug out her own books and notebooks. They sat silently engrossed in homework until Rand and Marcus came trudging up the hill.

"What are you two doing?" Rand asked.

"Homework," Guin said, a bright smile lighting her features. She slapped her notebook shut.

Cee looked up at Marcus, who wordlessly offered his hand to help her up. "How's the project?" she asked.

But Rand answered. "Fine," he said tersely, making the project sound anything but fine.

Cee turned to Marcus thinking she would have better luck reading him, but his expression gave nothing away.

29

Then Guin reached over and tapped Cee on the arm. "Tomorrow?"

"Uh…" Again she looked to Marcus and received a sudden, vivid image of a black box slamming shut, a brass lock clicking into place.

Swaying slightly, Cee stepped away from Marcus, and he in turn moved away from her. She realized she hadn't so much moved of her own will as been repelled, as if by the adverse end of a magnet. *Just like Rand at lunch.*

Fear struck through Cee like a bolt. Was Marcus pushing her away? If so, how? Why? What had happened during his meeting with Rand? She resisted the urge to reach over and grab Marcus's hand, hold on for dear life.

"Cee?" Guin asked.

Cee looked at her arm and saw Guin's hand was still there.

Marcus busied himself by gathering Cee's things from where they lay scattered on the grass.

"Yeah," Cee answered faintly. "Tomorrow."

Guin flashed that brilliant smile, then, tucking her pale hand into Rand's dark one, they walked off down the slope, the murmur of their conversation punctuated by occasional bursts of laughter. Cee watched them go, wondering that they didn't get in trouble for being so "physically familiar." And wishing she and Marcus could do the same.

Something bumped Cee's right arm, and she found Marcus holding her backpack out to her. She reached for it slowly, trying to sense any resistance between her and Marcus, but whatever barrier had been there was now gone. "But you felt it, didn't you?" she asked.

"Felt what?" Marcus asked, then, "Are you afraid it's going to bite you?" He shook her bag impatiently, and Cee snatched it out of his hand.

As they started home, Cee asked, "What will you regret?"

Marcus was silent for so long Cee wondered whether he'd heard her. Then he said, "I don't know, Cee. I don't think anyone can know what they regret until it's too late to do anything about it."

CHAPTER
FIVE

Any Pre-Morph showing signs of Telepathy will be removed for immediate training by the Brigade until the Brigade is reasonably assured of the safety of the population at large.

—Transformation Handbook

"CAN I ASK YOU SOMETHING?"

Cee's mother looked over from the pancake batter she was neatly dolloping onto the griddle, and in the second before the familiar smile, Cee thought she'd seen apprehension on her mother's face. But her mother said, "Of course!"

"Can you still do... the stuff you learned in school? Even though you never morphed?"

The smile stayed firmly fixed, but Cee saw little lines appear around her mother's eyes as if her face were being held up by taut wires. "Which stuff do you mean?"

"Like... Telepathy?"

Her mother turned her attention back to the stove. "Telepathy is strictly regulated, you must know that." She turned back around, this time with a plate stacked with fluffy pancakes. She brought it to the table, and she and Cee sat. Cee let a few bites go by before pressing on.

"Well, but any of the magic you learned?"

"My job doesn't really call for it. Few of ours do."

"But *can* you? You learned it, right? They can't take that away."

"I never really liked school," Cee's mother said. "Eat up or you'll be late."

CEE STARED at the back of Marcus's head throughout Al-Cal and gave herself a headache trying to read his thoughts. But there was nothing.

So she made it a point to accidentally brush his arm when they were at their lockers. Though Marcus shied like a startled colt, Cee felt nothing. Nor did she receive any mental images.

After school, she trailed Marcus to the library, where he planned to meet Rand. "What are you doing?" Marcus asked when Cee caught the door behind him.

"The library is for everyone, isn't it?"

He frowned and stopped walking, so they stood in the empty space beside the circulation counter. "Why are you staring at me like that?"

"Like what?"

"Like you're attempting to bore through my skull with your eyes."

"I'm practicing telepathy," Cee said. She tried to make her voice light, as if she were joking. "Trying to read your thoughts."

"That's illegal," said Marcus, "should its being immoral not be enough for you." The corners of his lips twitched. "And have you managed to... read anything?"

Cee drew a deep breath. "Yesterday, I—"

The library door opened again and Rand swooped in like a large, dark bird. "Have you heard?"

"I've heard a lot of things," Marcus said, his voice bland, and Cee wondered whether Marcus didn't especially like his Lit partner. Had what she'd felt yesterday been more about that than about her? "But if there's one thing in particular—"

"You'd know what I meant if you'd heard," said Rand. "They're not making it public because they don't want to start a panic, but there's something really wrong in the Far Eastern Wilderness."

"They who?" Marcus asked, just as Cee said, "Of course there's something wrong. Like, a quarter of it burned down."

"The Magi," Rand said, answering Marcus.

"Then where did you hear it?" Cee asked.

Mrs. Drury emerged from the frosted glass cave that was her office and came to stand behind the counter. She peered at them over her glasses. "This isn't a place to chat." She made the last word sound like a profanity. "Take your discussion into one of the study rooms."

Rand turned and led the way. Cee earned another frown from Marcus as she followed them inside. "What?" she asked. "I don't get to hear the news?"

"Close the door," Rand told her. "Edmund Dougherty came back this morning."

Cee and Marcus only stared at Rand, dumbfounded. Mr. Dougherty was the owner of a local café. His wife was running the place while he was with the Volunteer Corps.

"They're due to get a new foster soon," Cee recalled. "My mother mentioned it."

Rand shook his head and waved aside Cee's words. "Don't you see? He came back. Alone. On foot."

"How do you know this?" Marcus asked.

"Annice Bradshaw saw him."

"You're taking Annice's word for it?" Cee asked. Annice Bradshaw was a frizzy-headed loudmouth. "She was probably just making it up for attention."

"She said he was half dragging himself up the East-bound Road."

"They do live on that end of town," reasoned Marcus.

"Theirs is the last house," Rand said. "Or, from Mr. Dougherty's perspective—"

"The first." Marcus looked over at Cee. "Shouldn't you go? Guin will be waiting."

Cee wanted to ask since when did she care about Guin Dacre, but she couldn't very well say such a thing in front of Rand. So she responded by sitting down at the study room table, leaving the boys standing. She kept her eyes on Rand. "So then what happened?"

Rand took the seat across from her, clearly eager to continue sharing what he knew. "Annice saw Mr. Dougherty as she was leaving for school. She said he looked like he'd been chased through the woods by wild animals."

Cee glanced up at Marcus, but his expression remained impassive. "On foot, the Far Eastern Wilderness would be at least two days' walk," was all he said. "And that's the nearest border. From farther in—"

"Anyway," Rand went on, overriding Marcus's pending geography lesson, "Mr. Dougherty came to the house. Annice's parents let him in. Annice tried to hang around, but her parents sent her off to school."

"That doesn't prove there's anything wrong," reasoned Marcus. "Mr. Dougherty coming back like that is strange, perhaps, but—"

"But as Annice was walking up the Eastbound Road, two Administrative vehicles drove by, headed for her house."

"They sent cars?" Cee breathed.

"More than one," Rand emphasized. "Annice says she almost turned around and went home, never mind what her parents said."

"Why didn't she?" Marcus asked, sounding angry now, and Cee looked at him again. Marcus's mouth was set in a thin line, and his fists were clinched at his side.

Rand shook his head. "I don't know. She thought better of it, I guess."

"We should go." Cee stood up. "To the café, I mean. You could work on your project there, couldn't you?"

"Not really," said Marcus.

"Let's go get Guin first," said Rand. He stood, too, and led the way back through the library and out the back doors of the school. On the hillside behind the building, a lone blonde spot jumped to its feet and came half skidding down the grass to meet them. Guin launched herself at Rand, and he caught her effortlessly, laughing.

Beside her, Cee felt Marcus stiffen at such blatant flouting of the Code of Conduct. As Rand told Guin their plan, Cee reached out again with her mind and tried to feel Marcus while simultaneously kicking herself for being so ridiculous. But then something sharp and cold and blue-silver flashed behind her eyes, something like the edge of a knife, and Cee let out a yelp.

"Cee?" Guin asked.

Cee looked down. Guin's hand clutched her sleeve, just like the day before. "It's you," Cee realized.

"It's her what?" asked Rand.

"You can read minds," Cee said to Guin.

Guin's smile froze on her lips. "Telepathy is—"

"Carefully regulated," Cee finished. "But not uncommon."

Rand placed a hand on Guin's shoulder and gently steered her to face him. "Guin? Is this true?"

Guin's head dropped so that her hair curtained her face.

"Have you told anyone?" Marcus asked.

Guin gave her head a tiny shake, and her long locks rippled. Then they parted as she tilted her head and looked at Cee. "But how did you know?"

Cee glanced at Marcus; his expression was stern, and fear tightened her stomach. She and Marcus had always liked each other, even on the relatively rare occasions they didn't get along. But now Cee wondered whether Marcus would—could—come to dislike her. The idea inserted itself behind her breastbone, like an acute and invisible blade.

"When you..." Cee faltered. Swallowed. Tried again to make her voice work. "When you put your hand on my arm, I..." She glanced again at Marcus. "It happened yesterday, too."

Guin and Marcus appeared to understand, but Rand did not. "What happened yesterday?" he asked. "What's going on?"

"I only caught flashes!" Cee said, forcing herself to meet Marcus's gaze. "Nothing that made any sense. Nothing..." Nothing what? "Personal," she finished.

"It's all I ever get either," said Guin. "I'm not even trying, it's just every now and then I catch something, like I've cast a net I don't even know about." She noticed

37

Marcus's stony countenance, and hastily added, "But I've never gotten anything from you."

"What about me?" Rand demanded.

Guin pressed her lips together as if trying not to smile.

"Oh, come on!" said Rand. "That's not fair!"

"I'm sorry," Guin said, but she was giggling. "I guess we're just more in tune."

Cee watched Marcus closely for any sign that he was furious, disgusted with her, that they were broken beyond repair. But his frown seemed more thoughtful than angry, and his eyes were on his shoes.

"When they find out," Rand said. He didn't finish the thought. He didn't have to.

"Why do you think I haven't said anything?" Guin asked. "I didn't ask for it. It just happened."

"*Is* happening," Marcus murmured. He lifted his gaze, his green eyes stabbing into Cee. "And though telepathy is common enough, absorbing others' abilities is not common at all. And to be unusual... It will draw attention. Not necessarily of the good sort."

Cee let her breath out slowly. He wasn't angry; he was *worried* for her!

"But it's happened before," said Rand. "Right?"

They all looked at Marcus. If anyone knew, he did.

He didn't disappoint, only nodded slowly. "To my knowledge, there is only one creature with that ability, and..."

They waited. Marcus's features twitched, reminding Cee of how he looked when doing Logistics homework. It was the face Marcus made when he was sure an answer couldn't be right yet was just as sure he'd worked the problem correctly.

"And?" Rand prompted.

"And," said Marcus, "it's extinct."

T he Brigade will be extended the authority to hold and/or incarcerate any person or persons deemed a threat to the public until a Magistrate can be sent to conduct an Inquiry.

—Safety Brigade Charter

"Dracona." Cee stared into her untouched tea. The café was incredibly busy yet eerily quiet. The news was out, somehow, without anyone saying a word. Mrs. Dougherty stood rigid behind the counter while Magdalene Rodgers did most of the work. Every now and then, Mrs. Dougherty would blink and move a hand toward the stack of cups as if to brew something, but Magda was faster. She zipped between the register and the carafes and back again, almost literally running circles around her boss.

"You keep saying that," said Rand, bringing Cee's attention back to their table. They sat knee-to-knee at a tiny round, each of them hunched the way people did when they were cold, though the café was, in fact, stiflingly warm.

"It's not likely... Is it?" Cee asked.

"You keep saying that, too," Rand said.

"Poor Mrs. Dougherty," said Guin. "Where do you suppose Mr. Dougherty is now?"

Cee turned to look over her shoulder, but Marcus said, "Don't stare." So Cee went back to looking at her teacup.

"Even if Dracona still existed, which they don't," Rand added, shooting Marcus a look that dared him to disagree, "there would be no way to be sure Cee is one. Not before she morphs."

"You think they took him to the hospital?" Guin asked.

"Annice said cars, not an ambulance," said Marcus.

"Has anyone seen Annice?" Cee wondered aloud. She pulled her gaze from her drink, and the four of them exchanged a flurry of glances.

"Not since before lunch," said Rand.

Something cold settled in the bottom of Cee's stomach; it took her a minute to comprehend it was dread. "She was in Phys Fit."

"That was before lunch," Marcus pointed out.

"I didn't hear her in the cafeteria," said Guin. "Hear" was the operative word; Annice's voice carried through the thick of hallways and assemblies, an ever-present rumble like ongoing thunder.

"Well, they can't just take her," reasoned Rand.

Each of them shifted in his or her seat. The truth was, this was uncharted territory. Excepting acute illness and rare instances of violence (always a rumor from another town, never in Morrowville), someone being taken from their home was unheard of, the stuff of urban legend.

"They'd have done better to grab her before she went to school at all," Marcus remarked.

"Marcus!" Guin looked aghast.

He shrugged off her disapproval. "It's true. Now they will have the added chore of having to stop the rumors."

"There would be rumors either way," Cee said. "If Annice disappeared—"

"They would have been able to give out the word that she was sick or something," inserted Marcus. "*Before* she was able to say anything about Mr. Dougherty."

"Look at you, all conspiracy theorist," said Rand. He chuckled, but it came out half as a cough and his smile appeared uneasy.

"Marcus is brilliant," Cee said. "Smarter, probably, than anyone running this town."

More shifting, awkward silence as Guin and Rand ducked and bobbed their heads and Marcus sent Cee a side-long glance that she couldn't interpret.

Rand cleared his throat. "All right then." He looked at Marcus. "What should we do next, Mr. Brilliant?"

But it was Guin who answered. "We could check on Annice, at least. Cee and I could go to her house, say we'd heard she was ill."

Cee could not imagine many places she'd less like to go than Annice's house. Hospital, maybe, where Mr. Dougherty might be, or Holding, where Annice might actually be, though what they could hold her for was unclear. "It's getting dark," she hedged. "And for all we know, Annice will be at school tomorrow anyway."

They turned their collective eyes to the rapidly dimming windows. Guin gave a resigned sigh. "Okay. But if she's not back tomorrow, we'll go?"

Cee nodded and tried to feel confident that Annice

would be at school the next day. Then they rose and gathered their things and, with a backward glance at poor Mrs. Dougherty, exited the heat of the café and disseminated.

ANNICE WAS NOT AT SCHOOL.

Cee could not tell whether it was merely the absence of Annice's voice that made the school feel even more subdued, or whether everyone really was quieter than normal. Or maybe it was the way Guin nodded at her from across homeroom, a silent reminder of their pact, and the idea of going to Annice's house that dampened the day.

Rand and Guin joined Cee and Marcus at their lunch table, and Cee fleetingly wondered when they'd become a foursome and how and why. She missed being alone with Marcus; despite his promise to her father, he hadn't come to her house since the Volunteer Corps had left and was too busy with Rand and the Lit project to do homework with her. Lunch was all they had left, and now it, too, was being invaded. Cee pulled her shoulders in and hunched over her meal, feeling crowded despite the fact the table provided plenty of space.

"Have you heard anything?" Rand asked.

Cee stared at her food.

"We'll go over to her house after school," said Guin.

"Good," Rand said. "We still have our project to finish."

"I'm not sure what you hope to accomplish," Marcus said.

"Well, we'll know, won't we?" Guin asked. "That's something at least."

"But what do you want to know?" Marcus asked.

"Maybe..." Cee murmured.

Everyone at the table grew quiet and still. Cee felt their

43

eyes on her, the weight of their expectation, though she didn't look up.

"Maybe Guin will be able to..."

And Cee did look up then, and over at Guin, who was seated next to her but with a large enough gap that they wouldn't touch, not even accidentally. Had Guin planned that?

Guin grimaced but nodded at the same time. "It's worth a try."

And so Cee found herself at Annice's house that afternoon, standing just outside the white picket fence that demarcated the yard. It was in good repair, aside from the gate, which hung askew and showed signs of the paint having worn off in the places where hands were most likely to push, pull, and grab.

The house was empty. Cee could tell without having to get any closer. The windows were dark, not in the way of there being no lights on (though there were none), but in the way of abandonment. The red brick structure might as well have been a corpse.

There were no near neighbors. Unlike the tidy part of town the Klingers and Doyles lived in, with its rows of houses and lack of fences, the yards bleeding into one another unimpeded except by the occasional hedge, Annice's family lived on the fringes. Houses out on the Eastbound Road were set farther apart, and the air out that way hung thick with the smell of horses, cattle, and other livestock. In fact, Cee was almost certain she heard the soft clucking of chickens coming from the other side of Annice's house. With a pang that surprised her, she wondered who was caring for the animals if no one was home.

"Maybe they're just out," Guin suggested, but her voice was shaky.

"Out where?" asked Cee. Vacations were rare, requiring special permissions for travel, so Annice definitely would have mentioned if her family was planning one. And if the Bradshaws were out and about in Morrowville, they'd have been seen.

Movement on her right startled Cee; Guin strode decisively to the gate and pushed it open, the squeak of it seeming far too loud in the quiet neighborhood. In a split second Cee was right behind, opting to stick with Guin rather than remain alone. She followed Guin to the door, waiting a step behind as Guin rapped loudly. But of course there was no answer.

Guin pulled open the screen door and tried the knob. But even as Cee yelped, "Guin!" she saw that it was locked.

Undeterred, Guin started off around the side of the house. Cee stayed in her wake, balled hands tucked in her blazer pockets, determined not to touch anything. She kept her head ducked, eyes on the dusty ground, which is how she saw—

"Guin," she said again. They were behind the house now, and there was the chicken coop, a handful of birds scratching around inside. Guin was peering into windows. Without thinking, Cee went to a bag of feed that was leaning up against the back of the house.

"Guin." There was a scoop inside the feedbag.

Guin finally turned around.

"Look at the ground," said Cee. She tossed a couple scoops of feed into the coop. She had no idea how much chickens ate, when these had last been fed, what other livestock at the farm might be in need. But the chickens garbled in what Cee liked to think was some kind of gratitude.

"So many prints," breathed Guin as she surveyed the dirt. "It's like an army came through here."

But Morrowville didn't have an army, not exactly. It had Administrators, and it had the Volunteers (all gone, excepting the truant Mr. Dougherty), and it had the Safety Brigade. That was as much as they needed, *more* than they needed. "Preparation!" read the signs at the Brigade office, though what they needed to prepare for was something no one ever talked about. Cee had difficulty imagining any situation that would require that kind of force as a response. Yet here she was at Annice's abandoned house, and clearly something had happened that *had* required it.

"Maybe Mr. Dougherty is sick," Cee said, wiping her hands on her skirt. She was only thinking aloud, articulating the possibilities. "Sick enough that coming into contact with him..."

"Then they'd have to quarantine all of us," said Guin, "since Annice came to school that day."

"Maybe there's a time frame," Cee suggested. "And we weren't exposed to her long enough to worry."

"She was barely in Mr. Dougherty's company," Guin countered, and Cee sighed. They could spend all afternoon conjecturing. They had no facts outside of an empty house and over-trod ground.

"We should go find the boys," Guin went on.

Cee hesitated and cast a look over her shoulder at the chickens. A number of yards behind the coop stood a barn; it was closed up as if for the night. Guin saw the direction of Cee's gaze and said, "We can't. We don't even know how to—"

Abruptly, Guin's head swiveled in the direction of the house, and at first Cee wasn't sure why. But then she heard it: the thud of boots at the front of the house.

Cee's breath froze in her chest, and she turned wide-eyed to Guin, who stood motionless as a deer that senses a hunter. But standing there wouldn't save them, so Cee took two long strides and grabbed Guin's arm, only to be assailed by a series of rapid images. Boots, yes, and round wooden buttons on a coat, and a yellow bicycle leaning against a gate, no, *the* gate, the one here at the house.

Cee let go of Guin, but it took effort, like trying to release one's hold on a live wire. Only by concentrating on opening her fingers could Cee free herself from whatever was coursing through Guin.

And then Mrs. Montague came trudging around the side of the house. She wore her boots and her barn coat, even though the days were getting warmer. She stopped short when she spotted the two girls.

Cee felt air escaping her like a punctured balloon, a slow deflation. Mrs. Montague owned the next farm over, was the Bradshaws' nearest neighbor. Mr. Montague had passed away almost two years before, a sad thing because it meant Mrs. Montague would soon be transferred into a care facility and her farm would be given to another family. "Two years is the time it takes to grieve," Cee's mother had explained. "That's why we give families two years between fosters, too." Except in rare cases like the Doyles.

"What are you girls doing here?" Mrs. Montague asked. She didn't sound angry, only surprised.

Guin still appeared unable to move, so Cee pushed a smile onto her face and said, "Annice wasn't in school, so we wanted to check on her. And then the animals..." She gestured at the chicken coop. The birds had made short work of the feed and were still scratching around for any they might have missed.

"Sweet of you," said Mrs. Montague. "But the Bradshaws have gone on a little trip. I'm just here to see to the animals. I promised I would. You can help if you like."

Guin's eyes got wider and her nostrils flared; she looked wild, like she might start tossing her head like an agitated horse, send her mane of hair flying.

"Oh, we can't stay," said Cee. "We still have homework. We're just glad to know the animals will be okay." She reached for Guin's arm again but stopped. Jamming her hands back into her pockets, Cee strode out of the yard, trusting Guin to follow. She could feel Mrs. Montague's shrewd eyes on them all the way to the Eastbound Road.

CHAPTER

SEVEN

S tarlight: Kiss! Kiss! Bring the air between you to nothing!
    Dew: *Would they not suffocate?*
Starlight: *A most blissful asphyxiation.*

—"The Fey Wager"

THEY DIDN'T TALK. Their steps fell together as Guin came to walk beside Cee, an unintentionally syncopated march back to the school, inside and up to the library. Mrs. Drury was absent from the circulation desk, but there were a few students at study tables.

One of the study rooms had its door closed and blinds drawn; Cee headed in that direction, Guin hot on her heels. Cee flung open the door without knocking, then took a step backward as if knocked back by a physical blow. Her heel came down on Guin's toes, and Guin yelped, earning them nasty glances from the kids at the tables.

Cee was rooted, blocking the doorway. Guin craned around her for a look inside the study room. "Dear heavens."

"What are you doing here?" Marcus demanded at the same time Rand said, "Close the door!"

Guin shoved Cee into the room, stepped in after her, and did as Rand commanded. Only when the door was shut did Guin give into laughter. "What in the world?"

Marcus and Rand had shoved the long table as far to one side as they could and stood in the middle of the gray room, each dressed in what looked to Cee like a plain white sheet. Marcus had a silvery band resting atop his springy hair; more securely pulled down on Rand's head was ring of green plastic vines.

"We're rehearsing," Marcus said through clenched teeth.

Tears were leaking from the corners of Guin's eyes. "Rehearsing what?"

"We're doing a unit on Quiney," said Rand. "For our project, we have to perform a scene from one of her plays."

"You must be Starlight and Dew," Cee realized.

"You should pin that on," Guin told Marcus, pointing to his lopsided headdress.

"What are you doing here?" Marcus asked again.

Cee's and Guin's words tumbled over one another, but somehow Marcus and Rand managed to comprehend them. "You're sure the prints weren't just from the Bradshaws?" Rand asked once the deluge had trickled to a stop.

Cee and Guin exchanged thoughtful frowns, then each shook her head. "Didn't look like the same prints over and over again," said Guin.

"A lot of different sizes," Cee added. "Though the treads were similar."

"Standard issue," murmured Marcus, and when they all looked at him, he went on to explain, "A lot of the same boot in a variety of sizes points to the boots having been assigned footwear for a group of people."

"What group of people?" Rand asked.

Marcus shrugged. "The Brigade?"

"But Mrs. Montague said—" Cee began.

"Mrs. Montague would say whatever they told her to say," Marcus cut in. "And now she'll almost certainly tell them she found you sneaking around the place."

"We can't get in trouble for worrying about a friend," said Guin, but she was getting the frightened deer look again.

Rand's eyes drifted to the clock above the whiteboard. "It's getting late. We should head home." And when nobody moved, he looked at Guin and, gesturing at the sheet he wore, said, "We need a minute, you know?"

Cee turned for the door, but not before one last look at the draped Marcus, his skin almost as white as the fabric wound around him, his exposed limbs thin and sharp looking. "We'll wait for you out here."

Mrs. Drury had returned to her place behind the desk; her eyebrows went up as Cee and Guin exited the study room. Guin had been pulling the door closed after them, but apparently not quickly enough for the boys' taste, as there came a shove from behind that caused her to give a little hop forward. She and Cee stood awkwardly under Mrs. Drury's stare; the other students had gone, so they had the full benefit of the librarian's attention.

After a long moment of feeling at a loss, Guin whispered, "Who are Starlight and Dew?"

"You don't know the story?" Cee murmured, and Guin shook her head, sending her hair swaying. "It's one of

Quiney's most famous plays," said Cee, striving to keep her voice low, even though no one else was in the library. "About two fairies who bet another two fairies they can make two humans fall in love. Then the other two fairies are trying to make the humans hate one another."

"So Starlight and Dew are fairies?" Guin asked. "Are they the good ones or the bad ones?"

"The good ones, assuming you think making people fall in love is good," said Cee. She'd loved the illustrated children's version that had been in one of her books when she was little. But the more she thought about it, the more she wondered whether it was wrong of *all* the fairies to manipulate people like that.

"Well, love is good," said Guin. "So I guess falling in love is good, too. Since it's the creation of love, in a way."

The study room door opened, and Marcus and Rand emerged dressed in their school uniforms. Cee noted the excess of fabric, how it hid exactly how thin Marcus was. She stretched on her tiptoes to pluck a wayward bit of tinsel from his hair. He drew back at first but then grew still to allow it.

Cee leaned into the warmth of him. She so seldom had the opportunity to be this close. Even when they studied together, they never sat this close. "Within orb," she murmured.

"What?" Marcus asked.

Cee could feel his breath on her cheek. She swayed a little, lightheaded from the proximity.

Her ability to focus was impaired, her movements sluggish. As she teased at the tinsel, a tingling started in Cee's fingertips, small at first and hardly noteworthy, but it gathered strength and speed and shot up her arm, into her shoulder, up the side of her neck, and suddenly she felt faint. Her world tilted left. Arms, thin but strong, caught her before she could fall.

The tingling sensation increased, crawling up and down Cee's back as if she'd come into contact with a numbing agent. She rolled her head and looked up into Marcus's frowning countenance. Golden clouds skidded across his sea-foam eyes. The overhead lights created a flare, a halo around his messy hair. The bit of silver was still there.

"You..." Cee mumbled. Her lips were rubbery and did not want to cooperate. *Close your arms*, she thought. *Hold me.*

But Marcus was looking up and over at things or people outside her vision. "Rand, take her." He sounded desperate.

Cee felt her body being shifted into stronger, more solid hands. Almost immediately the tingling drained away to nothing as Rand set her on her feet. "You okay?"

Cee nodded and tried to catch Marcus's eye, but he steadfastly refused to look at her. "I don't know, I just went weak."

"I'm going to be closing the library soon."

Cee started in surprise at the voice so close behind her, and Rand put a steadying hand on her arm. Thankfully, there were no side effects to contact with him. Marcus's head whipped up, and Cee caught the swing of Guin's hair out of the corner of her eye as they all turned to look at Mrs. Drury. The librarian had posted herself right behind Cee without any of them having noticed.

Mrs. Drury's sharp eyes bored into Cee. "You're all right now, I trust." She didn't seem to be asking so much as stating, and Rand quickly removed his hand from Cee's arm before the librarian could cite them for breaking the Code of Conduct. But if Mrs. Drury noticed, she gave no indication.

Cee had the sudden urge to reach out and touch the old woman, to find out if there was anything in her worth absorbing. She flexed her fingers, and Mrs. Drury's gaze darted downward. "Go on, then," she said, and Cee thought it was an invitation to act on her impulse, but the others moved hastily for the door.

Mrs. Drury's glossed pink mouth twisted to one side as Cee was slow to follow her friends. "You don't need me to call the nurse, now do you?"

Cee broke free of the librarian's hypnotic stare and hurried to where Rand was still holding the door for her.

AFTER PARTING with Guin and Rand, Cee and Marcus walked in silence toward their homes. Cee started and stopped a dozen conversations in her head but was unable to bring the words to her lips. Everything she could think of to say felt fragile, or like something that would send Marcus running.

They were almost to Cee's house—she could see the glow of the light over the door—when Marcus finally spoke. "You felt something. When you touched me."

Cee thought about telling him how he carried light and warmth with him like a sun, and how she was colder when he went away. But she could too clearly picture the shuttered expression he most likely would give her if she did. Ever since Arlon's Relinquishing, it seemed, Marcus was pulling away, closing a door between them. So she only asked, "Do you feel that way all the time?"

Marcus looked away, off into the growing darkness. "It's starting."

Cee did not need to ask what he meant, so instead she offered what she hoped would be useful information.

"When I looked into your eyes, there was something..." Cee searched for the words. "Golden," she said. "Your eyes are green, but when you caught me, something golden swam through them."

Marcus frowned thoughtfully, and Cee knew he was working this new tidbit into his massive collection of mental data. "Several Clans exhibit golden eyes," he mused. "Felidae is the most common, but there are a number of others as well."

Cee considered. Marcus *was* very catlike in some ways. "Maybe you could catch and eat Arlon."

Marcus barked a laugh. "I'd have to be one of the larger cats, then."

Cee was glad to see him smile; it seemed he rarely did anymore. They stopped at the steps to her house, and as Marcus said goodnight and turned to go, Cee blurted, "We'll always be friends, right?"

Marcus turned back and regarded Cee, the porch light making his already pale skin corpselike. But the green eyes were as brilliant as ever.

"We will," Cee insisted. She needed to hear it from him. Did he feel colder without her, too? "Right?"

"I don't know, Cee," Marcus said, choosing his words with care. "It will depend on what Clans we turn out to be in, and the relationship between those Clans. We might not—"

"Don't," said Cee. She couldn't bear to hear him say it aloud, that they might not see each other again.

"I will always have fond memories of you, Cee."

It was the most she could hope for, but Cee wished for once Marcus was a better liar.

A Pre-Morph who does not transform before his or her twenty-first birthday will be classified Unaltered and will be provided a job and home by the Town or Community in keeping with his or her abilities, subject to evaluation.

—Magistrates' Guidelines

"How good are you at it?" Marcus asked.

The four of them were squeezed into Cee's room, much to Cee's mother's delight. Mrs. Klinger had ferried up fresh slices of pound cake topped with berries and cream and steaming mugs of hot apple cider, despite Cee's room being the warmest in the house.

Marcus's question was directed at Guin, whose doe eyes widened. "What do you mean?" Her voice cracked with the question, and she turned a pleading look on Rand, who sat beside her but was focused on flattening the remaining crumbs of cake with his fork so he could get them to his mouth.

"The telepathy," said Marcus. "You won't be able to hide it much longer. But before they find out, we might be able to put it to good use."

"Since when are you so calculating?" Cee demanded. She found herself on edge, trying to catch glints of gold in his eyes, but he'd barely looked at her all evening. Was he avoiding her? As much as he could while remaining in the same room?

"It's simple logic," Marcus said, unfazed, and eyes still on Guin. "We want to know what happened with Mr. Dougherty and Annice. The best way to find out would be to read their thoughts."

"Who is 'they'?" Rand asked as he set his cleaned plate aside.

"We've had this conversation," Marcus told him. "My guess is the Brigade. It seems they believe there may be some risk to the community."

"That's a big assumption," said Rand. "And even if you're right, we can't just send Guin into the Brigade office."

"It's not an assumption," said Marcus, his tone edged with rising exasperation. "It's *logic*. How many times do I have to say it?" He took a deep breath and collected himself. "The boot prints. There is only one organization in town that has the numbers and variety to produce them. The Brigade. Annice said there were cars. Again, a limited number of those in Morrowville. The Brigade has access to the Administrative fleet."

Rand pressed his lips together, and Marcus took his silence as assent. He moved on to the next point. "As for getting Guin in..." His eyes slid toward Cee. "You're good at magic."

Cee's jaw fell open and hung there a moment before she found the power to move it. "Well, yeah, I mean, some of it."

"You've got the highest marks in our level in Incantations," Marcus reminded her. "You were the first of any of us to charm a snake. You can light and snuff candles from across a room, you—"

"We get the idea," said Rand. "What's your point?"

"That, with Cee's help, we won't have to go to the Brigade. She'll bring them to us. One of them, at least. That's all we really need, so long as we get someone high enough in the ranks to know what's really going on. Then Guin can read him, mystery solved."

"Mystery solved," Rand repeated dryly. "Or we could just leave it alone."

"I don't think that's an option," said Marcus.

"Really, Mr. Brilliant? And why's that?"

"Don't call me that," muttered Marcus.

"I don't think I can just *lure* a Brigade officer," Cee blurted. "It's not like a snake."

"And I don't read people all that well, either," Guin added. "Mostly I get flashes." The others looked at her, and she squirmed self-consciously where she sat. "It's not like I'm *trying*, you know. It just happens!"

"And what happens when you do try?" Marcus asked. He locked his green eyes to Guin's brown ones.

A tiny flare went up in Cee, rising from her abdomen, through her chest and straight to her head like a wayward firework. *She* was Marcus's best friend. But he'd slammed his mind closed against her. What would Marcus dare share with Guin that he wouldn't share with her?

"He's right," Guin said thickly, eyes still fastened on Marcus's. "We have to find out what's really going on."

The air in the room suddenly felt oppressively heavy. Cee shot to her feet and went to the window, threw it open. When she turned back around, they were all staring at her.

"It's hot up here," Cee said. She looked at Guin, who now had bright pink spots high on her cheeks; her ears were flushed, too. "I think Guin is overheating."

The color in Guin's face brightened, and she jumped to her feet. "I have homework," she mumbled as she grabbed her book bag. "See you..." She was gone before she could complete the sentence.

Rand's bulk required him to unfold himself more slowly. "Wait up, Guin." He shot Marcus a dark look before departing, but Marcus failed to notice. He was staring at Cee's whitewashed paneling, though she could tell he didn't see it. His brow was slightly puckered, and after a moment he said, "I probably shouldn't have done that."

"Go home, Marcus," said Cee.

Marcus looked over at her, startled. She finally had his attention, but it was too little too late.

"Go," Cee said again, like someone shooing an unwanted stray.

"Cee..."

"Go away!" Cee shouted. She whirled around and gulped fresh air from the open window. Out in the shadows, something rustled and fluttered. An owl disturbed during its hunt for its dinner, perhaps.

She waited for him to try again. To say something, be determined to get through to her. To make a move, come stand behind her at the window. She ached for him to put a reassuring hand on her shoulder. Not that he ever would. That would be too "physically familiar."

After a minute, Cee realized the chill in the room was from more than just the open window and outside air.

When she turned around, she was alone.

WITH THE VOLUNTEERS GONE, Community Days were subdued, grown men noticeably absent from the crowd. Still, the women and children came, and the older men, and Cee wondered if she was merely imagining that the smiles were strained and fake, the chatter brittle and breaking rather than flowing smoothly as it usually did.

She was arranging the massive dish of pasta bake, turning it first one way on the table then another, as if the direction might make a difference to its taste, when a voice behind her said quietly, "This would be the perfect time."

Cee jumped and looked over her shoulder at where Marcus towered over her. "The perfect time for what?" she snapped. She was still carrying the awkward mixture of sorrow and anger he'd inspired in her two nights before, compounded now by a fresh surge of irritation at his having surprised her. He could at least look a little sorry for it.

But Marcus's face remained free of anything resembling concern or apology. He gave a small nod toward one of the Brigade members, identifiable by his uniform as he patrolled the common.

Cee turned away and continued to adjust the casserole dish. "We'd need Guin for that, wouldn't we?" When Marcus didn't respond, Cee looked back at him, only to find him staring off into the mingling crowd with a strange expression on his face that Cee couldn't decipher. She followed his gaze but could not figure out what he was looking at, if anything at all.

"Are you planning to have any?"

Cee turned and found Mrs. Montague beside her. The old woman was holding a plate filled with food. "The pasta," said Mrs. Montague.

"No," Cee told her, stepping back from the table. "I was just—" But Mrs. Montague was already scooping a helping onto her crowded dish.

"You'll be glad to know the Bradshaws' animals are all well," Mrs. Montague said as she spooned a heap of cheesy pasta right on top of the green salad occupying a corner of her plate. Cee idly wondered whether Mrs. Montague ate in layers, excavating her meal the way an archeologist would a site, discovering new flavors as she went.

As Mrs. Montague made her way down the table, Cee stepped back to get out of the way, only to walk right into Marcus. Warmth flooded her. A low hum filled her brain. She felt as if she were touching something that was vibrating at an extremely rapid rate.

Almost immediately, Marcus moved away a fraction, but the sensation stayed with Cee for several seconds before dissipating. She felt tiny cracks opening up inside her, as if a minor earthquake had jostled something awake. "Are you... close? To transformation?" she asked.

Marcus threw a glance in Mrs. Montague's direction, but she was mining grapes from an oversized bowl of fruit salad. Cee saw Marcus's thin fingers flex and suspected he would have liked to grab her, drag her off somewhere. The idea sent a thrill through Cee that she didn't entirely understand.

"Come on," he murmured and headed for a cluster of willows surrounding a small pond at a corner of the common.

Cee briefly considered ignoring him. What could he do then? What *would* he do? The cracks in Cee widened, and the waking thing uncoiled and stretched, begged her to hold back and find out how Marcus might respond to insubordination, and this desire shocked her. She wanted to stop and feel out what might be happening inside her, but Marcus was already walking away. With effort Cee tamped down on these strange feelings and followed in Marcus's footsteps.

Yet deep within her she could feel the dark thing slither.

Marcus stepped into the relative isolation of the trees, the curtain of their curved and swaying boughs. It was not completely private, but it was outside the general hubbub of running and shouting children and mingling adults.

"What are you doing?" Marcus asked as Cee joined him.

Cee stopped in her tracks. "What am *I* doing? *You're* the one who says I should entice a Brigade officer."

"Not entice," Marcus hissed. "Look, you can't go around talking about how I—" He waved a hand over his body, "when there are other people around."

"Who? Mrs. Montague? She's so old, she's probably deaf anyway." Cee stopped cold. She didn't understand where the words were coming from. They didn't sound like the kind of thing she normally said.

Marcus's expression bore out her suspicion. He stared at her as if she'd grown another head.

"I suppose it's okay for you to share how you feel with Guin, though, isn't it?" Cee went on. She stopped again and ground her teeth.

Marcus's face went from astonished to confused. "What does Guin have to do with anything?"

It was suddenly clear to Cee that the thing inside her did not like Marcus, and now it was rearing up and feeding on her growing anger and frustration. "And I thought you didn't even like girls," she said. *It* said. She would never talk this way to him. "But maybe it's just me you don't like." She spun on her heel to go, to get away before she ruined the little bit of friendship left between them. What was happening?

"Cee!" She could tell he was trying not to shout, to keep from drawing attention. "You know... You've always known..."

"I'm starting to think I don't know you at all," said Cee. She wanted to bite off her own tongue. She wanted to turn and run, but she was as rooted as the willows around her. Trying to move was like pushing at a stone wall, only the wall was inside her.

"Is there a problem here?" A Brigade officer was walking toward them, and Cee recognized Colin Finn. He'd been in school a few years ahead of them but had never morphed. Evidently, once Morrowville concluded they were stuck with him, Mr. Finn had been placed in the Brigade.

Inside Cee, the dark thing smiled and struck. "He made me come with him," Cee babbled. "Told me he wanted to show me something."

"What?" Marcus gasped. "Cee—"

Tears, hot and real, began spilling down Cee's cheeks. A heavy hand landed on her shoulder. "It's all right," Mr. Finn told her. "It'll be all right." He unhooked his radio from his jacket.

Time to try, the thing inside Cee whispered. Without fully understanding what she was doing, Cee lifted her head and looked Mr. Finn in the eyes. He froze, the radio in one hand and his other still on her shoulder as his visage went slack. Then Mr. Finn began to jerk erratically as if having some kind of seizure.

"Cee!" cried Marcus.

She could not look at him, could not break the connection with Mr. Finn without doing some kind of damage, of that much she was sure, even though she did not know how she knew or what would happen.

A thin stream of foamy drool began to trickle from the corner of Mr. Finn's mouth. An image formed clearly in Cee's mind: A room with paneled walls painted the color of pool water. There was black leather furniture and tall green plants in pots. And there was a window. With effort, Cee pushed forward through the vision so she could see out.

Morrowville's Central Common was a large, green rectangle in the middle of town. Main Street and Centre Street ran parallel along the long sides of the rectangle and were fronted with cafés, shops, and restaurants, and also housed a Brigade office and a few Administration branches. Now, Cee's mental picture showed her the bandstand from above, and she heard an echo of Commissioner Beaulieu as he began to make his weekly announcements. She started to turn around and see if anyone was in the room with her, but like a snapping elastic, all at once Cee found herself back inside her own body.

Mr. Finn's hand had slipped from her shoulder.

"Cee?" Marcus's voice was shaking. She'd never heard him sound like that before. Well and truly scared.

Mr. Finn was blinking like a man waking up. He looked at the radio in his hand as though he didn't know what to do with it.

Cee scanned the buildings around the park and tried to figure out what angle she'd been seeing from in the vision. Her gaze settled on a corner building topped with a gilded onion dome; the window under the dome had lacy curtains to each side, just as the one she'd seen, and as she looked, Cee was sure there was movement. Someone had stepped away from the glass. Or been pulled.

"Up there," Cee said.

Both Marcus and Mr. Finn looked in the direction of Cee's gaze. But while Marcus only added confusion to his frightened expression, Mr. Finn scowled. "What about it?" he demanded.

The creature inside Cee stirred. *He'll kill you when he gets the chance.* Cee narrowed her eyes at Mr. Finn, but the creature said, *No. The other one.*

She looked over at Marcus. It was late afternoon, and the sunlight guttered around him, dancing to the sway of the willow branches.

Give me a name, said the creature.

"Livian," said Cee without hesitation, and beside her Marcus's brows came down, punctuating a silent question.

"Look," said Mr. Finn, "I don't know what the two of you are up to—"

Cee turned her big blue eyes on him. "I told you, *he*—" a jab in Marcus's direction. *Why are you doing this?* she asked silently.

"Cee." Marcus's voice was shakier even than before.

I'm only doing what you've always wanted to do.

"Dragged me over here," Cee finished. *I've never wanted this! Stop!*

"That true, Doyle?" Mr. Finn asked.

"Not exactly," said Marcus, then with more surety, "No."

Mr. Finn's eyes darted from one to the other of them. "You know the Code of Conduct."

"Yes, sir," they chorused.

"I could run you both in for statements," said Mr. Finn.

"All right," said Cee. Marcus paled.

Mr. Finn sighed as his threat backfired. "How about I just escort you back to your mother?"

"And what about him?" Cee asked. "You're just going to let him go?" She wondered if Livian could purr. If so, he was doing it now.

Mr. Finn glanced around uncertainly. The families and conversing groups nearest the trees were beginning to dart looks in their direction. "Okay," Mr. Finn said, "let's take this over to the office."

CHAPTER
NINE

T he Brigade is entitled to use force if and when
necessary for the protection of the Community at
large.

—Safety Brigade Charter

As Mr. Finn took them around the edges of the gathering,
Marcus fell into step beside Cee. "What are you doing?"

"I saw..." The words clogged her throat. She wanted to
apologize, beg forgiveness, but nothing more would
come out.

They crossed Main Street and headed for the building
topped by the onion dome. Cee couldn't keep her eyes from
drifting up to the now vacant window.

"Without Guin this gets us nowhere," whispered
Marcus, and another flare shot through Cee, Livian's hot
breath charring her insides.

"You'll think of something, I'm sure," she said, all her regrets melting to nothing. "You always have an answer."

Mr. Finn led them into the building, the downstairs of which was painted the same color as the room in Cee's vision. *Aquamarine*, Livian told her, and when the information failed to provoke any response in his host, *to calm nerves and amplify psychic abilities.*

Cee wondered how many Brigade officers were psychic. Whatever had transferred from Mr. Finn when he'd touched her shoulder and allowed her to see that room... She was beginning to understand that even if someone never morphed, his or her education and talents might yet include magic. Possibly strong magic.

A woman with straight, dark hair was sitting behind the main desk. The rest of the office appeared empty. Cee guessed the brigadiers were out on the common with the rest of the town.

"Wu," Mr. Finn said, and Cee wondered if it was the woman's first name or her last, "put Mr. Doyle here in room A. Miss Klinger, come with me."

Marcus shot Cee another pleading look, but Cee turned her back on him and Wu and followed Mr. Finn down a hall to a door marked "B." He opened it and gestured her inside. Without being told, Cee took a seat at the table. Mr. Finn sat down across from her.

"Aren't you going to write any of this down?" Cee asked.

"Let's talk first, and then I'll decide what needs to go on the record. If anything."

Cee eyed him. Then her eyes floated upward to the ceiling.

"Tell me what happened," said Mr. Finn.

"I was putting out the pasta bake and talking to Mrs. Montague. You can ask her," Cee added. "And then Marcus dragged me off behind those trees and..." She pictured Marcus, sitting in a room like this one, hunched over the table and waiting. "What will you do to him?"

"That depends. What did he do to you?"

"Something happened. When he touched me." It was true, at least. "I think there's something wrong with him."

She expected Mr. Finn to laugh it off, and something in her—*not* Livian—wanted him to. She wanted Mr. Finn to send both her and Marcus back out to the common, to their parents, and have the whole thing forgotten. But Mr. Finn frowned and asked, "What happened? When he touched you?"

"He just... Felt weird. It was like his body was humming. Vibrating."

Mr. Finn stood up. "Wait here for a minute." He went to the door and, hand on the knob, asked her as an afterthought, "Do you want any water?"

Cee realized she *was* thirsty. She felt hot and dry inside and wondered if that was Livian's fault. But she didn't want to give Mr. Finn or his colleague Wu any more reasons to come into the room than they already had, so she shook her head.

"What are you?" she hissed to Livian the moment the door had closed behind Mr. Finn. "Where did you come from?"

You don't have to speak aloud, you know, said Livian. *And I've always been here.*

"No you haven't." Cee pushed back quietly from the table so that the chair made almost no sound.

What have they been teaching you? Nothing much, apparently. Nothing useful.

Cee tiptoed to the door.

Useless, the lot of them, Livian went on. *And that one you think is your friend. He's not, you know.*

"Shut up," Cee said under her breath.

They can't hear me.

"No, but I can." Cee eased the door open a crack. Marcus certainly wouldn't be her friend after today. What had gotten into her?

Livian had.

But what had set her off? Or him, rather?

He's dangerous, said Livian. *And will only get more dangerous if we don't get rid of him now.*

Cee couldn't see anything but the wall of the corridor. She pushed the door open a little farther and prayed its hinges were oiled. Sliding one foot past the other so as not to even make the sound of a footfall, Cee edged her way out of the interrogation room.

She looked left and could see the waiting area, the door onto Main Street, and a slice of the front desk, but not all of it, so she couldn't tell whether Wu had returned to her post. Then she looked right and saw the hallway ended in a high-set window. But right before that, there appeared to be a cut in the wall—the kind of break that might be a stairway. Walking as quietly as she could, Cee moved toward it.

She was almost there, was able to see the corner of the ebony stairs, when a shout went up on the other side of the wall. Whether it was pain or simply shock and surprise, Cee couldn't tell. But one thing she *did* know: It was Marcus who'd shouted.

Better yet, the dumbfolk will take care of him for us. Cee could feel Livian's satisfaction spreading through her like warmth from hot cocoa. *Where are you going?*

Cee had changed direction. No longer trying to be quiet, she all but ran down the hall, back toward the waiting area and front desk. Unoccupied. Behind the desk, a second corridor ran perpendicular to the one Cee had been in; at the corner where the halls met was a black door with a brass "A" nailed to it. Cee threw it open.

Wu stood over Marcus, her hands on either side of his head. Marcus was seated, his head bowed and eyes squeezed shut, shoulders lifted defensively. Cee's eyes widened at the sight of handcuffs encircling Marcus's thin wrists. There was no sign of Mr. Finn.

Neither Wu nor Marcus appeared to have noticed her entrance. Cee stepped forward, but Livian warned, *If you break the connection abruptly, it will do damage.*

I thought you wanted to hurt him anyway, Cee thought. She felt Livian shift inside her, coiling like a snake. *Are you a snake?*

We don't have time for this conversation, said Livian. *We should go now while we have the chance.*

But she couldn't leave Marcus. Guilt flooded Cee; how could she have done this to her best friend? And all at once she knew what she had to do. Dropping to her hands and knees, Cee crawled over to Wu and Marcus, reached out, and took Marcus's hands in her own.

Marcus's eyes flew open and met Cee's. Above them, Wu remained still, her eyes closed as she concentrated. Cee squeezed Marcus's fingers and hoped he understood how sorry she was. Inside her, she felt Livian heave a disgusted sigh.

Breathe on them. And when Cee made no move to act, *the handcuffs. Breathe on them.*

Cee grimaced and tried to remember whether she'd eaten anything smelly.

By all the ancient gods—

She opened her mouth and exhaled, doing her best to

aim for the chain that held the bracelets together. Her mouth felt drier than ever, and her breath came out unexpectedly hot; Marcus's wrists turned bright red, but at least they didn't melt like the handcuffs did. The silver rippled, sagged, and fell away, leaving a dark stain on Marcus's shirt cuffs and trousers.

Wu finally realized something was happening. Her eyes opened, and she strengthened her grip on Marcus's head. He gritted his teeth and curled in on himself.

Without thinking, Cee tightened her grip on Marcus's hands. It fleetingly occurred to her that she no longer felt the tingling sensation she'd come to expect from contact with Marcus, but she didn't have time to think about it. Instead, Cee felt something begin to flow out of her through her hands and into Marcus. "Livian?" she croaked.

No answer. But Marcus began to unfurl his body, slowly, and Cee could feel tremors through his fingertips, like an engine starting. The hum was back. The lights in the room flared suddenly brighter.

Wu made a sound like an angry cat as her hands were repulsed and she was thrown backward. She hit the wall hard enough to incapacitate her, at least for the moment.

Cee looked up at Marcus. She suddenly felt terrifyingly cold and empty, unable to think clearly. *Livian?* Even in her head, her words quivered.

Then Marcus leaned forward and kissed her.

His lips were as soft and firm as Cee had ever dreamed, and when he opened his mouth, she obligingly did the same. Heat poured into her, and the room started to spin. Reflexively, Cee tightened her grip on Marcus's hands. She would gladly have melted right into him, but he pulled away abruptly, his brilliant eyes wide with shock.

But it was Livian who spoke, if only in Cee's mind: *Fastest way back in. We should go.*

The tingling had built to a crescendo during the kiss but was ebbing quickly now that she and Marcus were no longer touching. Cee felt as though her entire body had lost circulation and now suffered the pins-and-needles sensation of fresh blood flow. She struggled to get to her feet.

Marcus stood and reached down to help Cee up. Against the wall, Wu was stirring. Slipping an arm around Cee's waist, Marcus propelled her to the door.

"I thought you didn't like..." Cee mumbled. With Marcus's arm around her, the numbness was returning.

"I don't," said Marcus, while at the same time Livian growled, *You weren't going to leave without him, though, were you?*

The Brigade office was still empty. Marcus was pushing Cee toward the glass doors and the dusky twilight beyond when Cee dug in her heels. "No!"

"What do you mean, no?" Marcus was tugging at her like one would an intractable mule.

"Upstairs! We have to—"

Wu appeared in the doorway of interrogation room A, swaying slightly on her feet. "Stop!"

Marcus thrust Cee through the door and across the street into the common where Community Day was just breaking up. Blankets were being shaken out, crumby dishes collected from the tables. Marcus steered Cee into the thickest point in the crowd and slowed his steps. "Act normal."

"Then let go of me," said Cee. "I can't feel my legs."

Marcus unwound his arm from her waist, and Cee tipped precariously for a second before finding her footing. Together they waded through the gathering, alert for any sign the Brigade was looking for them. But the few officers they saw appeared more bored than anything.

"Where did Finn go?" Cee wondered.

"I'm more worried about Wu," said Marcus, who checked behind them every few steps. "We can't go home. We need to talk."

"Marcus, I—"

"Save it," he said.

Don't let him get you alone, Livian whispered.

"Shut up," said Cee.

"What?" Marcus asked.

"Not you. There's something..." Cee searched for a way to explain or describe Livian, the problem being she wasn't entirely sure what he was.

Marcus saved her some trouble. "Oh, that," he said grimly. "We'll need to sort him out, too, won't we?"

Not if I sort you first, snarled Livian.

"He just saved your life," Cee said.

No he didn't.

"He didn't want to," said Marcus.

"That's your fault," said Cee. "You—you *hatched* him somehow."

Marcus spared her a peculiar glance. "Let's go to the trees," he suggested, and Cee understood he meant their private place near the school. "We can talk about it there."

Cee hesitated. "Livian says I shouldn't. That you're dangerous."

Cee expected him to protest, to assert he would never hurt her, but Marcus merely said, "You've named him." Something about his tone led Cee to believe it was a bad thing. "Well, does *Livian* have anything to say about how dangerous it would be to go home right now? Or to stay here, in full view of the Brigade office?"

Livian remained stubbornly silent, though Cee could feel the heat of his irritation spreading through her. She wanted to hit something, or someone, and she wasn't sure why. She wanted to argue, but reason won out, and she carved her way swiftly through the dispersing people, angling away from the Brigade office and toward the school. Marcus followed, using his height to scan the crowd for signs of motion in their direction. "What is she waiting for?" he murmured.

"They'll wait and do it quietly, like with the Bradshaws and Doughertys," said Cee.

They had made it to the far corner of the common when a familiar and breathless, "Hey!" sent them jumping out of their skins. Turning, they found Guin running after them, Rand taking long strides behind her but unwilling to do anything so undignified as jog. Inside Cee, Livian stirred with interest. *Venison.* Cee ignored him, though it was difficult; Livian's pull, his power, was strengthening at a rapid pace. Fighting him was like an ongoing wrestling match, and it was becoming exhausting.

"Where are you going?" Guin asked as she caught up to them. "We were looking for you, but..." She shook her head.

"We need to get somewhere private," Marcus told her, and when Guin opened her mouth, "No time to talk about why. Come with us and we'll tell you when we get there."

Livian hissed softly, and Cee took a deep breath in the hopes it would cool the burst of heat that surged through her at the idea of Guin sharing her and Marcus's special spot. As Rand caught up to them, Livian said, *This one will be an ally*, and without fully understanding why, Cee was compelled to step closer to Rand. He smiled at her, and a harsh kind of satisfaction flooded Cee. She smiled back. A startled expression crossed Guin's features, and for some reason this delighted Cee; Marcus merely frowned.

"Don't trust him, Cee".

"Who, me?" Rand asked, his brows lowering.

"He saved you," Cee said again.

"*You* saved me. He's the one who wanted me in chains."

"What are you talking about?" Rand demanded.

"I couldn't have saved you without him!" cried Cee.

"Shhh." In two strides Marcus had his hand over her mouth. "We're neither of us safe yet. Come on."

Don't let him touch you. But Cee couldn't help the tiny fireworks of pleasure that went off inside her, even as her face began to tingle under Marcus's palm. Her lips remembered the kiss, and having Marcus touch them again made her heart flutter.

Marcus removed his hand, the light of consternation refracting through his sea-green eyes. He drew back slowly from Cee, the way one might from a snake poised to strike, and started walking.

What is he? Cee asked silently as her cheeks regained feeling. *Which animal has that kind of power?*

Isn't it obvious? Livian sniffed, and Cee felt his contempt as a palpable thudding in her chest keeping time with her heart. *Your little friend there is a Magus.*

CHAPTER

TEN

E *arly signs of transformation may include, but are not limited to: changes in appetite, irritability, depression, headaches, insomnia, and a variety of physical changes that this handbook will go over in subsequent chapters. If you exhibit any of these symptoms, speak to your Transformation Coach right away.*

—Transformation Handbook

"Magus?"

Cee hadn't realized she'd said it aloud until the others swung to look at her. Marcus's mouth dropped open, but then he closed it and shook his head and continued walking. Guin darted an uncertain look at Cee, then at Marcus, and Cee found herself bringing up the rear with Rand.

"Mind filling me in?" Rand asked quietly.

Cee grimaced. "I don't entirely understand it myself,

but... Something is awake inside me, and it doesn't trust Marcus."

Rand's dark eyes focused on Marcus's back. "And he doesn't trust it, either," he surmised.

"Livian says Marcus is a Magus."

"Livian?" Rand's eyebrows lifted. "It has a name?"

Cee looked up, prepared for the same censure Marcus had shown, but Rand was smiling. She couldn't help smiling too. But after a moment her grin faltered. "I don't know what it is. Feels... snaky."

"Dracona?" asked Rand.

Smart boy.

Cee was so startled she almost stopped walking.

Rand misunderstood her hesitation. "No, I know it's not likely. But it is what *he*—" a nod in Marcus's direction, "said before. And if he is a Magus, maybe he knows something we don't."

"It's inside me?" Cee whispered. "How does that work?"

"I don't know," said Rand. "It's definitely not textbook. But then again, Dracona have been extinct for something like three hundred years."

I take it back. Not so smart after all.

Cee bit down on the various responses that sprang to her lips. Suddenly, all she wanted was to go somewhere quiet and safe and talk to herself. Well, to Livian. It felt like the same thing. Even that impulse gave Cee pause; usually she went to Marcus when she needed to talk. But this was a discussion he clearly wasn't open to having.

Did he know he was a Magus? If so, how long had he known? Why hadn't he told her?

Secretive. Liars, Livian hissed.

They had exited the common amidst a stream of Morrowville denizens, the increasing dark aiding their attempts to remain unseen. They stayed with the bulk of the people for a few blocks, but once the masses began to thin and trickle in smaller rivulets towards various neighborhoods, they broke away and slipped into the alleys where houses stood back to back, fences and hedges shielding them from view.

"Where are we going?" Guin asked.

They came to the end of the alley. It was the closest neighborhood to the school, but there was still a large field of grass to cross before the stand of trees. Marcus stopped and turned to Guin and Rand. "It's only fair to tell you... To give you the option... Cee and I are in some trouble, and if you're found with us, it's possible you will be, too."

"Possible," echoed Rand.

"Probable," amended Marcus.

Rand's gaze alighted on Cee. "This have to do with your friend? Livian?"

Cee tried to smile. "He likes you," she told Rand, "If it's any consolation."

"It's not," Marcus said.

"Hey, man," said Rand, "That's not for you to say."

Cee looked from Rand's warm, dark eyes to Marcus's flinty grey-green ones. "We're not equipped to run away," she half whispered.

Rand's eyes traveled to the trees. "You going in there?"

"It won't hide us for long," said Marcus.

Rand nodded. "We'll meet you in a bit." He reached for Guin's hand, which evidently startled her; she looked a question at Marcus, sent an uncertain frown in Cee's direction, then meekly allowed Rand to lead her away.

Cee shivered in the rapidly cooling evening air; it was still spring, and she hadn't expected to be out past sundown. With Livian awake in her and heating her insides, the air around her body felt that much colder by comparison. Marcus's stern features were melted by sympathy and he stepped closer to her, though he was careful not to touch her. Cee basked in the heat she felt wafting from him, the faint lamplight glow of him that he seemed unaware of.

"I'm sorry I'm not wearing a jacket," he said.

Cee shook her head to show it didn't matter. "Are you a Magus?" she asked, her voice sounding as if someone had scraped out her insides.

"We need to cross the field quickly," was all Marcus said. He studied the distance. "Even then they may still be able to follow our prints."

"Not in the dark," Cee said. The only lamps were those by the houses and up around Morrowville Prep; the field and trees were lightless. "But if we don't go soon..." She had no idea if or when the Brigade would get as far as the field, the trees, the school, but it wasn't so dark yet that the motion of two people running across the grass wouldn't be noticed.

Marcus looked at her, his eyebrows lifted and a small smile teasing his lips. For a minute he was just as Cee always pictured him, entirely himself. But then he said, "Did your friend tell you that?"

"I'm not a complete idiot," Cee snapped. "I don't need whatever it is to do my thinking for me."

"What about your talking?" Marcus asked, and Cee pressed her lips tightly together. "You know what it is," Marcus continued. "But it can't be trusted, Cee. Remember that.

"We're going to head for that gap on the left," he went on. "We start on three. One..."

Cee wanted to ask why she should trust him more than, quite literally, her own gut. She wanted to ask why other people morphed into creatures that could be trusted (well, except maybe for Vulpes) but she, for whatever reason, had hatched something inside her that was more like a parasite, something to be hated and possibly feared. And would she ever morph? Or would she simply live like this forever, with Livian feeding off her thoughts and feelings, making her say terrible things and exerting his control whenever he saw fit?

But there was no time for questions. Marcus reached "Three!" and set off at a sprint, his long legs carrying him like an antelope. Cee felt clumsy and plodding as she tried to keep up.

They reached the dark safety of the trees. Marcus switched from sprint to sure and swift steps. He wasn't even short of breath. Cee, on the other hand, was gasping; outside of battledore, Phys Fit had never been one of her strongest courses.

Cee followed the paleness of Marcus's shirt, his misty aura, through the shadows. "Starlight," she murmured.

Marcus glanced back over his shoulder. "What?" His voice was a harsh whisper, a reminder to keep her voice low.

"I was just thinking you won't be able to do your scene with Rand now."

"Yes, I'll have missed my chance at fame."

Cee was walking behind him, so she couldn't see Marcus's face, but from his tone she guessed he wasn't smiling. "This is my fault," she said. "I'm—"

"Don't bother apologizing," said Marcus. "It won't do us any good now."

Cee felt Livian rear up at the implied censure, and she

struggled to squash his desire to throttle Marcus before she could act on it.

"Fine," she said. "Then I'm not sorry." She turned on her heel to go back the other way.

A few seconds later, a hand grabbed her upper arm roughly and spun her back around. "Where are you going?" Marcus hissed.

"To tell them where and what you are," Cee spat. "To turn us both in. Let them fix it."

"There is no fixing it!" Marcus's voice sounded through the trees; he'd forgotten to whisper this time. He took in a deep and shaky breath. "It was bound to happen sooner or later," he said more quietly, though Cee could hear the strain in him. Her right arm was starting to feel numb from his grip, a combination of the physical contact and sheer constriction.

She peered up at Marcus, squinting to see in the near dark. His beautiful eyes had clouds of gold gathering at the edges of the irises. "There you are," she breathed. "Are you the Magus? I saw you before, in the library."

Marcus released his hold and stepped back. The golden clouds were crowding his pupils now, and he stared at Cee avidly in the interested way she'd always wanted Marcus to look at her—except this wasn't Marcus. The tilt of the head, the way he held his mouth, was different. Wrong.

"Do you have a name?" Cee asked.

He stared so long Cee wasn't sure he'd heard her, or whether he spoke English. Then slowly, as if using his tongue for the first time, he said, "Diodoric." Die-AH-door-ick.

Inside Cee, Livian hissed.

"Your serpent doesn't like me," Diodoric said.

"How does it work, two people in one body?" asked Cee.

She had a terrible mental picture of Marcus pinned down inside his own form, fighting for supremacy, clawing frantically for control.

"I'm everything he aspires to be," said Diodoric. "Eventually we'll be one and the same."

A strong, bitter taste burned its way up Cee's throat and flooded her mouth. "What do you mean?"

But the gold in his eyes was receding like a tide going out. "I can't," Diodoric murmured. "Not strong enough yet." An arc of gold like a shooting star fell across his left iris. "You're very pretty, you know."

Cee opened her mouth to demand what he meant by calling her pretty, and—more importantly, she supposed—what it would mean for Marcus if he and Diodoric became "one and the same." But now Marcus stood before her, all himself and scowling, and Cee lost her nerve.

Better off never changing at all, whispered Livian, *than becoming one of* them.

"And now I guess we know each other, truly, for the first time in our lives," said Marcus.

ELEVEN

*agus (pl. Magi) – a member of the ruling Clan responsible for making and enforcing the law*

—Concise Guide to the Clans

"You're not Diodoric," said Cee, "any more than I'm Livian."

"But I will be," said Marcus. "It's not like with Arlon, who will always be Arlon, even if he is an eagle. Once a Magus is strong enough to take his true form..."

Cee didn't ask how he knew all this. Marcus knew enough on his own, and she suspected Diodoric had been whispering in Marcus's ears same as Livian had begun whispering in hers. What she did ask was, "How long?"

Marcus's eyebrow quirked a question.

"How long have you known about Diodoric?"

Marcus turned and began walking slowly, deeper into

the trees. Cee kept pace beside him and wished she could hold his hand.

"I thought I was hearing voices," Marcus said at last. "I thought I was going crazy."

Cee's heart tightened. The idea of Marcus going through something so terrifying and never telling her... "Why didn't you say anything?" she asked.

"Oh, Cee," Marcus sighed, and for the first time in a long while she heard affection in his tone, "I couldn't do that to you. You rely on me to be perfect. How could I frighten you with the possibility I'm not?"

Cee tried to wrap her thoughts around Marcus's logic but kept coming to the conclusion that it was his vanity that kept him from being forthcoming about Diodoric. She didn't say it, though. Marcus was finally opening up, and she didn't want to do anything that might make that box slam shut again.

From the dark branches of the trees above them came the rustle of leaves, the scrabble of claws on bark, the flap of heavy wings. Cee wanted to ask Marcus more about Diodoric, but Marcus had stopped walking and was looking upward. Cee followed the direction of his gaze but couldn't see anything but the black on black of trees against the night sky.

Livian must have sensed something, however, because without conscious thought, Cee turned to her right just as Guin stepped silently through the opening created by a couple of conjoined oaks. *You're sure we can't eat her?*

Cee had to admit she was hungry; they hadn't eaten at Community Day.

Just let me...

Cee felt something push at her fingers from the inside as if trying to stretch them. Sharp pain seared her nose, mouth, face as Livian attempted to force her features forward into something longer and narrower. "Stop it!" Cee screamed. "What are you doing?"

Guin froze.

We can't eat her if we stay in this form.

Cee's shoulders were rising as if spires of bone were growing there. "I don't want to eat anybody!"

But we're hungry. There was genuine confusion in Cee now, but at least Livian stopped trying to transform her. She felt her body collapse into its familiar, normal shape while within her Livian swayed from side to side like a riled snake.

"What just happened?" asked Guin. She was rooted in place, and even in the dark Cee could see she was trembling. But Cee was shaking harder, her chest burning as if bile were boiling inside her.

"The dragon is getting stronger. Cee is on the brink of morphing."

Cee whirled and discovered a taller, thinner figure standing beside Marcus. Someone dressed in pale robes that gathered the little bit of light and held it, making him appear to shimmer and glow more so even than Marcus. "Arlon!" Cee exclaimed.

Arlon inclined his head, his long, dark hair swaying with the motion. "He's left some holes in your shirt."

Cee glanced at her shoulders and saw where the material had suffered for having the start of dragon wings pushed through it.

"You'll need Forma fabric," Arlon went on. "If you don't want to end up without clothes."

With a pang, Cee thought of how, for most Changers, this would be the moment their foster mother would begin work on robes for the Relinquishing. Word would go to the

Administrators and out to the Clan, ostensibly to be received with great joy. "I don't have a Clan, though, do I?" Cee realized. There was no one to take her in or teach her. She was utterly alone in the world.

Arlon glanced at his brother, and Marcus dropped his gaze. "The Dracona were wiped out by the Magi some three hundred years ago," said Arlon. "Or so we thought."

"Hey, what's going on?" Rand appeared behind Guin, a large duffel bag over each shoulder.

But Guin seemed incapable of speaking or moving, and Marcus only continued to stare at the ground.

"There must be *someone*," Cee said, thinking aloud now. "I had to come from *somewhere*."

"Arlon?" Rand asked whoever was listening. "What's he doing here?" And when no one answered, he asked Arlon directly, "What are you doing here?"

Marcus finally lifted his head. "We've been meeting."

Guin broke free of her stasis, and Cee noticed she was clutching a couple of grease-spotted white bags, the kind that came from the Morrowville Diner. Her stomach growled, or Livian did; it came to the same thing. Except it must have been audible because Guin froze again.

"You'd better feed it," Arlon advised. "Or you really won't be able to stop it from doing something you'll regret."

"He has a name," said Cee.

"You named it?" Arlon asked.

"Why does everyone act like that's a bad thing?" Cee countered.

"Names have power," said Arlon. "Once you give something a name, it becomes real. You form an attachment. That makes it harder to get rid of."

Cee took an instinctive step backward.

Movement on her right drew Cee's attention. Rand

stepped forward and snatched the bags from Guin's hands. "You said we should feed it, right?" He walked over to where Cee stood and dropped neatly to the ground with a grace his size belied. "Come on, then. Let's eat."

Cee sat, and after a moment Guin drifted closer and settled on Rand's other side. Rand handed around toasted sandwiches and fished bottles of water from one of the duffels. "You gonna eat?" he asked Marcus and Arlon.

Marcus shifted uneasily on his feet. "We should keep moving."

"To where?" Rand asked. He waved a sandwich at Marcus. "You won't get far with nothing to fuel you."

Arlon walked over—his robes made him appear to float, and Cee wondered absently whether he had shoes—and sat down beside Cee. After a moment, Marcus joined him and completed the circle by inserting himself between his brother and Guin. Rand handed each of them a wrapped sandwich. "I didn't know what you liked, so..."

Cee felt like she could eat just about anything and devoured the now tepid pastrami and cheese melt without really tasting it. Livian purred; Cee could feel the low thrum of it in her sternum.

"So why are you here?" Rand asked as Arlon picked at the lettuce in his sandwich. Had he always done that? Cee wondered. Or was it an adopted habit from living with eagles?

Arlon glanced at where Marcus was dutifully nibbling his dinner.

"You knew," said Cee.

"Knew what?" asked Rand.

"About Diodoric," Cee said.

Next to Marcus, Guin flinched. "You knew, too," Cee realized. "Am I the only one who *didn't* know?"

"I have no idea what we're talking about," said Rand around a mouthful of roast beef. "So I guess I still don't know."

"Marcus is a Magus," said Cee. "Or Diodoric is, and Marcus is, what? Hosting him?" She looked to Marcus, but it was Arlon who answered.

"Neither Magi nor Dracona have typical transformation cycles. We don't know much about Dracona," he admitted with a nod to indicate Cee, "and the Magi are somewhat secretive about it, but we do know that they don't change form so much as resolve into a new persona."

"Diodoric is Marcus's Magus persona," Cee told Rand.

"You've met him?" Rand asked. He cocked an eye at Marcus.

"A few minutes ago," said Cee. She asked Marcus, "What did it feel like when he...?" She wasn't sure how to finish the question.

Marcus answered by jumping to his feet. "We really should get moving."

"They've stopped for the night," said Arlon. "But they'll pick up again once there's enough light. I was circling," he explained when he saw Cee's confused expression.

They gathered their wrappers and bottles. "Where can we go?" Guin asked. Her voice sounded broken, as if someone had taken a hammer to her insides.

"*You* can go home," Marcus told her. "You'll only be in trouble if they find you with us."

"Well, I brought stuff," said Rand, patting a duffel, "so I'm not going home."

"They will notice your absence soon anyway, if they haven't already," Arlon said. "It may no longer be safe for you to go home.

"You should put distance while it's still dark," he went on. He rose. "I'll make one more circle to be sure it's safe."

"Are you allowed to help us?" Cee asked.

A corner of Arlon's mouth twitched. "Each Clan has its own rules about..." He sought the appropriate word and settled on, "*Attachments* to our previous lives." He glanced in Marcus's direction. "My circumstances were somewhat different from most. We don't usually have siblings, and it's even more rare to be dealing with a burgeoning Magus."

"You mean it's a political benefit to the Aerie to have a connection with the Magi," said Marcus dully.

Arlon placed a hand on his shoulder. "I mean someone I care for is in a precarious situation. The politics are beside the point."

Marcus looked up in surprise. Arlon stepped back and in one fluid movement that Cee thought should have been impossible, he threw open his arm only to have the sleeves of his robes form into feathers. In a blink, the eagle had soared up and out of their midst.

"He's gotten good at that," Rand remarked.

No one spoke as they crumpled the sandwich wrappers and meal bags, took last swigs of and capped their water bottles. Rand held a duffel out to Marcus, who ignored it, so Cee stepped up to take it.

"Blankets, more water, some snacks," Rand told her. "Won't last us more than a couple days, though, and that's if we ration. Where are we going?"

"To the Far Eastern Wilderness," said Marcus, his voice floating back to where they stood. "We need to find out what really happened."

CHAPTER

TWELVE

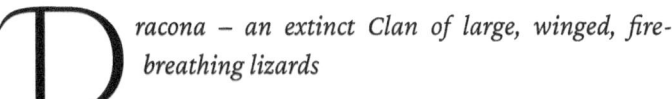 *racona – an extinct Clan of large, winged, fire-breathing lizards*

—Concise Guide to the Clans

"WE KNOW WHAT HAPPENED, don't we?" Rand asked.

At the same time, Cee said, "What about Annice and her parents and Mr. Dougherty?"

Beside Cee, Rand jolted, and Cee knew—or Livian did—before he spoke what he would say. *Don't let him leave.* Impulsively, Cee reached out and grabbed Rand's wrist as he said, "I'll get them. Where are they?"

Rand's eyes met Cee's, and he must have seen how frightened she was because he added, "I'll be fine. I'll catch up."

Cee felt Guin's big brown eyes searing the place where Cee's hand met Rand's flesh, and with effort Cee forced her fingers one by one to release their grip. She nodded wood-

91

enly at Rand's assurance while still seeking an argument that would deter him.

Marcus did Cee's work for her by demanding, "What's the point in rescuing them?" At Rand's scowl, Marcus pressed, "What would you do? Lead them off into the woods? They may not even be well enough for that. It seems unlikely you'll convince Mr. Dougherty to come back to the Wilds. The best way to help them is to go to the source."

"What source?" Guin asked, her voice faint and unsteady.

Marcus looked at her and his expression softened, and in that moment Cee wasn't sure if she wouldn't eat Guin after all. "We have to find out what drove Mr. Dougherty back to Morrowville. And why the town administrators would want to keep him from saying anything."

"In that case, why not just go get him? He's closer than the Far Eastern Wilderness," said Rand.

This time Marcus glanced at Cee. "You heard Arlon. We need to put distance—"

" 'Whenever they catch you, they will kill you,'" Cee quoted, the words rising suddenly inside her, a memory of a book she'd once read, something she'd found on her mother's shelf. Something she probably wouldn't have been allowed to read if she hadn't secreted it away, plugging the spot on the shelf with another book, one prescribed by the teachers but far less interesting. " 'But first they much catch you.'"

Both Rand and Guin appeared mystified, but Marcus gave a short, sharp nod as if the words made perfect sense.

"Go ahead and get them if you want," Marcus told Rand. "Mr. Dougherty and the others. But I don't know what you plan to do with them once you have them. Assuming you can get them out at all."

It was all but an outright dare, and Cee sensed Rand was apt to take Marcus up on it. She gave Rand her most pleading look, begging him with her eyes not to go. When Rand turned and saw it, his shoulders fell and the fight went out of him.

Well, *that* fight anyway.

Cee could see anger and determination continue to burn deep in Rand's eyes. He was picking his battles, and with a mixture of gratification and relief, Cee realized the battle Rand was choosing this time was her.

"If anything happens to them while were out tromping through the forest," said Rand, "it's on you."

Cee wasn't sure if he was speaking to her or to Marcus. Maybe it didn't matter. She felt selfish for wanting to keep Rand with her and guilty for the relief of having succeeded.

They pressed on, Marcus leading, Guin after him, and Cee and Rand as close to side-by-side as they could manage through the trees. Now and then Guin would glance back at them; Cee only knew it from the swing of Guin's long hair, the crescent of her features flashing at them and disappearing again in the dimness. More than once Rand reached for Cee's hand, guiding her over roots and under low branches, and Cee found his warmth and sturdiness comforting.

After a while, Cee realized Livian had gone quiet. She no longer felt hot inside. *Livian?* she asked silently, and she felt something stir, as if shifting in its sleep, but there was no other answer.

"What's wrong?" Rand whispered, and Cee jumped at the soft sound of his voice, which sounded loud after the silence. In the dark Cee wasn't even sure how Rand could tell anything was bothering her.

"Livian," she whispered back. "He's gone quiet."

"Do they sleep?" asked Rand.

"I don't know. Maybe."

"We've got to find you somebody who *does* know." And with a glance at Marcus, "And doesn't hold it against you."

Cee wanted to protest that Marcus didn't hold anything against her, that he was only concerned for her, but her throat went dry and the words got stuck.

Rand put out a hand and stopped Cee's progress, and her tongue came loose, ready to turn her objection in a different direction. But then she saw Marcus had stopped, and Guin, and Rand was only preventing her from walking into them. They'd come to the end of the trees; from here they would need to walk in the open to the Eastbound Road. That road was bordered by farms and open spaces on its way out of Morrowville. And while in theory they knew what lay beyond—they'd taken Geography, after all—in truth none of them was certain.

Marcus turned to address them. "We'll need to move quickly and hope to find more cover before daylight."

They nodded their understanding. If Marcus's estimates were accurate, it was two days' walk to the Far Eastern Wilderness, or whatever was left of it. Between that and where they stood, there was the road and, if the maps they'd learned from were to be believed, no other towns. But there were hills, and streams, and most likely a few clumps of trees along the way.

Cee wondered whether the Brigade would bother pursuing them once it became clear they'd left town.

The Eastbound Road was not paved, at least not this far out, but Marcus kept them to the verges anyway. They trudged through the thick, newly sprouted grass, and Cee could feel the evening dew begin to seep through the toes of her shoes. She tried to pick her feet up, but she was too tired, and finally resigned herself to wet socks. They passed a few thickets that would have served for cover, but Marcus insisted they keep going. "We need to use the darkness to our advantage," he told them. "We'll stop closer to dawn."

By the time the eastern horizon began to turn lavender-gray, Cee could barely keep her eyes open. Marcus turned away from the road, steering them toward a copse some yards north. Cee didn't think she could take one more step, much less make it across the gentle rolls of grassy earth, but somehow she did. It was only as they came to the trees that she realized Rand was supporting her elbow; she wondered for how long.

The birds, only just cheering the morning, fell silent as they entered the stand of trees. Guin, Rand and Cee waded in after Marcus, exhausted, and found a relatively flat and clear space to spread the blankets. Cee collapsed onto one, legs aching, and was instantly asleep.

It was Livian who woke her; like a fire kindled in her stomach, Cee felt something flare within her. She opened her eyes and was greeted by the dizzying stretch of trees above her, the sun flashing into her eyes now and then as the slight breeze pushed leaves aside. Cee lolled, disoriented and still tired. She would have gladly gone back to sleep, but then Livian hissed, *They are coming.*

"Who?" The word came out weak and poorly formed, her lips hardly moving.

But then she heard it, though what it was, Cee wasn't sure. She'd never heard anything like it, a steady thrumming that echoed like thunder but was far too regular for a natural phenomenon. Cee sat up and squinted against the sunlight; the breeze had picked up as though a storm were coming, and the tree branches tossed as if caught in a whirlwind.

To Cee's right, Rand woke and propped himself on his elbows. To her left, Guin remained undisturbed, but on the other side of Guin, Marcus jumped to his feet.

"What is it?" Cee asked. The sound was growing louder, a choppy noise, as if the air itself was being cut.

"I've read about these," said Marcus, his voice almost lost in the uproar of thrashing trees, "but I didn't think they really existed."

Rand jumped over Cee and shook Guin into consciousness, directed her to gather up her blanket. Marcus appeared frozen as he stared up at the bit of sky available to them, and Cee was the same; she felt powerless to move, eyes turned to the treetops.

Something dark passed above them.

Cee recalled a day at Lake Morrowville when she'd dived under the clear water and a boat had passed over her, briefly blotting the light. This was similar. The shadow passed, roaring, and its echo began to fade. *Is it another Dracona?* Cee asked silently. The idea both terrified and exhilarated her. On the one hand: Dragon. On the other: Family?

Guin and Rand were stuffing blankets into the duffel bags; as Rand pulled her blanket from under her, Cee rolled off and struggled to her feet, her leg muscles and sore feet protesting. Marcus continued to stand there, and Cee could tell by the way he cocked his head, and the way his brilliant green eyes darted from side to side, he was listening and thinking.

"We can't go anywhere yet," Marcus declared. "It's full daylight, and there isn't any cover."

"What was that thing?" Rand asked.

The blankets away, Guin began pulling out bottles of water and packets of crackers and distributing them. Cee took them automatically as Guin nudged them against her hand.

"A helicopter, I think," said Marcus as he accepted Guin's offering. He sank to the ground, and soon they were all seated in a circle, nibbling at what passed for breakfast, though based on the sun it had to be after lunchtime.

"What's a helicopter?" Cee asked while quietly prodding at Livian. He was awake in there, she could tell—his warmth filled her, and she sensed his alertness—but he was still and quiet.

"A flying machine," said Marcus.

Rand snorted. "No such thing."

Marcus didn't respond, and they continued to eat in silence until Livian said, *Again.*

"Again?" Cee echoed aloud.

"What again?" Guin asked, voice quaking.

Marcus looked at Cee from across their small circle, and she had the fleeting, breathtaking thought that this was what he looked like upon waking: the untidy hair and rumpled clothing offset by wide, clear eyes. Eyes that were getting wider by the second.

"They're coming back," said Marcus.

CHAPTER
THIRTEEN

H *elicopter (n.) – a flying vehicle sporting revolving blades, or rotors, that allow it to move both horizontally and vertically through the air*

—Halpern's Book of Imaginary Inventions

EVEN AS MARCUS SPOKE, that thrumming, chopping sound became faintly discernable. For a long moment, they all sat there, frozen, and stared at one another. Finally, Rand asked, "So what exactly is a helicopter?"

"A faster way for them to find us," said Marcus. The words broke their stasis and spurred them to action. Each of them tossed their bottles of water and whatever remained of their crackers into the duffels. But after that, they were at a standstill.

"We need to stay as much under the trees as possible," Marcus instructed.

"Who are they?" Cee asked. She couldn't imagine

Morrowville's Brigade in some kind of flying contraption. Driving a car was complicated enough, wasn't it? And why go to such lengths to find four kids?

Marcus shook his head, leaving Cee to assume he didn't know and wasn't willing to hypothesize.

The noise was getting steadily louder. Cee felt as if someone were pressing their hands against her ears and then taking them off again, rapidly. It hurt her head.

Marcus waved them out of the clearing they'd slept in and into where the trees were closer together. Still, as the coming helicopter began to whip the branches above them into frenzy, Cee couldn't help feeling exposed.

Let me help.

Cee started; she'd forgotten Livian was even there.

You're getting used to me, Livian explained. *That's as it should be. Now let me help.*

"Help how?" Cee whispered. The others couldn't hear her above the manufactured thunder. Each had flattened him- or herself as much as possible against the available tree trunks.

Will you let me out?

Cee's heart seized up at the thought of transforming. "I can't. I—I don't have any other clothes."

You'd rather die clothed than live naked? Livian sounded honestly perplexed, and Cee had to admit it sounded silly. Yet somehow it was true. Her eyes traveled to where the others were looking fearfully up to the sky as if waiting for lightning to strike, stopping finally on Marcus. "Why can't *he* do anything?"

Livian snorted, and Cee felt it as a short, hot blast in her chest.

Cee studied Marcus's tense, stricken features; was it possible he'd become even paler and thinner? Shadows under his eyes made them all the greener and more brilliant by contrast, and his springy hair moved with the force of the helicopter's approach.

He sensed her looking and turned, his lips a thin, ruddy slash. And suddenly Cee realized Marcus was frightened, truly frightened. It hadn't occurred to her that anything bad was likely happen to them, not really, but Marcus not only believed it *could* but that *it was going to*. Marcus, who'd reached the end of his powers of intellect... Cee had always trusted nothing bad could happen to her when Marcus was there. But this time he was the one who needed help.

"Do it," she said.

Marcus saw her lips move and looked a question at her, gave his head a tiny shake to show he couldn't hear her.

The roaring of the helicopter was almost directly above them now, and everyone ducked instinctively against the noise and whipping wind.

"Do it!" Cee screamed.

Heat spread through her. Cee's face elongated, her arms extended, her nails formed into claws, and her feet became suddenly very heavy. The bony spires erupted from her shoulders, and Cee was compelled to double over to allow the wings to grow.

Throughout, Cee fought the urge to resist, though her instinct was to do just that. The transformation was less painful than when Livian had tried before, possibly because this time she allowed it to happen. She wondered what she looked like, caught a glimpse of iridescent red scales, and realized her eyesight had become sharper; all the details of the trees around her impressed themselves upon her brain: the cracks and flakes in the bark, the saw-tooth edges of the leaves, and every little spot and insect thereupon.

How big was she? Cee realized she was at eye level with

roughly the middle of the trees. She looked down and saw her friends pushing themselves even harder against the trunks, making way for Cee's—or Livian's, she supposed—tail as it snaked by.

Yes, we're very pretty, said Livian impatiently. *But we haven't time for showing off just now.*

The massive wings began to move, slowly at first, gathering speed that put the force of the helicopter's artificial wind to shame. Cee realized she had no control over what was happening. It was all Livian, and she was housed inside him somehow, along for the ride.

It was equal parts thrilling and petrifying, bursting through the treetops and being free of gravity. Cee would have liked to spend more time experiencing it, but there was the helicopter, like a massive black bug, and Livian went right for it.

Cee supposed if she could adhere herself to a kite—this would be a similar sensation. Only kites didn't attack helicopters. They didn't have massive claws and teeth and jaws, and kites didn't get angry.

The helicopter pilot, when he spotted Livian, tilted away. But Livian was half again as large as the machine and far more agile. He ducked under and butted upward, knocking the helicopter further sideways. It was clear to Cee it would crash, but Livian was having too much fun to allow it. He reached out and grabbed the helicopter, began to crush it with his massive claws, careful to avoid the rotor.

Cee caught a glimpse of the pilots, two of them, their faces horror struck as the walls imploded around them. *Livian, no!*

Livian didn't even hesitate as he asked, *What do you mean, 'no'?*

Don't kill them!

You realize I'm in control now. I don't have to do anything you say.

Was that true? Could Livian decide to stay in dragon form, leaving her trapped inside him? Even as panic at the idea began to well up, Cee discovered they were touching down on the clearing near the copse. Livian set the helicopter down and, the rotor no longer functioning, peeled back the top.

Together they looked down into the machine at the two men cowering, their gibbering punctuated with yells that Cee supposed were meant to scare her and Livian away. Then Cee felt all the anger run out of Livian like water down a drain. Still, he cocked an eye at them and growled for good measure. The men curled into balls, arms over their heads. *Ridiculous,* snorted Livian.

From the edge of the thicket, Marcus, Rand, and Guin ventured out looking as stricken as the men in the helicopter. They crossed the grass, and Cee was sorry to see Marcus and Guin hanging back, uncertain, while Rand plowed ahead. He came right up to Livian's side. "Cee?"

Livian lowered his head and Cee looked Rand in the eye.

"Are you in there?" Rand asked. "Do dragons speak?"

No. Cee heard it, but of course Rand could not.

It's not safe to change form yet, Livian continued. *We must do something about* them. He raised his head again and stuck his massive nose into the opening he'd ripped in the helicopter. The men yelled some more. Livian withdrew, picked up the helicopter, turned it upside down, and shook. The yelling stopped as the men fell out onto the grass. They glanced up at Livian and rolled themselves into balls again.

Why do they keep doing that? Livian asked. *It won't help them.*

Livian finished crumpling the helicopter until all that remained was a ball of metal with bent blades sticking up at odd angles.

Panic threatened Cee once more; she didn't know what Livian was planning to do and couldn't stop him if it was something terrible. But then Marcus stepped forward. He glanced briefly up at Livian then turned his attention to the two men. "Who are you?"

The men unfolded themselves just enough to look at Marcus, though they couldn't keep their eyes from darting now and again to the dragon towering above.

"He won't hurt you," Marcus promised.

Oh, and I supposed he'd stop me if I tried? Livian snorted.

"I'm guessing it's going to be a long walk for you," Marcus went on. "You're not from Morrowville. Where *are* you from?"

The men unbent a little more, so they were sitting on the grass, now staring openly at Livian. Via Livian's keen eyesight, Cee could read name patches on the men's uniforms: Grantham and Hayes. Grantham was round-faced and sturdy looking, and Hayes was thinner and more angular. Marcus was right, they were no one Cee recognized from Morrowville.

"They're from Suttercliff," Guin said suddenly, and when everyone swiveled to look at her, she blushed. "They're trying so hard *not* to say it, it's, like, loud in their minds."

Rand reached over and squeezed Guin's hand.

"Are you a registered telepath?" Grantham demanded as he climbed to his feet. "They didn't say any of you were —"Livian leaned in a little closer, and Grantham took several steps backward.

"I'd say that's low on your list of worries at the

moment," remarked Marcus. "You were looking for us, but why? Why would anyone from as far away as Suttercliff be called to search for four kids from Morrowville?"

Grantham put his fists to his hips and appeared prepared to lecture if not threaten, but Livian growled from deep in his throat and gave Grantham second—and possibly third—thoughts. It was Hayes who wobbled to his feet and answered. "We were the nearest town with a helicopter."

"Not anymore," Rand murmured.

"We haven't done anything wrong!" said Guin.

"Says the unregistered telepath with a dragon for a friend," Grantham pointed out.

"I thought these were, uh..." Hayes peered up at Livian. "Extinct?"

"I pretty sure there's nothing illegal in one being a Dracona. Unusual, but not illegal," Marcus said.

"Destruction of public property, on the other hand," said Grantham, and Livian leaned in, his massive red snout inches from Grantham's own bulbous nose. Cee smelled the sourness of sweat and fear and tried to hold her breath against it, but she had no breath to hold.

This time Grantham did not move, only glared back at the beast. "I'm not afraid of—"

Cee was aware of Livian's intent only a split second before it happened, and even with more time she couldn't have stopped him. Admittedly, though, part of her *didn't* want to stop him. Part of her was just as irritated and offended by Grantham as Livian was, and when Livian opened his jaws and stuck out his tongue, drawing Grantham into his maw with it, that part of Cee was satisfied.

But a much bigger part of her was horrified. *Livian, no!*

Grantham was gone; Livian hadn't even chewed, just swallowed the man whole.

If she could have been sick, she would have been. But she had no physical form; she existed only in consciousness. She was free floating, like hot air contained only by the massive shape of Livian around her.

Cee was desperate to see the others' reactions, and Livian did her the courtesy of looking at everyone in turn. There was no screaming, just a throbbing silence. Rand and Guin wore identical expressions of horror, and Hayes was trembling, his mouth open in disbelief. Only Marcus appeared unmoved.

"I hope, Mr. Hayes, *you* have a healthy respect for the appetites of Dracona," Marcus said.

Cee caught a glimpse of gold in Marcus's eyes before Livian returned his attention to Hayes, moving his snout close to the man and giving him a snort that blew back Hayes's hair. Hayes let out a thin, high scream and collapsed to his knees.

"No!" Guin cried, bringing her hands to her face as if she couldn't bear to see the dragon eat anyone else.

Rand ducked around Marcus and Livian and took Hayes by the arm, half leading and half dragging him away, back toward the dirt track that was the Eastbound Road in that part of the world. "That way," Rand told him, pointing. "About a day's walk to Morrowville. Go. Now!"

Hayes stumble-ran for the road.

"You shouldn't have done that," Marcus told Rand.

"Done what?"

"Let him go. Now he knows about Guin, about the Dracona."

Rand stared hard at Marcus. "You think we should have killed him?" Then, "What's wrong with your eyes?"

"Nothing is wrong with them. And we could have tied him up, at least given ourselves more time."

Guin tiptoed over to stand beside Rand. "No, there *is* something..."

Get me a look at him, Cee begged Livian. *I need to see his eyes.* But around her, she could feel Livian beginning to fold. It was as if he could no longer hold his own weight and was pressing in on her from every side, suffocating her. The hot air balloon was deflating.

"It will take him a day to get back to Morrowville," said Rand. "By then we might be to the Far Eastern Wilderness, or at least very close."

Livian's head drooped, and as Marcus turned to look, Cee caught a glimpse of the gold radiating from around his pupils, stretching like a starburst through the green of Marcus's natural eyes. *Diodoric.* It was all she had time to think before the dead weight of the dragon snuffed her consciousness.

CHAPTER

FOURTEEN

S o that every Foster receives the attention and affection necessary to emotional growth, only one Pre-Morph shall be assigned to any given household at any time, unless the Placement Officer submits a case for exception. Such cases shall be reviewed and ruled on by the Magistrate.

—Magistrates' Guidelines

SHE WOKE WRAPPED IN A BLANKET.

"Sorry," Guin said, "but there was nothing left of your clothes."

Cee didn't have time to be horrified at the prospect of her nudity; she rolled over and was sick in the grass. The memory of Grantham came full into her mind—she'd *eaten* a person. The idea made her stomach heave again, but it was too empty to produce anything more. A bottle of water appeared, and Cee shakily took it. She sat up and looked around. They were back in the trees. "Rand carried you," Guin explained, and the horror did hit Cee then; a burning far greater than anything Livian could inspire flooded Cee's cheeks.

"Arlon was here," Guin went on. "He'll be back with something for you to wear."

Cee remembered Arlon telling her she'd need Forma fabric once she started morphing. The idea of walking around in the kind of cassock Arlon wore was not appealing. But better than a blanket, Cee supposed.

Thinking of the blanket made Cee aware of the scratchiness of the fabric, and all at once she itched all over. She wriggled uncomfortably and looked around, trying to think of something else.

The boys were nowhere in sight. "Diodoric," Cee remembered.

"The Magus," said Guin. "The one in Marcus. What about him?"

"That was him, with the golden eyes," said Cee. "You saw, didn't you?"

Guin's eyes went to the trees. "Yes. I mean, Marcus told me, you know, telepathically, but ..."

The bald admission of Marcus having willingly connected with Guin so personally shot through Cee like an arrow. She reached into herself in search of Livian, who she'd come to think of as anger personified, but found nothing. Inside she was cold and empty, filled with ash of a long dead fire.

A new panic crawled up Cee's throat. Was Livian gone?

"What's wrong?" Guin asked.

Cee shook her head, unable to voice her fear. Something told her she should be relieved at the prospect of being free of the dragon, but she wasn't, not at all.

Above them, something flapped through the canopy of leaves, and seconds later not one but two large eagles swooped, morphing into Arlon and a woman Cee did not know. She was a head shorter than Arlon, and more rotund than he, but had a similarly straight nose. Her dark hair showed glints of auburn where the sun struck it.

Arlon stepped forward, smiling, and a pang ran through Cee when she saw the way he reached back and took the woman's hand, drawing her forward. "Cee, Guin, this is Ernesta."

Only as Ernesta knelt did Cee notice she held a bundle of cloth in one hand. "I've brought you something to wear," she said. Cee's thoughts about the Aerie robes must have showed on her face, because Ernesta clucked. "No, not like ours. Each clan designs clothes that suit their mode of transformation. I'm not sure what's best for Dracona, but I tried to make something you'd at least like."

"Make?" Cee asked.

Ernesta's caramel-colored eyes crinkled, though her smile was a tad sad. "I'm sorry you won't get your ceremony. But I—we—" She glanced back at Arlon. "We thought you should have something special anyway."

"I'm going to find Marcus," said Arlon. He made a diplomatic departure, striding off into the thick of the trees.

Cee blinked rapidly and focused on the bunch of material in Ernesta's lap. Her hands, Cee noticed, were long and thin—surprising given Ernesta's somewhat soft, round shape—and the nails on them looked thick and strong. "Like claws," Ernesta agreed, and Cee looked up sharply.

Ernesta only looked back at her, kindness radiating from her eyes and smile. After a minute, Cee sighed and said, "Thank you. I may not need... I mean, I need the clothes, but... I don't know if I can transform again. I think...

I think Livian may be gone." She couldn't keep her voice from breaking over the last few words as her throat tried to close itself off.

Ernesta laid a hand on Cee's forearm where it extended from under the blanket, and Cee felt calm wash over her like a warm bath. She also saw flashes of somewhere high... A mountain? The tallest trees Cee had ever seen were there, standing straight and bushy as they crowded the steep slopes. It took Cee a moment to realize she was seeing the Aerie home territory.

"He's asleep," Ernesta said gently. "It took an awful lot of energy to do what he did. He'll probably be out for a while."

Guin's big, brown eyes danced from Ernesta to Cee and back again, and Cee felt her sense of warm peace fade against a fresh wave of Guin's visible anxiety and uncertainty.

Ernesta removed her hand from Cee's arm, and silence settled over Cee's brain. "Why don't we get you dressed?" the Aerie suggested. "And then we can eat."

The mention of food both made Cee's stomach growl and reminded her again of Grantham. Did he count as a meal? Cee put the back of a hand to her mouth, afraid she might be sick again.

"You shouldn't be reading her," Guin said, her voice uncharacteristically strident. "Not without her permission."

Ernesta paused in unfolding the clothes she'd bought, but her smile remained genuine and kind. "You'll learn," she promised. "When someone might be suffering, it *is* permitted, so long as you mean to help them."

Guin frowned as she considered. "Seems a bit loose."

"There's no tight way to rule something like telepathy,"

said Ernesta then added in a grim undertone, "Except to attempt to obliterate it altogether."

Cee drew in a breath to ask what that meant, but Ernesta was shaking out the dress she'd made. "I had to work on the quick, but it's Forma. Here, I brought a sweater, too, since it's still chill nights. But that's not Forma, so try to take it off before you morph."

Cee reached out and touched the material, which was a deep and lovely blue and silky soft against her fingertips. The dress was simple, sleeveless, in a wrap-around style that tied with a sash. Ernesta had added some stitched designs to the collar and hem, pearly white star-like swirls and spatters that made Cee think of the night sky. The sweater was a simple white cardigan with tiny iridescent buttons. Cee thought of her Dracona form and felt too cumbersome for such nice clothes.

"Come on, now, let's get you up and dressed," Ernesta cooed. She'd brought underthings, too, and sandals, all slightly too large, but better than nothing.

Ernesta held up the blanket as a kind of curtain and Cee dressed. She felt refreshed but also unworthy, and as Ernesta lowered the covering, Cee impulsively threw her arms around the woman. "Thank you."

"Of course, sweetheart." And one of those strong, lean hands stroked Cee's hair.

"Why are you helping us?" Guin asked.

Ernesta gently set Cee apart and said, "Marcus is Arlon's brother."

"So?" Guin persisted. "I thought Clans didn't interfere with—" She waved a hand.

Ernesta cocked her head, birdlike. "Do you feel as if we're interfering?"

"They're *helping*, Guin," Cee said. "Just be grateful."

Guin pressed her lips together, and Cee could see her jawline tense as she gritted her teeth. But she didn't protest further.

"Food?" Ernesta suggested. She draped the blanket over her arm and set off in the direction Arlon had gone. Cee was quick to follow; Guin trailed behind.

They found the boys seated in a patch of grass, and Cee was sure their expressions had been grave in the fleeting moment before they'd heard and seen her, Ernesta, and Guin come through the trees. Then they were suddenly smiling—at least, Arlon and Rand were. Marcus continued to look dour, as if he'd swallowed something foul. Yet he was first to rise when the women appeared, Arlon and Rand rapidly following suit as Marcus gestured the women into the circle as if offering them seats at a fine restaurant. Cee had always admired Marcus's manners, but just then she found them brittle and absurd.

Ernesta settled next to Arlon, and Cee sat between her and Rand, with Guin rounding to the far side to sit between Rand and Marcus. Cee saw Guin's own visage was solemn; she darted glances at Ernesta, her expressive eyes giving away every inch of her wariness so that Ernesta wouldn't even need to use telepathy to know how little Guin trusted her. Cee wanted to demand why Guin was so suspicious, but then Ernesta reached over and squeezed Cee's hand. It was small and quick, but Cee read the gesture clearly: *Not now. Give it time. Everything will be all right.*

Marcus saw the gesture, and Rand too, but though each raised his brows, neither said anything. Instead, it was Arlon who spoke, his voice oddly cheerful in the face of all the seriousness. "Well, now, who's hungry?"

He didn't wait for an answer, instead pulling out of seemingly nowhere a bag from which he extracted sandwiches, apples, bananas, one orange, and some bags of chips. "I know it's nothing fancy," Arlon went on, handing around the goods, "and you'll have to share the orange, but I assumed raw fish wouldn't be to your taste."

Or raw human, Cee thought, and her stomach flipped over again. She was starving, which seemed impossible since she'd eaten an entire person—how did that work, now that she was no longer the size of a dragon?—and at the same time she worried eating anything else might only make her sick again.

She caught Rand's eye and saw the sympathy in him, but it was laced with curiosity and questions of his own. Then a wrapped egg salad sandwich was being pressed into her hand, and Cee turned her attention to her meal, taking tentative bites to test her stomach.

They ate in silence for a while, and then Rand asked with a nod at Ernesta, "So who is she?"

Arlon smiled at Ernesta, and suddenly Cee knew the answer before he spoke. "Ernesta," said Arlon, "this is Rand, and of course my brother Marcus. Ernesta and I are mated."

Marcus coughed up a bit of tuna salad into a napkin.

"I'm sorry," Arlon said. "I should have prepared you."

"Mated? Already?" Marcus choked.

"I wasn't young for a morph, Marcus."

Cee glanced at Ernesta and guessed she was somewhat older than Arlon. "How did they decide?" she asked.

"Each Clan has its own way," answered Ernesta. "The Aerie elders keep a list of eaglets—that is, the children who go to be educated, the ones we hope will eventually morph and return. They plan well in advance which will be mated."

"What if someone never morphs?" Rand asked.

"I'm sure they have alternate plans just in case," said Arlon.

"Did you at least get to meet first?" Cee asked.

Arlon and Ernesta exchanged a smiling glance. "Yes," Arlon said. "And we're both very happy."

Cee could tell it was true. They oozed contentment, were relaxed with one another in a way she and Marcus had never been, even on their best days. But she wondered what happened if two people were mated and didn't like each other? Or if, like Marcus, someone wasn't interested in the opposite sex? Were they forced to mate anyway, for the sake of the Clan? *Could* you force someone to—? Cee stopped her thoughts before they could go any further.

Guin spoke up. "Do they decide whether you'll have any... eaglets?"

Ernesta nodded. "We don't want to overpopulate and tax our resources. So we take turns."

"Most Clans do that," Arlon added, as if fearing they would think the Aerie were tyrants.

Cee looked at Marcus, who was staring at Ernesta with open dislike. Moved to showcase Ernesta's better points, Cee said, "Well, it was very kind of you to make me this dress, Ernesta."

Marcus's green-eyed gaze swung Cee's way, and Cee stopped her breath as she tried to discern whether his dislike had just been extended. But Marcus's expression was inscrutable.

"Why don't you tell us what happened?" Arlon suggested. "That wreckage out there is going to draw some attention before long. Whoever sent those pilots will wonder what happened to them and come looking."

Cee had the sense Rand and Marcus had already filled Arlon in, but also that everyone was waiting to hear from her. A Dracona was unheard of, all but a myth, a footnote in history. Suddenly Cee felt her own rarity as a weight pressing down on her shoulders, and she slumped a little.

She told them about how it felt to be stuck inside the dragon's form, and about not being able to control Livian. Arlon nodded as she spoke and said, "Dracona are unique in that they harbor two distinct personalities. In all other Clans, each person is him or herself only, but Dracona..." And he shook his head as if it were beyond him to explain, or even comprehend.

"Magi are two personalities, too, though," said Cee, risking a glance at Marcus. "At least at first."

Arlon also looked at Marcus, and Marcus became absorbed with a bit of orange peel. "Yes," Arlon agreed. "But in Magi the two personalities eventually resolve into one. With Dracona," and he turned a sympathetic grimace on Cee, "it will always be two. Ideally, you'll work together, become a team in time. But it will take a while. It's new to both of you."

"Two resolve into one," Guin repeated. "But..." She, too, looked at Marcus, and the orange peel became the most interesting thing Marcus had ever encountered. "Really, it's more like one of them disappears, isn't it?"

"We can only go by what we've learned in school," said Arlon, and Cee sensed his reluctance. What *had* they learned about the Magi? That they were skilled at magic, of course, and had been elected as Head Clan because of it. Their powers were a burden, a responsibility, as well as a blessing, and the Magi used their abilities to the benefit of all.

But as far as their transition went, Cee knew little. How did a Magus morph? The most Cee had ever read about their transformation suggested a Magus began rapidly exhibiting abilities beyond his or her teaching. None of the textbooks mentioned hearing voices. No wonder Marcus had felt as if he'd been going mad. He'd had no resources to guide him.

A wave of resentment washed over Cee. How could the Magi knowingly leave a child to such a fate with no counsel? Surely each of them had been through it—which was probably exactly why they continued to put others through it as well. *Stupid pride, stupid traditions.*

A jolt went through Cee. Livian was awake.

"What if..." Marcus's voice was so low that Cee was moved to lean forward to hear, and she saw everyone else do the same. "What if a Magus doesn't want to adopt a new personality?"

Everyone sat back again, like a visible sigh.

"I'm not sure you have a choice," said Arlon. "Eventually, Diodoric will be powerful enough to... stay."

"Take over, you mean," said Marcus.

"It's not a hostile invasion," Ernesta said. "It's more a blending of two rivers into—" She faltered as Marcus pinned her with a *very* hostile glare.

"What would you know about it?" he demanded. Guin put out a hand to him, but Marcus leapt up and stalked off into the undergrowth. Rand started to get up as well, but Arlon held up a hand. "Give him a moment."

Rand settled back onto the ground, but he didn't look happy about it, and Guin continually glanced over her shoulder in the direction Marcus had gone, her hair perpetually swinging.

"How much farther to the Far Eastern Wilderness?" Rand asked.

"If you leave at sundown a keep a good pace, you might make it by dawn," said Arlon. "More likely midmorning."

Cee stood up and four heads swung in her direction. "I'm going after him," she said, and inside her Livian heaved a sigh. *You're going to have to learn to live without him at some point.*

Not yet, Cee thought. And, absurd and impossible as it seemed, she privately hoped not ever.

FIFTEEN

*B*ecause the Magi do not take a new physical form, a Magus' transformation is not as dramatic or obvious as in other Clans. Indeed, the initial transformation may be overlooked entirely. Only the keenest observers, or those closest to the Pre-Morph, are likely to notice the difference.

—Transformation Cycles by Clan

THERE WEREN'T PATHS; this stand of trees had been left to itself and consisted only of open and closed spaces, tall grass and patches of dirt. Cee walked out of the clearing where they'd eaten and was faced with a wall of trees, most of them the usual brown. But off to the right were two white-barked trees that leaned away from each other, forming a V with their trunks, a natural invitation to pass through.

We should just eat him and save everyone a lot of trouble, said Livian.

"Eating people isn't the solution to everything," muttered Cee.

It's the solution to a lot of things, Livian countered. *It would keep him from having to become one of them, and you'd get to be together... In a manner of speaking.*

"Oh, and so am I one with Grantham now?" Cee asked under her breath. She'd been walking slowly, quietly, as if sneaking up on something, though she wasn't sure why; Marcus wasn't quarry, nor was he dangerous.

Says you.

"Shut up." She came to the V and stepped through, only to hear something shift and rustle above her. Looking up, she spotted Marcus sitting against the trunk, his legs extended lengthwise along a branch some ten feet above. The fading daylight attached itself to his hair, his shirt, his pale face like a halo. "How did you get up there?"

Marcus shrugged as if it was not a question worth answering.

"You won't at least talk to me?" Cee asked.

"I'm tired," said Marcus, the words drifting on an exhalation of breath. "I'm so tired, Cee."

Cee searched for a way to reach him, to join him on the branch, but she couldn't see how Marcus got up there to begin with. There were no rocks to climb, no lower branches to pull up on.

"Like this," said Marcus, and he swung his legs around and, Cee thought, prepared to jump down. She gave a little yelp of protest, sure he would come crashing down and at the very least fracture his ankles. But then she felt herself rising through the air.

"Don't," said Marcus as Cee began to flail in surprise. When she was close enough, he reached down and took hold of her hands, pulling her up the rest of the way so she could sit beside him.

"You can fly," she said, her words coming in puffs as she caught her breath.

"*You* can fly," Marcus corrected. "Or your dragon can, at least. For me it's more like floating. And only very short distances so far."

"And you can make other people float, too."

"It's difficult. I'm not strong, you know. I could be stronger, but..."

"It would mean giving up," said Cee. "Becoming Diodoric."

Marcus nodded.

"Is that why you're tired? From fighting him?"

"I'm not ready, Cee. It would be easier to let him... But I don't want to lose myself. And he's... I'm not sure he's a good person."

Cee remembered Diodoric calling her "pretty" and privately thought he couldn't be *all* bad. But what she said was, "If he's part of you, he must have some good in him."

"I don't know how much a part of me he really is," said Marcus. "He feels like someone else entirely. Like your dragon does to you."

"He has a name," said Cee.

Marcus grimaced. "He was... impressive."

Is that all? Livian snorted.

"You're offending him," Cee said.

Marcus looked askance at her. "He talks to you?"

Cee nodded. "Doesn't Diodoric talk to you?"

"Not..." Marcus shifted on the branch. "He mutters a lot. He's very critical, always pointing out what I'm doing wrong or where I could do better. Where *he* could do better, and would do if I let him." He peered again at Cee, the dappled sunlight making his eyes beautifully translucent. "I don't suppose yours is like that."

"Mostly he wants to eat people," Cee sighed, then had to smile at Marcus's startled expression. "It's true! I'm not sure if he thinks it's the fastest way to get rid of a problem or if he's just always hungry."

Both.

"He also gives me a hard time about you," Cee went on. "I guess Dracona and Magi are not friendly."

"The Magi considered it to be in the best interest of pretty much everyone to get rid of the Dracona," said Marcus. "I'm not saying I agree," he added, drawing away as if Cee might bite him. "The history books are sparse on particulars, but it's generally thought the Dracona used up too many resources and were unpredictable in their behavior. They refused to join the Council of Clans or be held by any laws."

Lies.

Cee barely had time to register Livian's protest as Marcus continued, "But clearly they didn't get all of them. You must have come from somewhere."

All at once, Cee felt sick in the pit of her stomach. She wasn't sure if the egg salad had caused it, or Livian's slithering inside her, or the way Marcus had just casually implied she shouldn't exist. His detachment pained her, and she found herself saying, "He said I was pretty, you know."

Marcus's brow creased. "Who? The dragon?"

"Diodoric."

Marcus drew farther away, looking at Cee as if she'd bitten him after all. It was a mixture of surprise and self-satisfaction, an expression that said: *I hoped you wouldn't betray me but always knew you would.* Cee realized that

Marcus saw her as nothing more than a beast, or the host to a beast; either way, he was convinced of her base nature. She was wild whereas he was wise.

All at once, Cee wanted to slap him.

He sensed it. "You'd rather talk to him then, I suppose."

If you're not going to eat him, at least knock him off his branch.

Cee was seriously considering it when Rand appeared in the V of the tree trunks. She watched his head turn left, then right as he took a tentative step forward. Cee started to call to him, but Marcus reached over and placed a hand on her arm. Cee was so startled she nearly fell off the branch herself.

The warmth of Marcus's hand seeped through the knit of the cardigan, and Cee began to feel woozy. Her world tilted to the left. But then arms were around her, holding her steady.

"Careful."

It took effort to turn her head, and everything whirled as she did. Marcus accommodated her by leaning into her line of sight, and Cee saw the gold streaking through his green pupils. The final rays of sunset blazed behind him, forcing Cee to squint.

"If anyone can convince him, you can," Diodoric said.

Cee's lips could barely move; the numbness was making her heavy. "Convince?" was all she could manage.

"To Relinquish himself."

Cee wanted to pull away but didn't have the strength, and risked falling if she tried. She gave in to the heaviness in her neck and let her head fall forward against Diodoric. Below them, Rand was walking through the undergrowth, still looking left and right for any sign of them.

"Would you hate it if I kissed you?" Diodoric asked.

Rand looked up.

Livian? Cee pleaded, and inside her a warmth unfurled at her navel, spreading through her limbs. As her arms gained strength, Cee pushed Diodoric away from her, tipping off the branch in the process.

Rand moved fast despite his bulk and caught Cee as if she weighed nothing more than a football. His eyes flew up to where Marcus was steadying himself against the tree trunk then he gently set Cee on her feet and put one massive hand to her forehead. "You have a fever," he said.

Cee shook her head, incidentally nudging Rand's hand aside. "It's just Livian. I..." But she wasn't prepared to go through the whole story. She looked up at Diodoric. Even from a distance, she could see the gold in his eyes. He frowned down at them sullenly.

"What's with him?" Rand asked.

But something else had occurred to Cee. "You left Guin with Arlon and Ernesta?"

"Ernesta was talking to her about telepathy," said Rand.

"I didn't get the feeling Guin liked Ernesta much," said Cee.

Rand looked at her like she'd begun speaking a foreign language. "Guin likes everybody."

Cee wasn't convinced but decided to drop it as just then an eagle swooped through the trees, circled once, and landed on the branch beside Diodoric. Cee waited to see how Arlon would change, but the eagle remained as it was. She noticed Diodoric leaned closer to the tree trunk, away from the massive bird.

Rand noticed, too. "That's not Marcus."

"It's Diodoric," Cee confirmed. "He and Marcus— they're not getting along very well."

Rand cocked an eye in Cee's direction. "And how about you and your dragon friend?"

Cee could feel Livian perk up at being mentioned. "It will take some getting used to," said Cee. "But I think, in time, we'll figure it out."

"You trust him, then?"

Cee thought about it a moment then nodded. "He's helped me when I needed it. Like you."

Rand shrugged one shoulder and ducked his head on the pretense of scratching the back of his neck. In the tree, the eagle was eyeing Diodoric and stepping sideways toward him, forcing the Magus ever closer to the trunk. "What do you want?" Diodoric demanded.

Arlon let out a piercing shriek and extended his wings. As he did so, the feathers extended into robed arms, and all at once Arlon was sitting there in human form. The branch bent beneath the sudden change in weight.

"So you're Diodoric," Arlon said. "I've heard a lot about you."

"And I know all about you, of course," said Diodoric, his expression sour.

Cee watched, fascinated. She hadn't often seen Marcus and Arlon interact; so far as Cee knew, though they'd been raised together, the boys were not particularly close. Marcus never talked about Arlon, yet it seemed to Cee that Arlon was an affectionate older brother. How did he feel about possibly losing Marcus to Diodoric?

"You know as much as Marcus knows, I expect," said Arlon. "It's hardly everything."

"It's enough," Diodoric said.

Arlon's dark brows rose. "Enough for what?"

Diodoric appeared momentarily stymied. "What do you want?" he asked again.

"I only came to see if you were all right," said Arlon. "It's getting dark, and you'll need to be on your way again soon."

Cee glanced up and saw Arlon was right; the spaces between the tree leaves were turning a dusky lavender.

"Do you need help out of the tree?" Arlon asked.

Diodoric scowled. "Of course not. I got myself up, and I can get myself down."

Arlon looked into Diodoric's eyes for a long moment. "You're getting stronger," he said, and Cee couldn't tell if it was apprehension or satisfaction she heard in his tone.

"Not strong enough," muttered Diodoric, and Cee could see the golden light beginning to fade from his irises. It reminded her of a science film they'd once seen at school, one about an imploding star that swallowed up all the bright bits of the cosmos within its reach.

How far was Diodoric's reach, Cee wondered? He was swallowing Marcus, which was terrible enough, but who and what else might he consume?

Diodoric leaned back against the tree trunk and dropped his eyelids to half-mast. He appeared ready to fall asleep. In fact, he began to list dangerously to his right, at which point Arlon swooped in to catch him. The eagle transformed so quickly, Cee hadn't realized it had happened; one moment Arlon reached out with his hand, the next it seemed a massive bird was clutching Marcus and lowering him to the ground.

"What just happened?" Cee asked as Arlon reappeared in human form.

Arlon shook his head. "I don't know. Used himself up, I think. Rather like you did with the dragon earlier."

Livian snorted, which came out of Cee as a hiccough.

"How long will he be out?" Rand asked. He glanced up

at the rapidly darkening sky. "We can't really afford to waste any time."

Cee had another thought. "You can carry people?" she asked Arlon. "Why don't you and your friends just fly us to the Far Eastern Wilderness?"

Arlon smiled thinly. "People are too heavy for us to carry great distances. And we're not supposed to be involved."

"Involved in what?" Rand asked.

Arlon's smile became a grimace. "Whatever's happening out—"

Livian reacted before Cee realized; under his instruction, she turned her head toward the V in the tree trunks seconds before Ernesta and Guin stepped through. "There you are!" Ernesta said, though her pleasure dissolved at the sight of Marcus on the ground. "What happened?"

Cee scrutinized Guin, trying to discern whether she'd warmed to Ernesta at all, but she couldn't tell. Guin appeared solemn, but that was to be expected given her friend was unconscious. But instead of rushing to Marcus's side, or even staying beside Ernesta, Guin edged her way behind the plump woman to come stand beside Rand. Without looking, and seemingly without conscious thought, Rand slipped an arm around Guin's shoulders.

Something dark dropped through Cee, and she looked balefully at Marcus's prone form. All at once she wanted to kick him.

"Is he all right?" Ernesta asked, coming to kneel beside Marcus. She moved fluidly, gracefully for a portly woman, or maybe that was an illusion created by the flow of her robes.

Don't let her.

Cee was startled by Livian's apparent concern for Marcus, but she used his confidence to step in. "Let me."

Ernesta was visibly surprised but stood again, allowing Cee to kneel beside her friend. Marcus was as pale as ever, and heartrendingly beautiful in his sleep, lips slightly parted and long lashes diving along his cheeks. Cee wished *he'd* been the one who'd wanted to kiss her. She wanted to kiss him now, like a prince in a fairy tale, but she was a princess, not at all Marcus's thing, and anyway, everyone was watching. So she simply placed a hand on Marcus's forehead.

His skin was cool and clammy. Cee felt warmth begin to run from her chest down her arm and into her hand. *What are you doing?* she asked silently.

Livian didn't answer, but Marcus gave a little sigh that made Cee's heart want to burst. Marcus stirred, and Cee was forced to follow his head with her hand as he turned this way and that, fighting something in his dreams. Then, all at once Cee's body went cold. She felt as if someone had snatched away a blanket she'd been wrapped in.

Marcus, however, went still. Cee could feel the warmth radiating from him and understood. She only hoped they wouldn't need to kiss in front of everyone for Livian to return to her.

Marcus tossed his head once, twice, then stilled again. Cee's palm on his forehead grew searingly hot, as if Marcus were spiking an impossible fever. The warmth carried up Cee's arm and Livian curled himself back into his nest in her abdomen as Marcus's eyes opened. All green.

How do you do that? Cee wondered.

Palms, soles of the feet, and mouths, answered Livian. *Mouths are fastest, but...*

Cee wordlessly thanked him for not choosing that

particular exit this time around. Only then did she realize she still had a hand on Marcus's head; he was staring up at her with a small frown while everyone stood around them, watching. Cee hastily removed her hand and offered it to Marcus to help him sit up.

"I'm not woozy." She said it aloud without thinking, giving voice to her surprise. Marcus blinked at her, and Cee said, "I was touching you, but I didn't get..."

You will learn there is a difference between transmitting and receiving. When you receive, you are impacted. When you transmit, you are impacting others. In time you will be able to control the signals, both in and out.

Cee considered this. Being able to touch others without fear of how it might affect her? She definitely wanted to learn how to do that.

"How do you feel?" Arlon asked Marcus.

Marcus got to his feet, and out of habit Cee held up a hand for him to help her up. But he turned away from her, and it was Ernesta who took Cee's hand and helped her stand.

"Better," said Marcus. "We should start walking."

"Can't Cee's dragon fly us?" Rand asked.

Cee was about to answer that she didn't think she or Livian had enough energy for that, not after the helicopter that afternoon. And truthfully, Cee was worried the next time she morphed she might not be able to get control back. There was something terrifyingly claustrophobic about being inside Livian, and Cee worried there might come a time when, if he was strong enough, he might choose to remain in his full form, leaving Cee trapped within.

Now you know how I feel.

But it was Arlon who answered Rand's question. "You can't risk it, not even in the dark."

"Let's go get your things," Ernesta suggested, and the group began to straggle back through the V in the white trunks that almost seemed to glow in the dimming light.

Cee had taken two steps when someone plucked the sleeve of her cardigan. She turned to see Marcus's pale face shining in the same strange way as the trees and slowed her steps as Arlon drifted slowly past.

"Keep that damn dragon of yours to yourself," said Marcus.

He walked away, leaving Cee to catch up.

CHAPTER
SIXTEEN

*T*elepathy comes in numerous forms and strengths. It is estimated that 37% of the population has some telepathic ability.

—Transformation Handbook

THEY WERE BACK on the road as night fell, the two duffels filled with a few new provisions brought by Arlon and Ernesta, who promised to come check on them again the next day. As they flew off, Cee wondered where they went and whether they had to lie about what they were doing. Did the Aerie Clan know Arlon and Ernesta were helping them? Cee had the sense they did not, that such aid was forbidden, and that Arlon and his mate—her brain stalled briefly over the term—would be in trouble if it came to light.

With all this going through her mind, Cee was startled when Guin said, "There's something not right about it."

Cee turned to find Guin walking beside her. Guin's expression reflected the concern in Cee's, but based on her words Cee guessed Guin had a different reason for worrying. "What do you mean?" she asked.

"Ernesta..." Guin's voice trailed.

"You don't like her," said Cee. "Why? She was telling you about telepathy, Rand said."

"And you do like her because she made you a nice new dress," said Guin, her tone uncharacteristically severe.

Anger flared in Cee. "Look, I'm not going to have a Relinquishing, and this stupid dress is the closest thing I'm going to get to a ceremonial robe. I don't even know if there's a Clan out there for me to join! So, yes, I like that she made me a dress. Is that so horrible?"

Guin turned her big brown eyes on Cee. "I'm sorry..."

Ahead of them, Rand and Marcus had turned around and were coming back toward them. "You can't—" Marcus began, his voice a harsh whisper, but then he looked at Cee and something in his face broke, shattered into large, sharp shards like a ceramic plate. "Cee," he said. "You're crying."

Cee brought a hand to her cheek and discovered Marcus was right.

"What's going on?" Rand asked.

Marcus did not wait for an explanation. He reached and took Cee by the arm, walking ahead with her in tow. "What are you doing?" she asked.

"We can't stand around in the middle of the road," said Marcus. "And we certainly can't be yelling at one another. We have to keep walking. Quietly."

"Was I yelling?"

"Yes."

Cee glanced over her shoulder and saw Rand and Guin some yards behind them having a whispered conversation.

"She doesn't like Ernesta," said Cee. "Doesn't trust her for some reason."

"She didn't say why?" Marcus asked.

"Only accused me of liking Ernesta because she made me a dress," said Cee.

"Hence the yelling," Marcus deduced. "Not like Guin to behave that way, though," he mused.

"It must have been a shock to you," said Cee, "to suddenly be presented with a..." A what? Once someone left to join his Clan, you had no reasonable expectation of even seeing him again, much less knowing his mate. And most Pre-Morphs weren't raised with siblings to begin with.

"It did seem incredibly fast," Marcus conceded. "He's been with the Clan six weeks and he's already mated."

"You think they had a reason for rushing?" Cee asked.

Marcus shrugged, a short and quick movement that appeared defensive rather than nonchalant. "Each Clan has its own way of doing things. I only hope..."

Cee waited. When it became clear Marcus wasn't willingly going to give up his thought, she asked, "Hope what?"

She saw the green eyes dart in her direction as Marcus glanced at her from the corners of his eyes. "I hope the Magi don't do it that way."

"At least you have a Clan," said Cee.

"You will, too," said Marcus. "You didn't come from nowhere."

Cee thought of her mother and how she placed Clan children with Unaltereds. "They must keep records," she murmured.

"Yes," Marcus agreed. "And they must have a way of contacting the Clans for Relinquishing."

Cee hadn't much considered the process, everything that must go into it. The focus was on learning one's abilities, honing those skills, and of course Clan history and diplomacy. Well, as much history as any Clan was willing to divulge.

She remembered her Incantations teacher Mrs. Vargas talking about feminine magic being different from masculine. "But she never said we could morph into the opposite sex," she mused.

"What?" Marcus asked.

"Mrs. Vargas. Feminine magic. But Livian's magic must be different from mine, right?"

Marcus blinked and shook his head. "I don't know." The words came out hoarse, and Cee wondered what it cost Marcus to have to admit ignorance in something. But he was quick to add, "We don't know much of anything about Dracona."

"Or Magi, for that matter," Cee pointed out. "But at least you know there are others like you."

We are balanced, hissed Livian quietly. *This is how it is for our kind.*

Cee was so surprised she almost stopped walking. Marcus noticed, of course, and asked, "What's wrong?"

But Cee spoke to Livian, voicing the words aloud so Marcus could be included in the conversation. "You're saying a male human would host a female Dracona?"

Yes.

Cee explained what Livian was telling her. "Interesting," Marcus said. "I've never heard of that being the case in any other Clan."

"Guess I'm special in just every kind of way," muttered Cee.

"A dangerous thing to be," said Marcus.

"And you talk about it like you want to shove me under a microscope."

Marcus looked askance at her. "You've grown claws, Cee. I suppose it's not entirely due to the dragon, either."

Cee tried to decipher Marcus's words, his tone, his expression. Before Arlon's Relinquishing she would have been able to do so easily, but he had since become inscrutable. "And I suppose the changes in you are not entirely due to Diodoric?"

She watched the beautiful, smooth line of his jaw tighten as his teeth set. Then suddenly Rand materialized out of the darkness, a step behind but almost between Marcus and Cee, leading Cee to wonder whether Rand was intentionally separating them. Had he heard their discussion?

"We need to talk," Rand said.

Reflexively, Cee looked over her shoulder. Guin was walking a few steps behind, head down and arms folded. Cee knew she should probably fall back and walk with Guin, maybe even attempt to talk to her, but she didn't want to. She turned back to listen to Marcus and Rand instead.

"Who?" Marcus asked.

"All of us," said Rand.

"About what?"

"There's something wrong," Rand insisted.

"We know that," said Marcus.

"The Aerie," Rand said. "Guin doesn't trust them."

Marcus stopped walking. He turned and frowned at Guin as she approached, her steps slowing in the face of Marcus's obvious displeasure. "We don't have time for this," he said. "We need to keep moving while it's dark."

"You're the one who stopped walking," said Cee.

Marcus did not even spare her a glance; all his attention focused on Guin. "Why don't you trust my brother?"

Guin winced at the accusatory tone. "It's not him," she said. "I mean, it is him, a little bit. But it's *her* more."

"Ernesta," said Marcus.

"I can't read them," Guin said. "Well, I can't read anybody yet, not consistently, but with most people I at least pick up things here and there. It's like trying to get a com station. Mostly there's static, but every now and then you pick up a word." She glanced around at them as if seeking confirmation that they understood, and Rand gave a nod. "In this case, I usually pick up images. Random, not attached to anything. Sometimes there's a word..." Guin shook her head. "I'm not explaining it very well."

"You're concerned because you get nothing from them?" Marcus asked. "That's simple enough, I would think. Ernesta in particular is a telepath herself, so she knows how to shield her 'signal,' as you put it.

"And didn't she try to help you learn about your telepathy?" Marcus went on.

Guin chewed at her lip. "There was something... discordant. She was being so nice on the surface, but underneath I was sensing something else. I didn't get pictures or even words, just waves of feeling, I guess? Until she realized I had some telepathic power, too, and then she just closed off."

"That's not much to go on," said Marcus. He turned and began walking again. The rest of them stood in the road, unmoving.

Marcus made it several yards before realizing he was alone. He turned and scowled; Cee felt she could see it, even in the dark. Even at a distance, Marcus's pale skin seemed to glow just a little, as if absorbing the...

"Starlight," Cee sighed, and Rand gave her a questioning look but didn't say anything.

When it became clear, they weren't going to come to him, Marcus retraced his steps, his expression thunderous. "Now what?"

"You're pretty used to playing the leader, aren't you?" Rand asked.

"Somebody has to," said Marcus. "And you're the ones who chose to follow me. No one twisted your arms."

Guin's head bent on her slender neck, making her the picture of a drooping daisy bowing to high winds. The sight of her seemed to fire Rand's simmering temper to full boil.

"And maybe now we'll stop," Rand said. "We've put ourselves into a lot of trouble, and why?"

Guin's head lowered further, her long hair curtaining her face.

"We can go home," Rand insisted. "Stay out here if you want. Go live with your eagle friends, if they'll have you. Or find the Magi. Whatever. The rest of us can—"

"Cee can't," Marcus said quietly.

Cee rocked back on her heels; she felt as if a bolt had just struck through her.

"She's the reason I had to leave," Marcus continued. "And if they find out she's a Dracona..." He shook his head.

"You keep saying it like it's a bad thing!" Cee shouted.

"*I* don't think it's a bad thing," said Marcus. "Certainly it's nothing to be ashamed of. But it's not safe to be something the Magi exterminated."

"And you're a Magus," said Rand. "So why should she trust you? Why should any of us trust you?"

The green eyes settled on Cee, and she found it difficult to meet his gaze. "I won't leave you, Cee," Marcus said. "Unless you ask me to."

Cee reeled, swaying on her feet. This was what she'd always wanted, wasn't it? Then why did it feel wrong?

Sinister? She wanted Marcus to stay with her of his own free will, not because he felt responsible for her. And certainly not because she'd forced them into exile and he had no other options.

Guin lifted her head and reached to put a hand on Cee's arm, momentarily knocking Cee further off balance so that Rand was forced to steady her from the other side. Cee started to pull away from Guin's touch, but Guin's fingers wrapped around her forearm, and Cee felt the slow seep of understanding move through her mind. She didn't want to, but she made herself look Marcus in the eyes.

At first, she felt rather than saw. A warm wave washed over her. She was dimly aware of Livian hissing in protest. Then a vortex appeared at her feet, the same green-blue of Marcus's eyes. Cee was pulled under, the water—was it water?—closing over her while Livian thrashed inside her, desperate to rise.

Panic swelled in Cee, but she fought both it and Livian down and forced herself to *look*. Guin wanted to show her this. Why?

Cee was floating, surrounded by the green-blue. Every now and then gold flashed in the distance like lightning. Cee took a tiny, experimental inhalation and discovered she could breathe normally. The air smelled like Marcus's shampoo, cologne, whatever it was he wore. He never had told her.

In the distance, an image resolved: a black and barren tree with two large birds sitting in its branches. Arlon and Ernesta? Though Cee squinted, the distance made it impossible to tell.

"I don't understand," Cee murmured. Was this Marcus's mind? If so, how had Guin gained access? Were

Guin's powers strengthening? Had Ernesta showed her how to do this?

All the questions caused Cee's concentration to loosen. Suddenly the vortex was whirling around her once more, this time binding her arms to her sides. Livian began to struggle again, but it was unnecessary; the vortex—Marcus —was rejecting her, pushing her out. She bobbed to the surface and her eyesight cleared, going from the bright of the vision to the dark of the night in which they stood.

Inside her, Livian was snarling. Cee felt him as a churning, as if she'd eaten something disagreeable. That made Cee think of Grantham, and she doubled over, gagging.

Guin released Cee's arm while Rand continued to steady her as she heaved, panted, and caught her breath.

"Cee?" Marcus asked.

But Cee looked at Guin and gave her head a small shake to show she didn't understand what she'd seen.

"Do you want me to go?"

Cee turned to Marcus. His eyes were so luminous despite the darkness that she was afraid she might get sucked in again. But she held his gaze.

"No," she said. If the Aerie were a threat, it wasn't Marcus's fault. They were safer together. And even if Marcus—or Diodoric—was dangerous in some way, it was a risk Cee would gladly take.

On either side of her, Cee sensed apprehension. Maybe Guin was right and Arlon and Ernesta were not to be trusted. Maybe Rand was right and they should turn back. But they wouldn't—*she* wouldn't. Because she *did* understand something. She didn't need Marcus so much as he needed her. And she wouldn't leave him.

SEVENTEEN

T he Far Eastern Wilderness covers a little more than
80,000 square miles of the eastern interior. This area
is a Protectorate with no Clans inhabiting it. The
FEW is staffed with rangers from a variety of Clans, including
some specially selected Unaltereds. Visitors are required to apply
in advance for camping, hiking, and any other activities.

—Post-Fracture Geography

RAND AND GUIN closed ranks around Cee, apparently
meaning to walk on either side of her. But Cee stepped
forward to join Marcus. He glanced uncertainly at the other
two and jumped when Cee firmly took his hand. "We
should go," Cee said. "We're losing time."

Marcus stared at their clasped hands for a long moment
then walked forward, Cee keeping pace while Rand and
Guin once again took up the rear. Cee looked over her

shoulder once or twice and didn't like what she saw: Rand glowering, and Guin's lips set in a thin, grim line.

She would explain to them later, was thinking about how to do that, when Marcus murmured, "You're not faint?"

Cee remembered what Livian had said about receptivity. She didn't entirely understand it, but she knew in this instance her desire to aid Marcus meant her energy was flowing outward. With a start, Cee wondered if she could have blocked Guin earlier. Would she have wanted to?

"I'm fine," said Cee.

"Then what happened back there? When Guin grabbed you?"

But Cee wasn't ready to share her vision with Marcus; she wanted to talk to Guin about it first. She shook her head. "I'm not sure. Probably nothing."

"Probably?"

Cee didn't answer. The road was unpaved and uneven, and now and then they stumbled over unexpected stones in the dark. They walked in silence for what felt like forever, Cee merely relishing the nearness of her best friend and hoping he enjoyed being close to her as well. She waited for Marcus to drop her hand, but he never did.

If only they could go back to... When? What? Before Arlon left? Had that been the turning point? Cee tried to capture the memory of a perfect moment, but everything felt blurred, muddied, tainted by all the recent confusion. As if the present cast a shadow over the past, irrevocably tinting those happy times. Memories that should have blazed with color were now all sepia and ashen.

A thin line of indigo on the horizon was slowly turning cobalt while the vault of sky above them remained nearly black when Cee saw the darkscape ahead. It hadn't been visible at night, but as dawn approached, a long, low shadow remained, untouched by the coming light. At first, Cee thought it was a ridge of some kind, hills maybe. But as the sky rapidly lightened, she realized it was the uneven canopy of a very large forest.

"It looks fine," said Cee.

"On this side, perhaps," said Marcus. "And at this distance. But who knows what it looks like from closer or farther in."

Rand came up behind them. "What now, Mr. Brilliant?" he asked. "It's almost light, and we're out in the open."

It was true. They were on the road, open fields stretching to either side of them, misty in the cool grey of the morning.

"The nearest cover is the Wilderness itself," Marcus said. "We'll have to keep walking."

They lengthened their strides, walking clustered and quick like herded sheep. Guin pressed close to Cee's back, all but tripping on Cee's heels, and Cee sensed eagerness yoked to restraint, as if Guin was resisting the urge to break into a run. Rand turned his head continually, trying to see every direction at once. Marcus marched onward, eyes trained on their destination, though Cee felt tension run through him at the call of a bird flying overhead.

It took them an hour to reach the edge of the Far Eastern Wilderness, light steadily exposing them as they walked, so that by the time they arrived they were alternately creeping and rushing. As they drew close to the trees, Cee was surprised to see wrought iron bars topped with pointed fleur-de-lis. The fence was not visible until they were almost upon it, the dark bars blending into trunks and shade. The points came as high as Cee's chest but were unlikely to keep anyone or anything out. Or in. "What's it for?" she asked aloud.

Everyone seemed to understand the question, and as usual Marcus had an answer. "Only a boundary marker. When this land was classified as Wilds, they had to make it clear what was included in the designation. All Wilds have fences or walls around them."

Cee supposed they'd learned that in school, but she'd found no use for the information and had discarded it. Marcus, on the other hand, lived in firm belief that *all* information was useful, if not immediately then eventually. He hoarded it like treasure.

"Are there gates somewhere?" Rand asked. "Entrances?"

"Yes," said Marcus. "But who knows how long and far we'd have to walk to reach one. And they'd be staffed with rangers who would be best avoided." He approached the fence, which on his tall, thin frame came only to his abdomen. The bars were a hand's width apart. Marcus placed one hand between two bars and stepped experimentally onto the low crossbar that ran along the bottom of the fence. Cee remembered the way Marcus had lifted her into the tree the evening before and wondered if he would use that power to carry them over.

"Wait," said Guin. She pointed to the right where some yards away a massive oak jutted an elbow of trunk over the wrought iron spikes. It wasn't so far from the ground; by standing on the crossbar, even someone Cee's height might easily reach up and climb. Cee looked at Marcus and was certain he appeared relieved. Maybe he wasn't ready to share all his newfound abilities with everyone. The idea he would reveal them to her but not the others gratified Cee; they had a secret, something only theirs.

They walked along the fence to the tree, and Marcus

climbed up easily then held a hand down for Cee. Once Cee managed to get past him and down the other side of the trunk, which was slightly arched as if the oak were craning and straining to see around the other trees, Marcus helped Guin up as well. Then he followed Guin down, leaving Rand to climb up on his own.

"Well, there's nothing wrong here," said Cee as they stood amidst the trees. It was darker under the canopy, and colder, but there were no signs of fire or any other disaster.

Guin's eyes were wide, and she lifted her head as if smelling the air. "There *is* something," she said. They waited, and she shrugged. "I don't know what, exactly, but it's in that direction." She pointed off to the right.

"Northeast," said Marcus. No one bothered to ask how he knew.

"How can you tell?" Rand asked Guin.

"It smells wrong," she said. "And there's this feeling... I can't describe it. It's just all wrong. Makes my stomach..." Guin placed splayed fingers over her abdomen.

"Well, it's a place to start," said Rand.

Marcus's eyes turned skyward, and Cee wondered if he were wishing for Arlon and Ernesta to come guide them. After a moment of nothing happening, however, he started to walk in the direction Guin had indicated. He took three steps before Rand said, "Maybe Guin should lead. Since she can sense whatever it is."

Marcus's eyes met Rand's. "You sure you want her out in front like that?"

"I think she's pretty capable," said Rand. He squared his shoulders. "And she's got backup."

"I'm right here," Guin reminded them. She looked at Cee. "Cee will walk with me. Won't you?"

Cee tried to read the message in those big, brown eyes

but couldn't. "Sure," she said, irritated at the slight warble in her voice. With more confidence, she added, "Livian can usually sense things before I can anyway."

"Just don't eat anybody," Rand said. "At least not without fair warning this time."

Cee grimaced and joined Guin. They walked in quiet for some way, their attention devoted to navigating the roots and branches that littered the forest floor. Still, Guin moved quickly and nimbly; Cee felt like a lummox by comparison as she struggled to keep just behind her companion. Now and then Cee glanced back to check on the boys. Marcus walked with his head bowed as if watching his own feet, but Rand's eyes were everywhere as he acted lookout. Once he caught Cee looking and grinned. Cee's cheeks warmed, and she quickly turned around again, wishing she could blame Livian. But the dragon seemed to be asleep.

"What did you see?"

Cee gasped. Guin's words were quiet but felt like a shout in the silence of the forest. She focused on getting safely over a massive rise of roots before answering. "I'm not sure." She described the vision, the blue-green, the tree, the birds. "Was that what you picked up from Marcus?"

"No," said Guin. "It was what I picked up from you."

Cee almost stumbled over a jutting rock. "Me?"

Guin checked behind them to make sure Marcus wasn't close enough to hear. "You're sucked in by him. It's blinding you to the truth."

"I'm not *sucked in*," Cee protested. "He's my best friend."

"Think again about what you saw," said Guin. "That tree wasn't a tree."

Cee summoned the vision from memory, focusing on the claw-like tree. Black. Burned? It jutted from a sandy ground littered with black rocks. Or were those fallen bits of tree?

She tried to zoom in, but it was difficult. Something inside her resisted getting closer. Cee realized it was Livian; he was thrashing again, agitated, all but crawling up her throat. *Shh*, Cee thought at him. *What's wrong?* But Livian only continued to flail. He threw himself backward inside her, as if trying to force her back, away from the dream tree.

Not a tree. Or so Guin had said. Cee squinted at it, trying to make sense of its bizarre shape. The trunk was tall and thin, the branches barren. There were five of them, oddly splayed.

Five.

Not a tree.

A hand.

A massive hand, or rather, a claw. The tree wasn't just claw-like, it was a big, blackened dragon's claw with a leg for a trunk.

The two birds shrieked from one of the digits, and Cee backed away, out of the vision and back into the forest. It took her a moment to realize they'd stopped walking. The others stood around her, frowning.

"I don't understand," Cee whispered, her eyes on Guin. "They want to kill me?" Livian turned circles in her gut, making her queasy.

"I don't know what they want," admitted Guin. "But something isn't right."

"What's going on?" Marcus asked, his gaze bouncing from Cee to Guin and back.

Cee turned to him, her lips trembling. "How much do you trust Arlon?"

Marcus's brows lowered like darkening clouds. "This

again? He's my brother. I don't expect you to understand what it means to have a sibling."

Guin opened her mouth, her expression making it clear she planned to argue, but Rand held up his hands. "I think we all need some rest. Let's find a place to make camp."

They all looked to Guin who turned her head slowly left to right and back again. Finally she nodded to her left. "There's good cover over there. Or we can risk the clearing I sense that way." She pointed right.

"A clearing would be more comfortable," said Marcus, "but we don't know where the Volunteers are, or rangers, or who else is in the woods. Probably best to stay covered."

They blinked at him. Then suddenly Rand grinned and clapped Marcus on the arm. "There, now. That's a bit more like it. Democratic."

Marcus's face gave nothing away. "Are we putting it to a vote?"

"I think he's right," Guin said, though the words sounded as if they were being dragged unwillingly from her mouth. "Cover would be better."

Rand nodded. "Okay. Cee?"

"Me?" It came out squeaky, and she cleared her throat. "I don't—"

Clearing, sighed Livian.

Cee frowned. "Why?"

"Why what?" Rand asked.

"Livian wants to go to the clearing," said Cee.

I can't take off through these trees.

"Take off? Who says you're taking off anywhere?" Cee asked aloud.

Faster than letting the venison lead us around.

"You'll be spotted," said Marcus.

"He wants to fly over the Wilds and see where the

damage is," Cee explained. "That way we'll know which way to go."

"Let Arlon and Ernesta do that," Marcus said.

Guin opened her mouth then clamped it shut again.

"Yeah, assuming they arrive and can find us," said Rand. "If we're deep in the woods..."

"True," said Marcus. "Maybe we should go to the clearing."

Guin threw up her hands. "Please, just pick a direction!"

"The clearing," Marcus said firmly.

"Fine," said Guin. She turned right and marched off.

Cee worked to catch up. "How can you sense it? The clearing and the cover and all that?" she asked.

"I don't know," Guin admitted. "Maybe this is another emerging skill?"

"Livian says you're..." Cee stopped short of saying "venison." "Cervid, I think."

Guin turned her big, brown eyes to Cee, and Cee wondered how any of them had failed to see it before. "Really? Can he tell what others morph into?"

Sometimes, Livian replied, and Cee related his answer.

Guin glanced over her shoulder. "What about Rand?"

Cee hiccoughed, her diaphragm spasming. It took her a minute to realize Livian was laughing.

"Are you okay?" Guin asked.

"Yeah," Cee managed after another hiccough. "I don't know about Rand. I'm not sure Livian does, either."

Oh, I know.

Cee waited for more, but the dragon remained smugly silent.

Guin's face was crestfallen. "Not Cervid then."

"Oh, Guin," said Cee, "you knew that was unlikely. At least you're not mortal enemies like..."

Guin looked up sharply. "You're only enemies if you let them dictate the rules to you. Maybe you two are the bridge that will create peace between your Clans."

"You sound like my dad." The thought of Erwin Klinger pushed sharply through Cee. He was out there somewhere in the Wilds; she might even see him soon. Cee wasn't sure how she felt about that. Nervous? Excited? Would he be angry with her for traveling out there? Proud of her for having morphed?

"Anyway," Cee went on, "you're the one showing me visions designed to make me *not* trust Marcus, aren't you?"

"It's not Marcus," said Guin. "It's not even his brother, not entirely. But that bird girl of his..."

"What did she tell you? About telepathy?" Cee asked.

"She gave me some tips on focusing, tunneling in to what I want to see and hear. And also how to block out all the extraneous noise. How to block others from reading me, too."

"And you picked up nothing from her, I guess," said Cee.

Guin shook her head. "Nothing more than impressions."

"Unfavorable impressions."

"You saw them, perched on your bones."

"Were they my bones? Livian's bones?" Cee questioned. "Maybe there are other dragons out there. There must be, right? Else how did I get here? And I'm not even sure those birds were Aerie. Even if they were, who's to say they were Arlon and Ernesta?"

Guin didn't answer. They'd arrived at a break in the trees, and she stopped walking, coming to stand between two trunks. Beyond was a clearing Cee found surprisingly wide. Suddenly she was very aware of their being exposed.

Marcus and Rand came to stand behind them. "Nap time?" Rand asked.

"We shouldn't all sleep at once," said Marcus. "I'll take the first watch."

Rand smiled. "Hoping your friends will fly by?"

"It'll be dangerous for them," Marcus said. "They aren't supposed to be helping us." His eyes slid toward Guin. "They've taken a great risk."

"So they say," said Guin. "For all we know they're under orders."

Marcus's visage clouded. Cee inserted herself into the fray. "I'll stay awake with you," she offered. "Two and two?" She turned to Rand with a silent plea in her eyes.

Rand obliged by nodding. "Sounds good to me. I could definitely use some shuteye." He swung the duffel he carried from his shoulder and stepped into the clearing. Without sparing either Cee or Marcus a glance, Guin followed.

"She's a Cervid," Cee told Marcus.

"I know."

"You do?"

Marcus seemed unable to look at her. "Diodoric told me."

"Livian told me," Cee admitted.

"And what about him?" Marcus asked with a nod toward where Rand was laying out a blanket in the grass.

But she was too embarrassed to confess Livian wouldn't tell her.

Soon. Maybe tonight.

Cee was so startled she gasped, causing Marcus to look at her strangely.

"He hasn't told you," Marcus surmised.

"You know?" Cee asked.

"You guys coming out here or not?" Rand called.

Marcus grimaced, and Cee knew he thought Rand should not be so loud. She was inclined to agree. So to prevent more shouting, Cee walked out into the clearing, Marcus beside her.

"Blankets all laid out," Rand said. "Want something to eat? Some water?" He held up some bags of chips, and Cee gratefully accepted one along with a water bottle. Marcus took the offerings more reluctantly.

"Got to eat, man," Rand told him.

"Rand, what do you know about the Kornyx?" Marcus asked.

Rand cocked an eye at him. "Like from the fairy tales? Why?"

"Just curious."

Rand squinted thoughtfully. "You sure you don't need to sleep the first round?"

"I'm fine," Marcus assured him, though as he settled onto a neighboring blanket, he seemed awkward at best. Cee moved to Marcus's other side; she noted Guin had chosen the blanket on the far end, putting Rand between her and Marcus.

It was going to be a lovely day, and under other circumstances this would have been a fun outing. At least, Cee assumed it would have been. For her and Marcus it would have, if they could have holed up in the midst of the trees near the school, hiding out from the world. With a pang, Cee realized those days were over, gone forever. They would never be that way again, so easy with one another. Marcus himself might soon be lost to her, replaced by Diodoric. Cee's chest clinched at the idea, and the tears that prickled under her eyelids surprised her.

Guin looked over from where she sat and their eyes met.

Cee thought maybe she was supposed to go talk to her some more. But then Guin lay down on the blanket and rolled over, putting her back to everyone.

Inside Cee, Livian huffed. *Eat your chips. I'm hungry.*

Are you ever not hungry? Cee wondered.

I need to eat to gain my strength.

That gave Cee pause. If she didn't feed him, would Livian go back to sleep? At the very least, would he not be able to take full form?

No, you'd just die of starvation.

Cee opened her bag of chips and began to eat.

"If you two are okay..." said Rand.

"Get some rest," Marcus told him.

Rand was asleep within minutes, his breathing deep and steady. Marcus turned to Cee. "You can sleep, too, if you want."

It felt like a dismissal, which pained Cee. She had hoped Marcus would want time alone with her as much as she did with him. She missed their time together, just them. Her feelings must have shown because Marcus's features creased with regret. "It's not..." He sighed. "It's just that *he* comes out more when we're alone."

Cee blinked. "Why?"

Marcus shrugged. "Being alone with me has no effect on your dragon?"

"Well, he... doesn't like you," Cee reluctantly admitted. "But he's not driven to do anything about it."

"Only because he's not strong enough yet," said Marcus.

"He's helped you!"

"Keep your voice down." Marcus scanned the line of trees across the clearing. "Yes, he helped me. Because of you. He needs you. And you think you need me."

"No," said Cee. "I mean, I did think that. But now I think *you* need *me*. And Livian."

Marcus actually smiled, and the sight warmed Cee in a way Livian could not. "I'm impressed. You finally figured it out." But then his face grew serious. "But don't put yourself at risk for me, Cee."

"I'm the one who put you at risk. That stupid stunt at Community Day... What was I doing? Because I sure wasn't thinking."

"It's too late to be sorry for it, so don't dwell," said Marcus. Cee noticed he didn't say he forgave her, nor did he try to justify her actions. She guessed that was only fair. It wasn't in Marcus's nature to be falsely compassionate.

Moving on, Cee asked, "What was that Wu woman doing to you?"

Marcus grimaced. "I'm not sure. Nothing good. It hurt."

"I didn't know anyone in the Brigade had powers like that," said Cee.

"Just because you don't morph doesn't mean you don't have powers," Marcus said. "They went to school and learned the same things we have."

"I asked my mom—" Cee was cut short by the sharp cry of a bird. There was an answering cry and two eagles dropped to the grass a couple yards away, transforming upon touchdown.

"Good of you to make yourselves visible," Arlon said as he approached, Ernesta trailing behind him. Marcus's brother settled himself on Marcus's blanket, and Ernesta looked a question at Cee, a silent request for permission. Cee felt a rush of turmoil in her stomach, a sea bobbing inside her. But it was rude to keep Ernesta standing, so Cee gave a quick nod and the Aerie took a seat.

"If you'd been in the woods we might not have found

you," said Ernesta. From the sleeve of her robe she pulled out a sack. "You'll need more than chips," she said, handing Cee a sandwich then glancing over at Rand and Guin. "They're asleep?"

"We're taking turns," said Cee.

"Smart," Arlon said. "The easiest path is around the perimeter of the forest. Still a number of trees but not as thickly grown."

"Where is the damage?" Marcus asked. He was holding a sandwich but appeared uninterested in eating.

"Northwest of here," said Ernesta.

Marcus looked at Cee. "We were going the wrong way."

Cee's gaze traveled to where Guin slept. "We were going north."

"Northeast," Marcus said.

"The smell or—or whatever she was sensing... It's probably all over the place," said Cee. "Maybe it's hard for her to tell. She's only just learning, like any of us."

Marcus looked unconvinced but didn't argue.

"She was guiding you?" Ernesta asked with a nod toward Guin.

Cee nodded, but something stopped her from imparting that Guin was a Cervid. Instead, Cee said, "She seems to have a kind of connection to the forest, an ability to sense things in it. She knew this clearing was here without seeing it." Cee shot Marcus a pointed look.

"You're right that the smell of the damage can easily have drifted," said Arlon. He looked at his brother. "Your friend isn't trying to lead you astray."

Cee held her breath, waiting to see if Marcus would mention Guin's dislike of the Aerie, but Marcus only fidgeted with his sandwich.

When it became clear Marcus wasn't going to speak,

and probably wasn't going to eat either, Arlon said, "I'm not entirely sure what you hope to accomplish. The Volunteers will learn soon enough of what happened in Morrowville, putting you in just as much danger here as there."

"We need to find out what Mr. Dougherty... What happened to him," said Marcus.

"Why?" Arlon asked. His tone was gentle, like a doctor examining a wound and trying not to cause the patient any discomfort.

Marcus shook his head and took a bite of sandwich, though Cee suspected it was only to give himself an excuse not to talk.

"Where else could we go?" Cee asked. Arlon looked over at her. "We can't go home," she said, "and now even people from other towns are after us. They'll know one of us is a Dracona. This is all we have."

Ernesta patted Cee's hand. "We'll do our best to help. Marcus will be ready to join the Magi soon enough, and I doubt they'd suffer one of their own to be delivered to a Municipal Brigade. If there's any justice to be served, the Magi will do it themselves, within the Clan."

Marcus swallowed hard, his expression suggesting the bite of sandwich had not gone down easily.

"As for the rest of you..." Ernesta shot Arlon a worried look.

"I know of no Dracona," said Arlon. "But perhaps if you're able to keep him in you could pass as an Unaltered. It would mean facing whatever punishment for this adventure, but I'm not sure there's an alternative."

"As for the dragon," Ernesta added, "the one the helicopter pilot will say he saw, he doesn't necessarily know it was you, does he?"

"He never saw Cee," said Marcus, his green eyes sparking with understanding. Cee's breath caught in her throat; the expression was so very Marcus, the look he got when he solved a homework puzzle. "Though if he had his wits about him, he might could identify her by process of elimination."

Cee deflated.

"Of course," Marcus went on, "Mr. Dougherty can't know Cee's a Dracona. She didn't even know until a couple days ago. And if he saw what I think he saw—if he came back babbling about a dragon—that means there must be another one."

Cee's pulse quickened. "You think...?"

"We keep saying you had to come from somewhere," Marcus told her.

Arlon and Ernesta exchanged troubled glances. "Let's gather some facts," Arlon said, "not go on a tear of conjecture."

But Cee couldn't stop her heart from soaring at the notion there might be another Dracona out there, that she might yet have a Clan—even if only a Clan of one. Better that than returning to Morrowville to face whatever punishment they would deem suitable for her bizarre behavior and subsequent defection.

Marcus's eyes were still gleaming; Cee knew he was on her side in this, adding his hope to hers. Despite everything, they were still friends. Nothing could sever that deep bond.

At least, Cee hoped not. It wasn't something she was keen to test much further. "What about Rand and Guin?" she asked. "Where can they go?"

Both Arlon and Ernesta turned to regard the two sleepers. "If they morph soon," said Ernesta, "they'll be able to join their Clans."

"If not," Arlon said, "they will probably have to return to Morrowville as well."

Cee didn't much like the way Arlon assumed she would be returning to Morrowville but she didn't say anything.

"You should rest now," Arlon went on. "Ernesta and I will take turns, one of us circling and the other staying here."

Cee looked down the row of blankets to Guin's narrow back. Guin wouldn't like waking to find the Aerie present, but Cee for one welcomed the guidance and the help. She bolted down the remainder of her sandwich and lay back. For a moment she enjoyed the bright blue sky, and then she was asleep.

EIGHTEEN

*A*ndrasthenes *awoke, the great bird perched upon his person, its claws cutting deep into his chest, and knew he was caught.*

—Andrasthenes and the Kornyx

LIVIAN STIRRED, nudging Cee awake from the inside. The sensation was a strange combination of tickle and indigestion. Cee blinked her eyes open and was surprised to find the sky above her, which had been blue mere minutes before, was rapidly darkening.

It hadn't been mere minutes, of course. She'd slept several hours; they all had. Cee rocked herself into a sitting position on the blanket, trying to dispel the weight of slumber.

"Well, there's one of you awake at least," said Ernesta. She was sitting in the grass near the foot of Cee's blanket. "I hope it wasn't me that woke you?"

"No," mumbled Cee. "I..." She put a hand to her abdomen and wondered if this was what it felt like to be pregnant. Livian rumbled, coiling and uncoiling, unaccountably agitated. But for some reason Cee was reluctant to relay that information to Ernesta. Instead she thought, *What's wrong?*

Livian didn't answer, only continued to slither.

Ernesta saw Cee's gesture and asked, "Hungry again? I wouldn't be surprised. When Arlon gets back, I can—"

She *was* hungry, but Cee said again, "No. I mean, don't go to any extra trouble. Should we wake them up?" She gestured to Marcus on the next blanket over, and Rand and Guin beyond.

"I'd like to chat, just you and me, if you don't mind?" Ernesta made it sound like a question, and her lips turned up in a smile, lines appearing at the corners of her eyes. "You're not in such a hurry to take off into the woods again, are you?"

Cee looked over her shoulder at the trees' shadows growing thick with coming night. No, she wasn't in any rush to go in there.

"The dragon you carry," Ernesta said, drawing Cee's attention back to her.

"Livian," said Cee. She could feel him scratching at her stomach lining. Was he trying to get out?

"You can't control him," said Ernesta.

Cee didn't know what to say to that, so she didn't say anything.

"He *ate* someone, Cee," Ernesta continued. "Creatures like that, they require massive resources. And a lot of strength on the part of their hosts."

Cee chewed at the inside of her cheek. "I'll get stronger. We're still just... figuring each other out, I think."

"When he was in full form, how was it for you?" Ernesta asked.

"Suffocating," Cee admitted. A tiny drizzle of sorrow fell through her; poor Livian probably felt the same way now.

"And powerless," Ernesta said. "You couldn't make him do what you wanted, nor were you able to force him to abandon his form. It was only when he had no more strength of his own that he let go."

"He's not bad!" Cee insisted. "He's not some pet that needs obedience training."

"He really rather is," said a voice in the darkness.

Cee started; she hadn't seen or heard Arlon drop to the grass some feet away, but he walked toward where they sat, robe trailing and gathering evening dew along its hem. He dropped neatly down beside Ernesta, his movements so graceful Cee felt clumsy just by sitting there.

"If the Magi discover you're a Dracona," said Arlon, "they will in all likelihood try to destroy you. However," he added as Cee opened her mouth to protest, "if you go to them in human form and ask for their help, there's a chance they can put your dragon to sleep. You'd be able to live quietly."

"As an Unaltered," Cee surmised.

"There are worse things," Arlon said. "And it's not a bad life. You've seen for yourself how Unaltereds live. You would be free to marry whomever you choose—"

"So long as he's also an Unaltered," Cee muttered.

Arlon went on as if she hadn't spoken. "Could foster children. Maybe even work with your mother in placing them in good homes."

"You'd have your pick of a number of jobs," Ernesta put in. "You're a smart and talented young lady, after all."

"Marcus needs to join the Magi," said Arlon. "The

sooner the better. Think about it? You could accompany him, and both of you could get the help you need."

Cee nodded. She *would* think about it, of course, but she mostly wanted Arlon to stop talking about it.

"And now," Arlon said with a glance at the nearly dark sky, "it may be time to get everyone up and moving."

As Cee rose and began shaking the grass from her blanket, she realized Livian had grown still. *What's wrong?* she asked again.

They are liars, Livian hissed. *But they are not entirely wrong.*

What does that mean? Cee wondered. Then something occurred to her. *You can leave my body. You've done it, entering into Marcus.*

Only with Magi. And not for long. I cannot live indefinitely without my natural host.

Cee's shoulders sagged. So much for that idea. It was strange to think that in the short time since Livian's awakening she'd grown used—attached, even—to him. While Arlon's recommendation seemed logical, Cee found herself reluctant to put the dragon to sleep. Not just because she didn't want to live as an Unaltered, but because it would feel like putting a piece of herself to sleep as well. Which, Cee supposed, was exactly what euthanizing Livian would mean—deadening a part of herself. A part she never knew she had, but now that she'd discovered it, she couldn't imagine feeling whole without it. Without *him*.

While Cee ruminated, Arlon and Ernesta managed to get the others up and moving. Marcus stepped over and held open a duffel bag for Cee to toss her blanket into. "Ready?" he asked. "It's going to be very dark in there."

Cee frowned at him. "I'm not scared."

"No, I know. But we're going to have to stay close

together to keep from losing anyone." Marcus zipped the bag closed and pulled it over his shoulder. Rand joined them, carrying the other duffel, followed by Guin, who appeared reluctant to draw close and instead lingered behind Rand's bulk.

"We can't stay any longer," Arlon told them. "We're already pushing the believable, and we wouldn't be much use to you in that tree cover anyway." He pointed his chin toward the dark crowd of oaks.

"Just keep heading northwest," Ernesta said. "You won't be able to miss the camp."

"Camp?" Rand asked.

"The Volunteers," Marcus explained. "They will be camped near the damage."

"The Magi are there," said Arlon. "Directing the efforts."

Again Cee wondered the Magi didn't just use their powers to fix it themselves, but she didn't say anything.

"Which way is northwest?" Rand asked.

"That way." Guin pointed toward what looked to Cee like the absolute darkest part of the forest.

Rand frowned. "I thought we were going that way." He gestured in the general direction they'd been walking earlier.

"That's northeast," said Marcus, his voice tight.

"You could go that way," Ernesta said. "The path there, such as it is, runs along the perimeter of the Wilds. It would take you longer, but you'd get there eventually."

"It's less tree-y," noted Cee. Though there was no escaping the trees entirely—it was a forest, after all—the direction Guin had been guiding them was the closest thing to unobstructed the Far Eastern Wilderness had to offer. Short of an actual clearing, which Guin had also found. Cee couldn't shake the feeling they were wronging

Guin in some way by listening to Arlon and Ernesta. Guin had done her best, and had proven her skill to some extent.

"How much longer?" Marcus asked.

Ernesta and Arlon exchanged a look. "It's different for us," Arlon said with an apologetic smile. "As the bird flies and all."

"Might be safer to go the long way," said Rand with a glance at Guin. Her face was inscrutable.

"The Magi will be able to help you," said Arlon, "but only if you reach them before the Brigade, or whoever else has been sent out after you, reaches you."

"You're saying take the short route," Marcus said.

"It's only a matter of time before they catch up," Arlon told him. "The less time you give them for that, the better."

Cee recalled Arlon saying Marcus should get to the Magi as soon as possible. Marcus was becoming increasingly unstable, divided as he was against himself. Cee wanted to see him get better, but she also feared the Magi's interference. Surely they would seek to establish Diodoric, and then Marcus as Cee knew him would be gone.

Never mind what the Magi might to do her and Livian.

"We really must go," Arlon went on. He placed his hands on Marcus's shoulders. "We'll try to be back tomorrow, but if you're in the woods we may not find you."

Marcus nodded his understanding.

"When next we meet," Arlon continued, "you may be... changed."

"I hope not so changed that we can't still be brothers," said Marcus.

Arlon smiled, but his lips trembled. Cee thought he might be close to tears. Arlon released Marcus and stepped back, giving them all a general farewell. Then he and

Ernesta made graceful sweeps of their arms, transformed, and were gone.

Marcus rounded to face the others. "Shall we?"

"Should we vote or something?" Rand asked. And when Marcus gave him a blank stare, "On which way to go."

"We'll go the short way," said Marcus.

"Just like that," Rand said.

"You heard what Arlon said," said Marcus.

"Yeah, I heard what he said. His *recommendation*." Rand looked from Cee to Guin. "What do you think?"

"I'll go whichever way you want," Guin answered dully.

"And Cee, I know, would agree with me," Marcus said. "So, short way it is."

"Hold on," said Rand. His dark eyes landed on Cee. "Is that true? You just go with whatever Marcus says?"

Cee opened her mouth and surprised herself by groaning aloud. "I really don't—"

Go the short way.

Cee's mouth snapped shut.

"What is it?" Marcus asked.

At the same time, Rand asked, "Don't what?"

"Livian says the short way," Cee told them.

"Why?" asked Rand.

Cee waited for Livian to answer, but he didn't. She shook her head. "I don't know."

"I wouldn't normally side with the dragon," said Marcus, "but this time, I think he's right." He turned toward the shadowy stand of trees. "Everyone, stay close. As they say, the best way out is through."

MARCUS LED, Cee behind him, then Guin, with Rand as rear guard. They walked single-file and as close as they could without tripping on one another, though that happened sometimes anyway.

Once they entered the trees, Cee was amazed at the near pitch black. Ahead of her, Marcus was swallowed up; she could not even see his white shirt. She resisted the urge to reach out and grab hold of him, instead following the sounds, his scent, the little bit of heat she was able to detect coming off of him. These weren't things she would normally have been able to sense, but Livian was alert, lending her his abilities. Cee could feel him stretching into her ear canals and nostrils, a layer of warmth spreading through her as though Livian had laid himself flat against her insides. She only wished he could see in the dark.

Of course I can see in the dark.

Cee nearly stopped walking, which would have caused Guin to run into her. But she managed to find her footing in time to keep things moving relatively smoothly. *Then why can't I see in the dark?*

You want to see through my eyes? Cee's eyes began to burn, and she blinked rapidly trying to moisten them.

Marcus's white shirt blazed, as if it and his pale skin were drawing to them whatever faint light was available. It was similar to what Cee had seen before, when she'd associated the phenomenon with the Starlight character in Quiney's play. She'd thought it was something special in Marcus that had caused it, but it turned out it was something special in her: Livian.

Not entirely me, Livian grudgingly admitted.

What do you mean? Cee asked silently.

You used to see light around him all the time, even before me, the dragon remarked. Cee waited for more, but Livian offered no further insight.

She had no opportunity to think on it. The darkness

around them took form. Cee could now see Marcus fairly clearly; the ground and trees were more difficult to discern because they were darker in color. But it was better than nothing, certainly an improvement on the night blindness from before.

The path, if it could even be called that, was dipping downward, and dampness emanated from the soft ground, which was perpetually carpeted in leaves regardless of season and smelled of sweet decay. Moss dripped from branches like long, flowing hair, its silvery color making it more visible to Cee's enhanced vision. Marcus nearly walked into some but stepped around it at the last minute. Cee did, too, but she heard Guin inhale sharply behind her and imagined she had failed to avoid the tendrils.

It occurred to Cee to wonder how Marcus had known to evade the moss, how he even knew where the path was. She hadn't been able to see anything until Livian had lent her his eyes. Maybe Diodoric had similar abilities? Cee was about to ask when Rand began coughing. Not just one or two hacks, but a coughing that started small and got louder and more belabored until they were forced to stop and wait for it to pass.

Except it didn't pass. Even with Livian's sight, Rand's dark skin made him difficult for Cee to see clearly, but she could tell he was doubled over, hands on the knees of his jeans. Guin had a hand out as if she were trying to figure out where Rand was, maybe so she could thwack him on the back.

Marcus pulled a bottle of water from his duffel and shuffled forward, easing past Guin, who jumped back, startled, as Marcus passed her. Marcus murmured something to her and bent to try and get the bottle into one of Rand's hands.

But the coughing had taken on a strange squawking tone; it no longer sounded human, more like the harsh caw of a bird.

Yes, Livian purred. *I told you it would be soon. The darkness brought him out.*

"Who?" Cee asked through frozen lips.

Marcus realized it then, too, and stepped back, away from Rand.

"What's happening?" Guin asked. "Rand?"

Cee wasn't sure she could have made sense of what she was seeing even if it had happened in broad daylight. Rand's dark hair, which Cee only saw as bluish glints in the dark, got longer. But it was no longer hair; it was feathers. His straight nose lengthened to a great, sharp, black beak. His arms—

All at once, Cee realized what was about to happen. "A blanket!" she yelled at Marcus. "Get a blanket ready for him!"

Rand's shirt was ripping apart as enormous wings formed. His jeans fell and pooled at his feet as his legs thinned. But his shoes were a loss as gigantic claws pushed through the leather.

Unlike the Aerie, who when transformed became the size of a normal eagle, Rand was a human-sized...

"Crow?" Cee asked.

"Kornyx," said Marcus.

"Kornyx?" Guin echoed shakily, her head turning this way and that as she tried to pinpoint sound. "That's just a fairy tale."

"Tell that to Rand," Marcus said.

The childhood stories flooded back into Cee's mind, tales of the huge nocturnal blackbirds that presaged war and death. The Kornyx were Death's servants, if one believed the really old myths, the ones with gods and goddesses roaming the earth. But they were just that—myths.

And so are dragons, Livian reminded her.

Rand was almost impossible to see, being as black now as the air around him. Only now and again did Cee catch a flash of the inky eye, the blue-black plumage. Worse than the dark, though, was the quiet. The coughing and squawking had ceased, and Rand was utterly silent.

How do we turn him back? Cee asked Livian.

Why would you want to? Livian countered.

Cee wasn't sure how having a legendary death bird benefited them, or how *being* a legendary death bird benefited Rand. She watched as the bird lifted first one foot then the other, shaking its legs free of the jeans and what was left of the shoes. Marcus swooped in and gathered the discarded clothing, stuffing it into his duffel. Rand's duffel appeared to still be caught on one of the Kornyx's wings, a blue spot against the black void in Cee's vision.

"Rand?" Guin whispered, her hand still reaching, searching the darkness. The Kornyx dipped its head against Guin's outstretched fingers, and Guin hiccoughed a sob as she stroked the feathers.

The Kornyx cocked its head and nipped at Guin's sleeve. Despite its large, sharp beak, it was careful to catch only the fabric. It tugged, then released, then took a somewhat wobbly, march-like step forward.

"He wants us to keep going," said Marcus.

"How can you tell?" Guin asked, her tone strangled and shrill. "How can you even see?"

The answer came in the form of meteors of light falling across Marcus's pupils like shooting stars. The Kornyx noticed and rustled its feathers, hopping sideways away from Marcus.

Natural enemies, Livian explained.

"Who?" Cee asked aloud. "The Magi and Kornyx?"

Kornyx sided with Dracona in the war.

"What war?" Cee remembered nothing in history class about a war.

Marcus shifted from one foot to the other. "We should keep moving."

"What's going on?" Guin asked, her voice rising, becoming more strident.

"I'll explain later, as much as I know," Marcus promised. His eyes fired again with golden sparks. "It's even more likely the Magi could give us a more complete story, though—"

The Kornyx gave a little hop and a rasping caw.

"I thought as much," said Marcus.

"You understood that?" Guin asked.

"I don't speak Kornyx, but it's pretty clear he doesn't want anything to do with the Magi."

"*Nothing* is clear," said Guin. "All I'm receiving is... panic. Rand is stuck in there!"

Can you communicate with him? Cee asked Livian.

Take the venison's hand.

Cee reached over and grabbed Guin's hand. Startled, Guin made to pull away, but Cee held on.

Open. Receive, Livian instructed.

Cee wasn't sure how to do that, exactly, but she thought back to all the times it had worked before, the way she'd picked up Guin's telepathy. Was that what Livian meant?

In any case, it worked. Cee was flooded by the sensation of being confined somewhere dark—not the woods, which were certainly dark, but still felt open. No, this was like being cocooned in a black blanket, unable to fight one's way out. Cee's pulse leapt, and she broke out into a sweat. She labored to suck in air.

Now send, said Livian.

Send what? How? The panic was overwhelming. Cee struggled to gather her thoughts. Was Guin sensing all this too?

Livian tightened inside Cee; it felt like he was circling her heart, willing it to slow. As Cee calmed, she began taking deep breaths. With each exhalation, she sent Rand thoughts she hoped would calm him—images of a full moon in a starry sky, a memory of a rainbow she'd once seen—though she had no idea if he received them.

He must have because the sense of panic subsided. Cee released Guin's hand. *Where did those thoughts come from?* she wondered.

I chose what would appeal to the Kornyx as well as your friend. They will have to learn to bond as we have. The Kornyx likes dark things; that is his natural habitat. Your friend, however, seems to prefer more color.

Cee wasn't sure how Livian could know what Rand would like, but there was no time to pursue the conversation. The Kornyx was dancing from foot to foot, but as he rocked back and forth, he appeared to be growing smaller, collapsing. It took Cee a moment to understand, but then she shouted, "Marcus! The blanket!"

Marcus was ahead of her, as usual, already pulling the blanket free of the duffel. He tossed it over Rand, now human again, though Cee glimpsed a couple large, black feathers as they fell to the dark earth.

"What's going on?" Guin asked again.

"Rand is back," Cee told her.

"I know," said Guin. "I can tell. But what's going on?"

169

Marcus brought out Rand's jeans, the only bit of clothing that had survived the transformation.

"You can tell?" Cee asked Guin.

"Rand's thoughts... Is he awake?"

"Barely," said Marcus.

"I'm awake." Rand's voice was a low, thick rumble. Sluggish. Marcus did for him what Ernesta had for Cee by holding the blanket up as a screen while Rand dressed.

"Why can you see and not me?" Guin asked.

"Livian is helping me," said Cee. "And I'm guessing Diodoric is—"

"Yes," Marcus said.

"I can see, too," Rand said. "I couldn't before, but..."

"Probably because you're a Kornyx," Marcus told him. "They see in the dark." He held up the remains of Rand's shoes. "Not sure if it would be better or worse to try using these."

"I'll go barefoot," Rand decided.

The blanket returned to the duffel. Bottles of water were passed around. "Are you fit to keep going?" Marcus asked Rand. "Morphing expends a lot of energy. Do you need to rest?"

"No," said Rand. Then, as if remembering his manners, "No, thank you." He reached over and took Guin's hand. "I got you," he told her.

A lump crawled up Cee's throat. She risked a swift glance at Marcus, but he was busying himself with the duffel, getting the water bottles tucked away.

What about the Cervids? Cee asked Livian. *Which side were they on in whatever war it was?*

None.

NINETEEN

N o Clan shall interfere with or trespass upon another,
nor shall Clans form alliances for the purpose of
menacing other Clans. All treaties between Clans
are subject to review and approval by the Convention of Clans.

—Code of Clans

NONE?

Not everyone fights. Some refuse to take sides. Livian's tone
made it clear he did not condone such behavior. But Cee
considered Guin's naturally gentle nature and understood.

Rand took the lead this time, and Cee supposed his
Kornyx vision probably bested both Livian's and Diodoric's
in the dark. Rand walked with Guin in tow, Cee following,
and Marcus relegated to caboose. Despite her heightened
sight, Cee could barely see Rand in the dark; his shirtless
skin blended into the shadows. Just as well, Cee thought,

since the Code of Conduct did not allow for bare chests. Cee wasn't sure she wanted to see one.

Except she kind of did, a little.

Cee shook her head, as if telling herself no, and focused on not stumbling. What counted as a path through the trees sloped gently downward, and Cee began to wonder if the Far Eastern Wilderness was somehow a gigantic bowl in the earth. It was a gradual descent, yet before long there was the definite sense of land and trees rising behind them like a hill. Livian turned circles in Cee's abdomen, muttering in a language she didn't understand, but she had the general notion he didn't like the lay of the land.

She still hadn't decided what she would say to the Magi. Nothing? Or would she ask for their help as Arlon had suggested?

They will know, Livian told her. *When they see you, they will know.*

Of course they would. She couldn't hide what she was, not from them. The issue was one of compliance... or defiance.

In the dark, Guin's long, blonde hair swung, and Cee caught the glint of her dark eyes as Guin glanced backwards. Did Guin detect her turmoil? Cee wondered how strong Guin's abilities were, what Ernesta had told her.

Slowly, Cee became aware the trees were beginning to thin. There was a sense of space opening around them, like a crowd drawing back or a curtain opening. Cee had found a story once in a really old book—it told of a sea parting to allow people to walk through. That's what it felt like the trees were doing, letting them through.

And then the world fell away entirely.

Rand stopped and threw an arm out to bar anyone

moving past him. Guin stepped up to stand beside him, and Cee and Marcus moved forward to crowd behind them.

Inside Cee, Livian grew quiet, though he seemed to be quivering.

What Cee had begun to think of as a bowl was now more like a crater. Though it was dark, with Livian's help she could see the wasteland that lay before them. She wasn't sure if it appeared monochromatic because it was night or because there really was only gray and black, a great charred hole in the middle of the forest.

Beside her, Marcus let out a little moan.

"Well, Cee," he said, "I think we know now where you came from."

"WHAT DO YOU MEAN?" Cee demanded. Livian's trembling was now a near earthquake in her innards.

"A dragon did this," said Rand. "It must have been. Right?"

Guin's legs resembled Cee's shaking stomach, and she moved her head from side to side. "It smells wrong," Guin said. "But it's all smelled wrong."

"Does it smell like a dragon?" Marcus asked.

Guin's nose twitched. "Hard to tell with Cee standing here. Sorry," she added, and Cee assumed the apology was aimed at her, "but ever since you morphed..."

Cee hadn't considered her transformation might change her, what? Scent? Was that how the Magi would know? And others as well? Suddenly the pros of having a dragon inside her were outweighed by the cons.

"How bad is the damage? How far does it go?" Cee asked. If a dragon had done this, she was guilty by association. The worse the destruction, the greater her culpability.

"I can't see the end of it," said Rand. "I mean, aside from where we're standing, it's—" He shifted closer to Guin to give Cee a better view. "How well can you see?"

"Well enough." Her voice sounded small to her own ears. Truth was, she wished she were as blind as Guin in that moment.

They stood at the margin of what could only be described as a blast zone. The monochromatic landscape stretched away into the darkness, and she wondered if, come daylight, she'd be able to see the other side of it. Perhaps not. Perhaps like the parted sea in that story, the destruction was so vast they would have to cross without knowing where they were going to end up or what waited on the other side.

Of course, crossing it meant being out in the open for who knew how long.

"Where are the Volunteers?" Cee wondered.

Guin shook her head. "I don't smell them, but it may just be this smells stronger."

"But do you sense them?" Rand asked.

Guin was still for a long moment. "There's something off that way," she said finally, pointing off to the right.

"Northeast again," said Marcus, his voice laced with irritation.

"If we'd gone northeast to begin with, we would have gotten there without having to cross this crater," said Guin.

"We may not have to cross it," Rand said, forestalling the pending argument. "We could just skirt it, stay in some cover."

He was right, Cee saw. Though the trees were certainly thinner and many were damaged around the site, there were enough to cover them if they stayed along the edge of the basin.

"It will take us longer," remarked Marcus. "And may make it more difficult for Arlon and Ernesta to find us again."

"They'll find us easily enough," said Rand. "And they know where we're headed. Though," he added with a speculative squint at the sky, "I wouldn't say no to them dropping some breakfast our way. Morphing makes you hungry."

"At least you didn't eat anyone," said Cee. The memory of it made her stomach roil.

"I did have a strong craving for snakes," Rand admitted.

They stood in awkward silence. Usually, when someone morphed, they went off with their Clan and that was that. But in their unique circumstances, none of them knew what was expected, what was okay to say or ask.

Suddenly, though, Cee wanted to talk about it. She wanted to compare notes with Rand. She wanted to not feel alone.

Because Marcus, much as she loved him, didn't count. He wasn't going to morph the way she or Rand had.

Guin was the first to speak, her voice a thin whistle in the dark. "Did it hurt?"

Cee and Rand exchanged glances. "It was heavy," Cee said. "For me, anyway. Like wearing an oversized coat that weighs several tons."

Livian huffed.

"And for me, it was more like being smothered in a blanket. Not heavy—in fact, I felt lighter than normal—just... confining," said Rand.

"You seemed so panicked," Guin said.

"It's scary the first time," said Cee. "When you're not expecting it. The time I fully transformed, though, I did it on purpose. To stop the helicopter."

175

"You didn't eat the guy on purpose, though," Rand said. Cee thought he sounded a tad uncertain.

"No. I couldn't stop him. Livian, I mean. I couldn't control him, and that's what worries me."

More silence, but it felt good to have said it aloud. After a minute, Rand said, "Mine is named Taranis." When they all looked at him, he shrugged. "I don't know how I know. I just do."

"Does he talk to you?" Cee asked.

Rand paused as if listening then shook his head. "Not so far."

"That's odd," said Marcus, his first entry into the discussion. "Both Cee and I... met, if that's the word, our morphs before ever transforming."

"But you don't morph," Guin said.

Marcus only stared at her. It was then Cee realized the sky had begun to turn gray; they could see again. She snuck a glance at Rand's bare chest then bounced her gaze away, simultaneously embarrassed and intrigued.

Rand noticed the lightening sky as well. "We should start moving," he said.

"Or find a place to camp, if anyone needs to rest," said Marcus.

They decided to go a bit farther before stopping, and opted to skirt the damage rather than attempt to cross it because there would be no way to camp without being seen. Rand continued to lead the way, and Cee fell back beside Marcus, her eyes darting periodically to Rand's strong back then away again.

"Do you?" she asked Marcus. "Morph?"

"You've seen for yourself," Marcus said, his lips pursed as if tasting something sour. "I'll only ever be me. Except not me anymore."

Cee could taste his bitterness in her own mouth. "I don't want you to change," she told him.

Marcus looked surprised. "Why not?"

Cee was equally surprised he had to ask. "Because I—I like you the way you are."

"Even though I would never like you the same way?" Marcus asked.

Cee decided not to answer that one, mostly because she wasn't sure of the truth herself. The memory of Diodoric's intent stare, his request to kiss her, fizzled through Cee's core. Would she like it if...?

Cee became very aware of Marcus's gaze, his tiny frown, and forced her thoughts aside, though it was surprisingly difficult, like pushing at something heavy. She scrambled for a train of thought. "But do you have any choice? In whether to change, I mean."

"They'll make me, I'm sure," said Marcus. "And... Part of me wants to." He sighed. "I should be glad to be a Magi. I *am* glad. They'll teach me so much—"

"You're already brilliant."

Marcus continued as if Cee hadn't spoken. "And it's a privileged Clan. With a lot of responsibility, of course, but that comes with the job. Every Clan has its part to play—"

"In accordance with its skills and talents," Cee finished. That dictum had been drilled into them early and frequently. "And Magi have the most skills and talents."

"I'm sure Dracona have many as well," said Marcus. "You've already exhibited a few."

Cee's gaze traveled over to the black and gray wasteland. "And maybe there's someone to teach me after all."

Marcus grimaced. "Not if the Magi have their way." Though he still sounded like himself, when he looked at her, Cee saw the threads of gold stretching through the green of his irises.

"Did Diodoric tell you that? How does he know?"

"How does Livian know the things he knows?"

Cee frowned; she hadn't thought of that. *How* do *you know?* she asked silently. But Livian didn't respond. Cee could feel his warmth radiating from her chest through her limbs. Maybe he'd gone to sleep?

"I won't be able to hide him from them," Cee sighed.

"No," Marcus agreed. "But if you promise to behave..."

"Arlon said the Magi could possibly put Livian to sleep or something."

"You don't sound convinced."

"I'm sure they have plenty of power," said Cee. "I'm just not sure it's something I want."

"You've grown attached," said Marcus.

His tone needled Cee. "Yes," she said, "just like you knew I would. Too bad you and Diodoric can't also find a way to bond."

Marcus's face cleaved with hurt at her sharp words. "There is no compromise for me. No teamwork solution. Bonding with Diodoric means becoming him, completely, forever."

"Well, maybe the Magi can put *him* to sleep then," snapped Cee. She quickened her steps, putting Marcus behind her, though she felt bad almost immediately. Marcus's situation was much more complicated than hers, and at least he hadn't eaten anyone. In fact, Marcus—and Diodoric—had only tried to help in every circumstance. Could she really say that about herself or Livian? The events of Community Day, the very reason they were in trouble, testified that she could not.

Cee slowed down and waited for Marcus to catch up to

her so she could apologize. Ahead of her, Rand and Guin had their heads bent together and were still holding hands. Cee thought about holding hands with Marcus two nights before, how nice it had been and natural it had seemed. They were supposedly mortal enemies, but maybe their friendship would be the bridge between the two Clans. Just like her father had always said.

Marcus still hadn't caught up, so Cee turned around to tell him she was sorry, that she hoped they still had a future together as advocates for peace, that she would always love him no matter who he became. But there was no one to tell.

Marcus was gone.

TWENTY

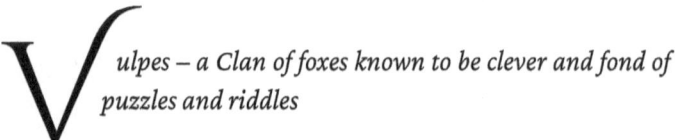

ulpes – a Clan of foxes known to be clever and fond of puzzles and riddles

—Concise Guide to the Clans

"Rand!" Cee didn't even turn around; she just kept staring at the emptiness behind her.

A moment later both Rand and Guin appeared at her shoulders. "What?" Rand asked, then, "Where's Marcus?"

"I don't know," Cee said. "He was behind me, and then he wasn't."

Rand looked up, and Guin's eyes went to the trees. The sky was light, the trees beside the blast site charred and widely spaced, as if a few had fallen during the destruction. Any movement, any flash of color would have been easy to see. There was nothing.

"Did you hear anything?" Rand asked.

Cee shook her head. She mentally prodded Livian, but

he only shifted and resettled inside her. Lending her his eyesight had evidently taken a lot out of him.

Guin shook her head too. "I don't smell or sense anything," she said. "But it could be that whatever happened here is just louder."

"Louder?" Cee asked.

"I don't know how else to describe it," said Guin. "Everything I'm picking up, it's all from—" She threw a hand toward the gray crater of land.

Rand's eyes were still on the sky. "Arlon and What's-her-name?"

"I would have heard them," said Cee, privately hoping that was true. "Why would they take Marcus anyway?"

"Why do they do anything?" Rand asked, and Cee had to admit he had a point. Friendship was well and good, and brotherly love probably even better, but it was just as likely the Aerie had an agenda.

"Maybe they plan to pick us off, one by one," said Guin.

Cee didn't particularly want to dwell on that possibility. "None of us heard, saw, or sensed anything," she said. "Livian didn't even stir, and he usually knows things before I do." She looked at Rand (trying hard not to stare at his smooth, muscular chest), but he didn't offer any information on behalf of Taranis, and Cee didn't feel comfortable asking outright. If her and Livian's relationship were any example, it might take a while for Rand and Taranis to come to trust one another and learn to work together.

"Which means," Cee went on, "we're dealing with something or someone pretty stealthy. Powerful, even."

"You mean the Magi," said Rand.

"Unless Marcus left of his own accord," put in Guin. And when Rand and Cee stared, she shrugged. "He's a

Magus, right? He could be pretty stealthy if he wanted to be, I'm sure."

Rand turned to Cee. "He was walking with you."

"Behind me." Cee hated the way her voice quavered.

"Right behind?" Rand asked.

"I'd gone ahead." Now she spoke in barely a whisper.

"You fought," said Guin. Cee looked sharply at her, and she added, "I don't have to read your mind to be able to tell."

"It wasn't a fight. We were just... talking. And you know how Marcus can be."

"Too smart for his own good," said Rand.

"Not smart enough in some ways," Guin countered. Rand looked confused, but Cee was glad Guin understood. Marcus was brilliant in all the ways that allowed him to do well in school, and he had what Cee's mother called "pretty manners," but when it came to dealing with people, his need for honesty and clarity often outweighed his diplomacy.

"Anyway," Cee said, "I felt bad about... About something I said, so I turned around and..."

Rand frowned in the direction of the trees. "Not like him to walk off in a huff, though, is it?"

Cee remembered the streaks of gold in Marcus's eyes. "Not like Marcus, maybe, but how much do we know about Diodoric?"

They stared at each other for a long moment. Then Guin said, "If we move away from the disaster site, I might have a better chance of picking something up from him."

"Unless he's, I don't know, shielding himself or something?" Rand said. Both he and Guin looked at Cee.

"How should I know?" Cee asked. "I mean, I don't know how strong Diodoric has gotten, or whether Marcus could fight him, assuming he wanted to." Marcus's comments led Cee to believe he did want to fight, and she prayed silently that he would—and could—hold out. But if Diodoric was getting stronger, who knew how long Marcus could last? A sudden, chilling fear shot through Cee like cold water on a hot day: What if she never saw Marcus again? And their friendship ended with a stupid spat?

Rand sighed. "We should go in anyway," he said. "Standing out here in the open now that it's full light... Plus, we could all use a rest."

Cee couldn't imagine resting with Marcus lost, but she didn't argue. She wanted to be doing something, even if it meant simply picking a direction. So she nodded, and they ventured toward the tree line.

At first it wasn't so different from being near the destruction; the trees were gray and dead, many leaning, some having fallen on their brethren like rotten and crooked teeth. But a few yards in, the bark began to be healthy again, the trees strong and proud, and the smell of ash was replaced by springtime. The cover was almost too good, creating a hush and making the warm day much cooler. Cee pulled her cardigan more tightly around her and felt sorry for Rand not having a shirt.

Guin's long, blonde hair flew left and right as she turned her head in search of a scent, or whatever it was she used to find things in the forest. "Even if he's masking his thoughts, I should be able to—" Guin stopped abruptly and cocked her head. "Some birds are disturbed."

"Where?" Rand asked.

Guin pointed. "That way."

"Closest thing we have to a lead," Rand declared. "Let's go." He took two steps then hesitated and looked at Guin. "Maybe you should lead. Since you, you know..."

Guin stepped ahead, and Cee noticed the careful, cautious way she navigated through the trees. Just like a deer.

She comes from that, but she will never be that.

How long have you been awake? Cee asked. *And what do you mean by that?*

But Livian didn't answer either question, instead saying, *There's another one.*

Another one what?

Guin's steps were getting slower, and Cee knew they were close. But to what, she wasn't sure and Livian wasn't telling.

They came to a loose ring of a dozen trees around a small clearing. There wasn't much grass because the tree branches met overhead and cut off most of the sunlight. Without a word, they spread out, each peering up into the leaf-crowded branches that were bright with new growth, but careful to keep one another in sight as well. Above them birds hopped and twittered, and Cee had the insane urge to reach out and catch them, though she knew she never could.

Breakfast, said Livian.

"Good luck with that," Cee muttered. "Because I'm not eating another living creature for you."

I'd do it myself if you'd...

Cee could feel Livian pushing at her insides as if testing the size and shape, and whether there was any give. "No," she said.

Thump. Thump. Thump. He was throwing himself against the interior of her chest. It felt like a sledgehammer trying to break through the obverse of her sternum.

"Stop it," Cee told him through gritted teeth.

I want out.

"No," Cee said again. "And if you keep doing that, you'll do permanent damage. Which would mean never coming out again. Ever."

The thudding subsided, but Cee could feel Livian's resentment radiating along with his natural heat. She slipped her cardigan off and tied it around her waist. "Now help me find him."

Livian remained stubbornly silent.

"Remind me never to have kids," Cee sighed, moving on to peer into yet another tree.

On your right, Livian sighed. *Your other right*, he added when Cee turned to her left.

If she hadn't been looking for it, she might never have noticed the way the trunk of the tree to her right was gilded in rust on one side. It took Cee a moment longer to realize this rust-colored thing was not part of the tree but behind it. Cloth. Clothing. Something—someone—was hiding behind the trunk.

"Who are you?" Cee asked. She tried to sound authoritative but her words came out as a harsh whisper.

The bit of cloth swayed as the person behind the tree shifted. Livian let out a low growl, and Cee was startled when she realized she was growling, too, quite audibly.

A sharp nose and ochre-colored eyes emerged from the far side of the tree. Cee detected no fear and no menace in the features, only mild curiosity. She started to call to Guin and Rand, but the person—it wasn't immediately clear to Cee whether it was male or female—put a finger to its lips then gestured for Cee to come closer.

Livian swished in Cee's stomach, but she stepped forward to join the stranger, drawn as though by an invisible cord. She saw as she rounded the tree that he was, well, a *he*, and the russet-colored cloth was a cloak worn over otherwise very average denim trousers and a green and white rugby shirt. His hair was almost the same color as the cloak. Cee guessed he was older than her, but not by more than a handful of years.

"Who are you?" Cee asked again.

"Valentian," he answered.

Cee waited for more but nothing was forthcoming, so she asked, "Valentian who?"

He frowned at her and shook his head as if her question made no sense, or perhaps was simply not important. "You're the dragon," he said.

Livian reared and Cee took two steps backward, but Valentian reached out and grabbed her wrist. "I won't hurt you," he hissed with a quick glance around the tree. Cee followed his gaze. Guin and Rand were finishing with the circle of trees, and Rand began looking around as he realized Cee was missing, too.

"Cee?" Rand called.

Cee looked at Valentian. He tightened his hold on her. She stepped out from behind the tree, towing him with her. "I'm here!"

She could see Rand's relief as his massive shoulders dropped. Then they went up again as he spied Valentian. "Who're you?"

Valentian stopped short, and Cee nearly snapped backward in his grasp. "No one said anything about a Kornyx," said Valentian.

"Who's no one?" Rand demanded.

Guin came to stand beside Rand. "He's a Magus," she said.

"A Magus?" Cee asked.

At the same time, Valentian said, "Of course I am. But,"

he added, "they don't know I'm here." He looked at Cee. "You have to go."

"Go where?" Cee asked.

"Anywhere." Valentian's expression was tight with concern. "You just—you have to go."

"Why?" Cee insisted. "Why do you even care? I thought the Magi—"

"Why should we trust you?" asked Guin. Her dark eyes narrowed as if she were peering into Valentian's thoughts, then snapped wide again. "He's shut me out."

"You can't go around invading people's minds," said Valentian. "It's rude."

"We still don't know who you are," Rand said. "What you are, maybe, but not who."

"His name is Valentian," Cee offered.

"Why is he dressed like that?" Rand asked.

"I'm standing right here," said Valentian.

A thought struck Cee. "Can you sense other Magi?" she asked. "We lost our friend... Why *are* you dressed like that?"

Valentian threw up his hands, releasing Cee in the process. "Look, no, I'm not a missing persons... And you just —you need to go. Now. And I need to go back to the camp before they find out I'm out here. And we all dress like this."

There was a long silence. Cee felt Livian huff behind her sternum.

Finally, Rand asked, "But seriously, why cloaks?"

Cee shot him a warning look and turned to Valentian. "We can't leave without Marcus. Or... Diodoric." Her voice wobbled slightly on the last word as a fresh wave of fear crested over her heart. What if Marcus was gone for good? What if Diodoric was the only one left? He might share Marcus's memories, but it would never be the same.

"Why are you trying to chase us away?" Guin asked. "We were going to the Magi for help."

Valentian looked at Guin as if she'd said they were going to sprout wings and fly, though Cee reflected two out of the three of them were actually capable of that. "Help?" the Magus echoed. "They're not going to help you."

Cee felt like her heart was being wrung of blood. "We have nowhere else to go."

She was startled when Valentian took her hand and squeezed it. "I'm sorry. But if you go to the Magi, you're only saving them the trouble of finding you."

"But what about Marcus?" Rand asked.

Cee shook her head. "We'll go if we have to, but not without Marcus."

Valentian scanned the determined expressions and sighed. "Where did you last see him?"

"Why are you helping us?" Cee asked. "Can't you get in trouble?"

They picked their way through the trees with seemingly no method to their search. Guin claimed she was unable to smell or sense anything beyond the damaged forest, and Valentian refused to explain his abilities, assuming he had any. But every now and then he would pause and change direction and, for lack of better options, the rest of them followed him.

Valentian hesitated at Cee's question then abruptly turned right, wending through tightly spaced trunks. "Yes," he finally answered. "Bad enough there's a dragon, now a blackbird too."

Cee glanced back at the others. "You mean Rand?"

"If that's his name. He could do with a cloak himself."

Valentian stopped walking. "We're coming too close to the camp." He frowned over at Cee. "You were going to the Magi, you said. Would your friend have gone to them on his own?"

"Well, he is one," said Rand.

Valentian forced air through his teeth in a long hiss.

"He's becoming one," Cee put in hastily. "He's—he's fighting it, actually." She hoped he still was.

"How close is he to Resolving?" Valentian asked.

Cee, Rand, and Guin exchanged glances. "No idea," Rand said.

"But you've met the Magus?" Valentian pressed.

"Yes," said Cee. "He couldn't stay long the first time, lasted a little longer the second."

"It will happen more frequently, with the Magus in control for longer stretches of time, until the original personality is absorbed for good," said Valentian.

"Absorbed?" Guin asked, her voice wavering.

"That's how we describe it," Valentian explained. "In the Clan, I mean."

"Do you remember your original personality?" Cee asked.

Valentian scrutinized her with those odd, ale-colored eyes. "Of course. But it's more like remembering someone I used to know a long time ago. I'm not that person anymore."

"Not even a little?" asked Guin. "No tiny part of— of whoever you were... remains?"

Valentian glanced down at himself. "Well, I look the same. Except my eyes used to be hazel."

"And that doesn't bother you?" Rand asked. "To just become someone else entirely?"

"This isn't about me," Valentian said abruptly. "We're

looking for your friend, but it seems to me he may have gone to the Magi camp, which is the last place you should be anywhere near."

"He wouldn't have gone without us," Cee said. "Not willingly." She looked to Rand and Guin for confirmation only to be greeted with doubtful faces.

"It's his Clan," Rand said with a shrug.

"And he wanted to go there," Guin added.

"And maybe he thought better of putting you in that kind of danger," Rand went on.

Cee recalled her last conversation with Marcus, telling him she wasn't sure she wanted to give Livian up. Had he taken her at her word and gone on to the Magi without them? Without even saying goodbye?

Rustling from the undergrowth drew Cee's thoughts to the immediate moment. Rand tensed, ready to fight, and Guin's eyes widened, but Valentian, Cee noted, remained calm and impassive as a large red fox stepped through the crowd of trees to join them. It looked at each one of them in turn, ending with a long stare at Valentian.

"I know," Valentian said, "but their friend..." He threw up his hands.

"You're talking to a fox," Rand pointed out. "And it hasn't even said anything."

The fox stood up on its hind legs and began to grow taller.

"Vulpes!" Cee exclaimed.

The woman who emerged was petite, with sleek red hair and blue-green eyes that tilted at the outside corners. She wore faded jeans that had seen more wear than possibly intended and a lacy white tunic top with some-what more holes than the lace accounted for. She was almost certainly older than any of them by five to ten years at Cee's estimation.

"Beverly," Valentian said, "this is Cee, Rand, and uh..."

"Guin," Guin supplied.

Beverly nodded to them then turned to Valentian. "You were supposed to take them the other way."

"They've got a missing friend," Valentian told her.

"I know," said Beverly. "He's in the camp."

Cee's breath stuck in her throat. Marcus *was* with the Magi!

But then Rand asked, "Why should we believe her?" and Cee's heart sank. He had a point. Everyone knew Vulpes were sly and untrustworthy. What did this one hope to gain by telling them Marcus was in the Magi camp? Was there a reward for their capture? This fox could clearly use new clothes.

Cee eyed Valentian with fresh suspicion. They didn't really know him. Why should they trust him either? Especially if he fraternized with Vulpes?

Valentian and Beverly appeared to have some silent conversation, their eyes locked on one another. Both Cee and Rand turned to Guin reflexively. Guin's brow puckered and she gave a tiny shake of her head. "He's a Magus. I can't get anything."

"Her?" Rand asked.

"She's strong, too," Guin said. "Or maybe he's shielding them both."

"What does your gut tell you?" Rand asked, and when Guin turned her wide eyes on him, he said, "I trust your instincts."

Guin smiled for the first time in days, and Cee felt her heart fall into her feet. She suddenly felt very alone.

What about me?

Cee draped her surprise at Livian's abrupt revival in anger. *What* about *you?* she demanded.

Not alone. Never alone.

Cee sighed. She couldn't explain to Livian that despite his constant presence, the loneliness she felt stemmed from something else. Something even she didn't understand.

But then a glimpse of Rand's and Guin's intertwined fingers made it clear—her solitude was born from a lack of companionship. Outer companionship, to be exact. Someone to hold hands with and...

"You have to go." Beverly planted herself in front of Cee. "Your friend is with his Clan now. Where he belongs."

"But where do we belong?" Cee asked. "As far as I know, I don't have a Clan." She glanced uncertainly at Rand. "And we don't know if he's even supposed to exist."

"Hey!" said Rand. "I mean, true, but still."

Beverly and Valentian had another, shorter silent argument. Finally, Valentian sighed. "I can explain a few things," he offered, "but I'd rather get farther away from the camp first."

"No," said Cee. "I'm not going until I'm sure about Marcus." When Beverly appeared ready to protest or lecture, Cee added, "I'll go if and when I'm convinced it's the right thing to do. Not before."

Beverly shrugged one thin shoulder. "That's fair."

Valentian took one more look around at the trees, assuring himself of their relative seclusion, then said, "Okay then. Sit down."

CHAPTER

TWENTY-ONE

N o one shall appear in public without appropriate attire. The area from the sternum to the mid-thigh is to be covered at all times while in public view. Bare arms may be allowed so long as shoulders are covered.

—Code of Conduct

CEE, Rand, and Guin settled themselves on the ground facing Valentian and Beverly like pupils awaiting instruction. Valentian swept his cloak aside and sat across from them. Beverly, however, remained standing, arms crossed, occasionally looking over her shoulders at the trees. Cee wondered if Beverly were expecting someone, or maybe just trouble.

Valentian's lips twisted as though words were marbles in his mouth that he must feel out and move into the correct order. After a minute, he said, "You don't have a Clan, Cee."

Cee exhaled slowly, trying not to show how hard the declaration had hit her—like a punch to her diaphragm. She felt as if she'd been doused in icy water.

Rand threw a verbal life preserver. "How do you know?" he asked. "How did you even know we were in the woods? Why should we trust you?" His eyes went unabashedly to where Beverly stood, and Valentian's gaze followed. Beverly pointedly continued to stare at the trees.

"The Vulpes told me," Valentian admitted. "They're not what you've been taught," he added swiftly. "No one Clan is all good or all bad. And, Cee..." She reluctantly met his gaze. "Just because you don't have a Clan doesn't mean you're the only Dracona."

Inside Cee, Livian swished in what Cee assumed was glee, though it gave her heartburn. "So there are others?" she asked.

"It might be best to start at the beginning," sighed Valentian.

"Yeah, do that," said Rand.

Valentian took a deep breath. "The Clans were formed—"

"Wait, whoa," said Rand. "Is this a history lesson or what?"

"It's stuff you need to know," Valentian told him. "And the more you interrupt me the longer it's going to take. Which means the more danger we'll all be in." He paused a moment then began again. "The Clans were created about eight hundred years ago by scientists who were doing genetic work. The world was really different then, but..." Valentian shook his head as if to toss off unnecessary tangents. "What matters now is that the Magi are descended from those scientists, and the Dracona are a mutation of the Magi Clan."

Cee tried to absorb this but couldn't. Valentian's words didn't make sense to her.

Guin sought to clarify. "So Cee is a Magus?" she asked.

"Genetically, yes," Valentian answered. "But the Magi have a policy of not tolerating mutations in their line. So you see why you need to go."

Rand barked a harsh laugh. "Not tolerating? Come out and say it. Your people kill their own kind."

"So did the Ancients," said Valentian. "The Greeks left babies on mountains." He was greeted with blank stares. "Never mind. Yes, the Magi kill Dracona. They believe Dracona use up too many resources and are too destructive, too unpredictable."

Cee flashed back to the moment Livian devoured Grantham. She remembered the insane accusations she'd made on Community Day, the very reason they were all in trouble to begin with. Destructive and unpredictable. Maybe the Magi were right.

"But you don't agree," Rand surmised.

His words surprised Cee and pulled her out of her spiral of self-loathing. Or Livian loathing anyway. But hating Livian meant hating herself.

"We don't think mass extermination of a species is the way to solve the problem," Beverly said.

"The two of you?" Guin asked.

"There are more," said Valentian.

"How many more?" Rand asked.

"Enough," Beverly answered.

"Enough for what?" Cee asked. Life had always been narrow and planned, a straight line. Now she felt like that path had been washed away and she didn't know which direction to walk. She had no Clan, but there was what? A

195

group of rebels secretly meeting? To what end? Cee's quiet and peaceful world was being swept away.

Valentian and Beverly exchanged brief glances before Beverly said, "It doesn't concern you."

"Yet here you are," Rand pointed out, "trying to throw us out of the Far Eastern Wilderness."

"We're trying to help you," Valentian insisted.

Rand stood. "Well, you figured out where Marcus is and got us close enough to rescue him, so thanks for that."

"What makes you think he wants to be rescued?" Beverly asked. "He's a Magus. And now he's with his Clan."

Rand ignored her and turned to Guin. "Can you navigate from here? Tell where the Magi camp is?"

Guin frowned up at him, then turned her worried dark eyes on Valentian. "You would leave the Magi if you could, wouldn't you?"

Valentian visibly started, as if Guin's words had been an arrow striking him. He opened his mouth to respond, but Beverly cut in with, "Don't."

"Don't what?" Rand asked. "Tell us the truth?"

"Tell you more than you need to know," said Beverly. "Because if you're going into the camp and they catch you, the less you know, the less you can tell them." She tilted her head and considered Rand. "At the very least you could try stealing a shirt."

Beverly's words had an unexpected effect on Cee; she felt a blaze of anger rise through her, though she wasn't sure why. She only knew Beverly had no right to comment on Rand's... lack of clothing. Or look at him that way.

Could eat a fox, Livian suggested.

"I just might," Cee murmured, earning her odd looks from the others.

"Or I could go for one of those stylish cloaks," said

Rand. He reached down to help both Guin and Cee to their feet, giving them each and hand and lifting them as if they weighed nothing.

Valentian stood as well, his expression grave. "I wouldn't. Steal a cloak, I mean. I wouldn't even try sneaking into the camp if I were you."

"Right. You want us to run away," said Rand. "But we aren't going to. So what's your next best advice?"

Cee was all too aware of the way Beverly's appraising gaze lingered on Rand. She glanced at Guin and saw flintiness in the usually soft brown eyes that told Cee her friend noticed it too. And liked it as little, maybe less, than Cee did.

"Why do you keep looking at him like that?" Cee demanded.

Beverly's eyebrows lifted and a corner of her mouth twisted upward. "Sorry. I've just never seen a Kornyx before. I thought he'd have more feathers."

Cee looked at Rand, who was squinting thoughtfully at the Vulpes. Then Valentian cleared his throat, and everyone's attention returned to him. "If you insist on..." More marbles in his mouth as he searched for the phrase he wanted. "This course of action," he went on, "then at least wait until dark."

Cee, Rand, and Guin had a silent conversation, all cocked heads and furrowed brows, ending in small nods. "Sounds fair," Rand finally declared. "We could use the rest anyway."

"Marcus has the other duffel," Guin pointed out.

"We can at least get you something to eat," said Beverly, and when Valentian looked startled, she added, "You want to help them, right? They need to eat."

Both Cee and Rand looked up at the slice of sky above them, then met gazes and laughed.

"What?" Beverly asked sharply, at the same time Valentian hissed, "Shh!"

"We're like baby birds," Rand told Cee, his grin brilliant in his dark face.

Valentian's face appeared sharper as his features pinched in with confusion and concern. Cee wondered whether all Magi had such noble noses and high cheekbones. Her own nose was straight enough, though not nearly so large. It hit her then: she and Marcus were the same Clan after all. The same and yet enemies.

But Marcus would never really be her enemy. Would he? Cee pictured his stony face whenever he was displeased and a shiver ran through her.

Valentian was still waiting for an explanation. "We're used to the Aerie bringing us meals," Cee said.

"The Aerie? Why?" Beverly asked.

Another quick and wordless conversation before Rand answered, "Marcus has an older foster brother. He's Aerie."

"He's been helping you," Valentian deduced.

Cee looked to Guin, whose head drooped so that her hair masked her expression. Was she tired and hungry or trying to hide how she felt about the Aerie?

Guin's head lifted just enough for her to meet Cee's gaze, and Cee realized Guin could read her thoughts.

She's getting stronger, Livian sighed.

That's good, right? Cee asked silently then immediately worried Guin had heard her. Could Guin hear Livian too?

Not that strong. Yet, said Livian. *I can shield you, but you wouldn't like it.*

"Why not?" Cee voiced the question aloud without thinking.

Valentian and Beverly exchanged glances. "I don't know," Beverly said, evidently in answer to Valentian's unspoken thought. "I'll have to ask around. But first we should get them food. I don't think the eagles are flying today." She threw another look at Rand, and Cee was almost certain she winked before suddenly a fox was diving into the undergrowth.

"I've never seen anyone morph that fast," said Rand, his tone tinged with admiration.

"She's been doing it a long time," said Valentian.

"And it's not like you've seen so many morphs, either," Guin added.

Cee blinked in surprise at Guin's unusually astringent manner. But if Rand noticed it, he didn't let on. He was still looking at the spot where the Vulpes had disappeared.

"How many blankets are in your duffel, Rand?" Cee asked. As intended, her question broke the strange crystalline stasis that had briefly frozen around them—Rand's interest in Beverly, Guin's visibly rising irritation. Rand turned his attention to the contents of the bag, and Guin relaxed slightly, though Cee still sensed tension in her. But Guin had been tense and nervous ever since they'd left Morrowville, so this was as near to normal as Cee could hope for.

"Two," answered Rand. "And some water." He handed over the half-full bottle and extracted the blankets but paused before laying them out. "We good with here or...?"

His question was aimed at Guin. Her nose twitched and she turned her head left then right. "This should be fine," she finally declared.

Cee read the question on Valentian's face and explained, "She sort of can do that."

Livian gave a huff that Cee realized was a laugh. *With*

eloquence like that it's a wonder you didn't need me to speak for you sooner.

"Shut up," said Cee, and Valentian drew back slightly. "It's my—he—"

Case in point.

Your eloquence is the reason we're in trouble to begin with. Cee tried to put power behind her words, as if she could punch Livian with them.

We'd be in trouble anyway, Livian pointed out. *Simply for existing.*

"I should go back," Valentian told them. "But I'll return around dusk to check on you."

"Are you going to help us find Marcus?" Rand asked.

Valentian shifted his weight from one foot to another as if standing on something hot. "I'll see what I can find out about where he is," he conceded, the words coming out slow and reluctant.

"Will you have a chance to talk to him?" Cee asked.

Valentian gave her a sympathetic look. "Unlikely." His expression melted into a frown. "And chances are he won't want to leave, you know."

"You don't know Marcus," Cee said. "Even if he wants to stay with... Well, he'd still want to say goodbye."

Cee could read the doubts on Valentian's face, could pinpoint the moment he chose to keep them to himself. All he said was, "Get some rest. Beverly will bring food, and I'll be back later." Then he disappeared into the trees.

Cee, Rand, and Guin stared at one another over the two blankets. "Girls on one, boys on the other?" Rand finally suggested.

"Someone should stay awake," said Guin.

"I will," Cee offered. She was exhausted but equally sure

she wouldn't be able to sleep. She kept thinking of Marcus —or was he Diodoric now?—surrounded by sharp-nosed people with amber-colored eyes, all of them wearing cloaks the color of dried blood.

S **tarlight:** *She wears fireflies in her hair, a glorious crown of night!*

—"The Fey Wager"

THEY'RE RIGHT, you know. He probably fits right in with the Magi. Most likely won't want to leave. Might even still be angry with you. Might also believe Dracona should be eliminated.

Cee leaned back against the tree and stared up into the bright holes between the leaves. She couldn't tell if the words were Livian's or her own. They were starting to blend together. Would they eventually become one entity? That wasn't how Dracona worked, though, was it? The Magi transitioned from one to the other. But the Dracona remained two separate personalities. Sugar and water versus oil and water. Cee wasn't good at Al-Cal, but she knew that much.

We were first. Definitely Livian this time. *They don't want anyone to know that, but we came first genetically. Then they refined their process and became what they are now.*

"Great," Cee muttered. "I'm a throwback."

An original. Undiluted.

"Whatever."

Being from the same Clan should have made Cee feel closer to Marcus. She should have been elated. Instead she felt farther from him than ever, the crack between them yawning into a chasm. If they'd been two different Clans, they might at least have formed a diplomatic bond of friendship. As things stood, however, no bridge could be built.

"That's not necessarily true."

Cee jolted where she sat. She hadn't realized her eyes were closed, hadn't heard anyone coming, but leaning to her left to look over her shoulder she saw Beverly sitting in the undergrowth. Beverly's knees were up, her arms draped around them. "How long have you been there?" *And how did Livian not smell or hear you?*

Beverly gave a one-sided shrug. "Not long. And I rolled in the dirt. *As a fox*," she added tartly when Cee's eyes swept her clothing, which was battered but not dirty. "We're good at keeping quiet, and rolling in the dirt makes us smell like the forest."

Lights went on in Cee's mind like stars winking to life. "So you can sneak up on Dracona. On Magi."

"On some. Not all." Beverly inched closer and swung around a knapsack Cee hadn't noticed.

Some help you are, Cee thought at Livian. *Shouldn't you be on top of these things?* But the dragon didn't answer.

Beverly pulled out paper-wrapped squares that Cee had

come to dread. More sandwiches. But beggars couldn't be choosers, and the growl in her stomach that might have been Livian reminded her it had been a while since her last meal.

Can you trust it? Livian asked.

Since when do you turn down food? Cee countered.

Since it came from a Vulpes.

Cee's hand, already extended to accept the sandwich, closed reflexively.

Beverly's eyebrows inched upward. "If you're worried I stole it, well yes, I did."

"From where?" Cee asked.

"The Volunteer camp. But I figured you wouldn't want me to bring you a dead squirrel."

Maybe, said Livian.

Cee took the sandwich. "The Volunteers are close to here?" She thought of her dad and the other men of Morrowville, minus Mr. Dougherty. Did they know where he'd gone? And why? "What happened here anyway?"

"Forest fire."

"We know that," said Cee as she picked loose the paper wrapping. A strong smell of chicken salad wafted out, and Livian did a wriggling, impatient dance in her abdomen. "But what caused it?"

"A dragon."

Suddenly Cee wasn't hungry any more. She felt as if a lead weight had plummeted through her and landed in her stomach, making it difficult to breathe.

Beverly watched her closely. "It's not fun to be demonized, is it? You should eat," she added. "And then sleep. I'll keep watch."

Eat, Livian agreed. *And then we should find our kin.*

The Magi are our kin, Cee reminded him. *And they want to kill us.*

But there is another Dracona.

That burns down forests. Not the kind of family I'm looking for. Cee took a tentative bite of sandwich. The taste woke her appetite once more and soon the chicken salad was gone, along with a baggie of carrot sticks Beverly had also taken and that reminded Cee of Marcus. Tears pricked her eyelids as she ate them, making her feel miserable and stupid.

"You love him, huh?" Beverly asked. Cee started and stared, forcing her eyes wide to keep the tears from falling. She hoped her expression was severe enough to keep Beverly from prying any further, but the Vulpes said, "He doesn't love you back?"

"He's my best friend," said Cee.

Beverly nodded. "So he loves you as a friend, but not..."

"He doesn't like girls." The words came out raspy, harsh.

"Aaah," Beverly said. "Well, at least it's not you." And when Cee's mouth fell open aghast, "I mean, it's not something about you in particular that's keeping him from—Besides your gender, that is." She heaved a sigh. "Never mind. Pep talks aren't my thing."

"Clearly," muttered Cee. She looked over at where Rand and Guin slept. Though each had a separate blanket, they had rolled in toward one another, as close as they could be without actually touching.

"He's probably just cold," Beverly remarked, following Cee's gaze.

"Then why didn't he wrap the blanket around himself?" Cee retorted. She wished Beverly would quit reading her thoughts and leave her in peace.

"Good point. And I don't have to read your thoughts to tell what you're thinking. Your face says plenty."

"But you are telepathic?" Cee asked.

"It's more common than you think."

Cee sighed. "Then I'm in the minority."

"You're special in a lot of ways," said Beverly. "You're an extremely rare creature, and if what they say is true, you can be telepathic any time you want just by reaching out and grabbing someone who is. Yeah?"

Cee wasn't sure telling a Vulpes about her abilities was a good idea. She gave a small shrug. "I picked it up off Guin a couple times," she admitted. "But it's hardly worth being Clanless and hunted to be able to..." She waved a hand.

Beverly studied her a minute. "The dragon in you have a name?"

Cee shifted where she sat, again uncertain how much she should disclose. "Livian."

"And is he worth protecting?"

Cee frowned, confused. "What do you mean?"

"I mean, if you could cut him out of you and go on with your life, have some normal, regular life, would you?"

Cee squirmed a bit more. "The Aerie said the Magi could put Livian to sleep."

"If that's what you want, then march on in there and ask them," said Beverly. "No need to wait until dark. Just go." She eyed Cee. "But that's not what you want, is it?"

"I don't know," said Cee. The whole conversation felt like a trick, a trap. She should have known better than to talk to a fox.

"We don't get to choose what we are. We only get to choose who we become."

While Cee attempted to untangle whatever sly and hidden meaning the Vulpes had intended, Rand stirred and sat up. Cee watched him blink away sleep. When he turned and saw her and Beverly, he eased to his feet and, careful not to wake Guin, came over to where they sat.

"You should sleep," he told Cee as he sat down beside her.

"And you should eat," Beverly told him. "Oh, here." She pulled a t-shirt from her bag. "They don't grow them quite so big where I'm from, but I got the largest I could find."

"Purple?" Rand asked as he slid it on.

"More of an indigo," said Beverly.

"Purple," Cee decided. "But it looks good on you." In fact, the shirt clung to Rand's muscular figure. Cee thought she it would be a relief to have him covered, but the shirt almost made her more embarrassed than when his chest was bare.

I thought you liked them tall and skinny?

Livian's words brought a blush to Cee's cheeks, which in turn earned her curious looks from Rand and Beverly. "I think I will go rest," Cee mumbled. She jumped to her feet and scrambled for the safety of the blanket. Unlike Rand, she wrapped it around herself like a cocoon. She fell asleep to the low rumble of Rand and Beverly talking, only fleetingly wondering whether it was safe to leave them alone together before exhaustion claimed her.

Up. Get up.

Cee struggled to open her eyes. They didn't want to obey. She was so tired she felt like she could sleep another ten hours and still not get enough rest.

She'd been sick once—only once—and made to stay home in bed for four days. Her body had ached, weighted with fatigue despite her lack of activity. That was how Cee felt again at that moment. Except instead of a soft pillow behind her head, she was aware of every bump, stone, and root in the ground under her blanket.

Up!

Finally Cee managed to force her eyelids apart. She immediately thought she must be sick after all because she was seeing spots. No, lights.

Fireflies.

It was dusk and there were a dozen fireflies hovering in the air.

"Oh," Cee breathed.

She was so taken with the sight she failed to notice Guin was no longer beside her. It took Valentian leaning into her vision to shock her into bolting upright. "You're back," she said rather stupidly.

"So are you." Valentian offered Cee his hand to help her up. The gesture made her think of Marcus, and fresh purpose spurred Cee to her feet.

"Did you see him?" she asked.

Valentian grimaced. "Saw him, yes. I wasn't able to speak to him though."

"Is he okay?" Cee pressed. "Is he...?" She wanted to know if Marcus was still, well, *Marcus*, but realized Valentian wouldn't know the difference.

"He seems very comfortable," Valentian said. The words were slow, hesitant, like a toe dipping into water.

Cee narrowed her eyes as if doing so would allow her to see the truth in the Magus's words. "You're saying he doesn't want to be rescued. But you can't know that because you haven't actually spoken to him."

"You won't get close enough." Now Valentian's words were urgent, rapid. "He's—he's Sabine's son."

"Who's Sabine?"

"Leader of the Magi." Beverly's voice came out of the gathering darkness between the trees seconds before she stepped into view. "They call her the Mother."

"But in your friend's case, she is his literal mother," Valentian put in.

Cee glanced around, looking for Rand and Guin to back her up but they were nowhere to be seen. Her heart crawled up her throat. Where were they? Had these two done something to them? And now she was alone, two against one...

What about me? Livian asked. Cee felt him yawn and stretch inside her. *Could totally eat them.*

"Oh, for the love of—" Cee muttered.

You never want to eat anyone. We're going to have to come up with a compromise if this relationship is going to work.

Cee doubted there would ever be a circumstance under which she'd willingly eat another person. Or let Livian eat them. Not that she would have much say in the matter should Livian take form and decide to do just that. But in that moment of panic, as she faced two potential threats, Cee had to admit the built-in safety of an inner dragon was nice. The only question was how quickly she could morph if it came to that. Could they get her first?

Cee could feel Livian attempting to take advantage of her fear by pushing at her insides, trying to take shape. Valentian and Beverly frowned at her, but not in a way that led Cee to believe they meant her harm. More like consternation. Did they sense her internal struggle?

Ask first, Cee decided. "Where are—?"

Rustling from behind Cee caused her to turn around. Guin appeared from among the trees. Despite the rapidly encroaching dusk, Cee could see the worry in Guin's doe-like eyes. "I lost it."

"Lost what?" Cee asked.

209

"The Kornyx," said Beverly. "His trail anyway."

Cee kept her focus on Guin. "Rand?"

"He was coughing again, and then..." Guin shook her head.

"They come out at night," Valentian said. "Once it started to get dark..."

"He was barely strong enough to morph last night," said Cee. "He can't have gotten so much stronger in a day. Can he?"

They looked at one another, but no one offered an answer.

"You tried to follow him?" Cee asked Guin.

"I thought he would land, transform back." Guin's voice was high and thin with concern. "Then he'd need someone. But I lost the scent of him. He was too fast."

"He'll find his way back," Beverly said. "Kornyx have keen eyesight, a great sense of direction."

Cee looked down at where her abandoned blanket lay piled in the dirt. "Did he take the duffel?"

ONCE THE BLANKET was folded and packed away into Beverly's knapsack, Cee declared, "It's dark enough now. We should go."

To which Valentian replied, "I told you—"

And Guin cried, "But what about Rand?"

Abrupt silence settled over them. The fireflies continued to wink, ever brighter in the growing gloom.

"I'll go on my own if I have to," said Cee. "I can't leave until we've at least said goodbye." Her voice cracked over the last few words, revealing the fragile structure underlying her determination. She had to see Marcus one more time. She couldn't let their last words to one another be an argument.

And if she found Diodoric instead of Marcus? The idea created a fresh lump in Cee's throat but she forced it down. She could only take things one step at a time.

First step: Get to the Magi camp and find Marcus.

Despite her bravado, she couldn't do it alone. She didn't have the ability to sniff out the correct direction, and she didn't know where in the camp Marcus was being held.

We could fly, Livian suggested.

And be seen, Cee thought. She didn't know what powers the Magi had, but she didn't want to test them. If they had eradicated the Dracona before, one little dragon wasn't likely to pose much of a problem.

Who's little?

But Cee had already moved on to another thought. "What happened to it?" she asked.

"To what?" Valentian asked.

"The other dragon. The one that caused all the destruction."

Valentian shook his head. "I don't know. We haven't been able to find it."

Cee felt air come out of her, slow, like a pinprick in a ball. It took her a moment to name the feeling: relief.

I thought you didn't want that kind of family, Livian hissed.

I'll have to take what I can get. Or go it alone. Cee wasn't sure which would be worse.

"How do you not find a huge dragon?" Guin asked, startling Cee from her thoughts.

"If it stays in human form..." Beverly let them figure out the rest.

"But the Magi can sense a Dracona, can't they?" Guin

insisted. Her brow was puckered with contemplation. "Even I can smell one." She glanced at Cee. "Sorry."

Cee resisted the urge to sniff at her underarms. "Is it bad?"

"No, just different. I could tell, when we met at Community Day—"

"This is fabulous," declared Beverly, "but hardly pertinent." She looked at Cee. "You're not going to leave until you see him, right?" Then she turned to Guin. "And I'm guessing you won't go anywhere until you have your feathered friend back." Finally, she looked to Valentian. "So?"

Valentian slumped, shoulders hunched, head hanging, and placed his face in his hands. It was clear to Cee this was more than he'd bargained for. He wasn't that much older than them, after all, and he'd only been trying to warn them off. Help them. But they refused to be helped that way. Instead they were demanding assistance Valentian was reluctant, possibly unequipped, to give. Aid that could get him into serious trouble or worse. This realization made Cee feel selfish, and for a moment she wanted to pat Valentian on the back and tell him she understood, that he could go on and never mind them. They'd find their own way.

Don't be nice to him, Livian warned.

At least you're not suggesting we eat him, Cee reasoned. *You must be warming to him.*

After a minute, Valentian lifted his head. His ochre eyes met Cee's. "I can get you close enough to see him, but I can't promise you'll get to talk to him."

Cee nodded that she understood while silently vowing that if Valentian at least got her to the camp, she could do the rest, hopefully at no risk to the others.

We'll do the rest.

Livian's confidence boosted Cee's own, and she felt his energy flood her limbs. She wanted to take off then and there, and the urge to fly came on so strong and so suddenly she almost shouted aloud. What would it mean to live free, able to transform and fly without worry? Would she ever know that feeling?

We will know it, Livian assured her.

Cee hoped he was right.

TWENTY-THREE

Anyone found trespassing on a Clan's territory will be dealt with by that Clan in accordance with their Clan Code. The Trespasser is given right to counsel and appeal of the offended Clan's Code via the Magistrate.

—Code of Clans

"WHAT ABOUT RAND?" Guin asked.

Valentian exchanged glances with Beverly, and she was the one to answer. "We don't have a way to track something flying that fast and in the dark."

Guin's face crumpled with despair.

"He'll come back," Cee said. "The Kornyx sleep during the day."

Tears welled in Guin's eyes. "But what if they land... who knows where? And Rand can't find us? Or if we leave to go find Marcus, what if Rand comes back here and we're gone?"

"Once they land, and in the light of day, we'll have a better chance of locating him," Valentian said gently.

"Or you can stay here," said Cee. "We can bring Marcus back this way."

Valentian looked sharply at her, and Cee could see the argument forming in him about how they were not planning to bring Marcus anywhere. But before he could say anything, Beverly asked, "What is wrong with these fireflies?"

There were only a dozen of the insects, which alone was strange; usually, Cee thought, they filled the air by the hundreds. And as Beverly pointed out, these ones were behaving abnormally as well. They'd been hovering while the four of them talked, but now the fireflies came together in a sort of ball, one in the center of the others.

Suddenly, the outer fireflies flew backward and the one in the center began to transform.

"Insecta," Cee breathed. She glanced at Valentian to see whether this was a good thing or a bad one, but his expression was inscrutable. Were all Magi so stony faced?

The most beautiful woman Cee had ever seen stood in their midst. She had long, caramel-colored hair and eyes that were a strange green-yellow like a cat's. Her dress was the same color as her eyes, trimmed in black, and seemed to glow. The remaining fireflies drew close to her, hovering around her head like a starry crown. "I am Hekaterine." She spoke in an oddly stilted way, as if unused to language.

Valentian bowed. "You honor us, Your Majesty."

"Your Majesty?" Cee echoed, and the Insecta's phosphorescent eyes moved in her direction, her lips curling downward in a way that made her far less lovely.

"To what do we owe this pleasure?" Valentian asked as he straightened.

"We have been looking," Hekaterine answered. "For signs of the dragon."

Cee forced herself to stay perfectly still under the considering gaze of the Insecta queen.

"And have you found any?" Beverly asked.

Cee began breathing again as Hekaterine's eyes turned toward the Vulpes. "No. We found you instead. Why are you here?"

Cee noted that Livian had gone utterly still inside her as if hiding. She wanted to ask him which side the Insecta were on, but she was too afraid in case Hekaterine or any of the other fireflies were telepathic.

Beverly gestured at Cee and Guin. "We found these two in the forest without permits. We were escorting them back out."

Hekaterine peered at Cee then Guin. "Why are you here?" she asked again.

Cee's mouth went dry; her tongue glued itself to the roof of her mouth. She was both grateful and surprised when Guin answered, "We wanted to help."

"Help." Hekaterine made the word sound foreign, like something she'd never heard of.

"The Volunteers," Guin explained. "We're just as able as any men. Probably more able than some."

Cee's eyes widened at the note of genuine self-right-eousness in Guin's tone. She caught Beverly looking at Guin somewhat approvingly.

"But we got lost," Cee added. "And then..." She waved a hand at Valentian and Beverly.

Hekaterine considered Cee a moment longer then turned to Valentian. "We will take them out of the forest. Me and my men." One long, thin hand motioned toward the hovering lights above her head, and Cee waited to see them morph but they remained as they were.

Valentian bowed again. "A kind offer, Your Majesty. But we can't ask you to put off your own duties. This," he pointed at Cee, "is beneath your notice."

Cee squelched the natural protest that rose inside her at his words. Livian, too, was agitated by them; Cee could feel him tremble with outrage, struggling to remain still and unobserved by Hekaterine's piercing eyes. Indeed, the Insecta queen shot a quick look at Cee as if sensing something, but after a moment she relented. "Have them out quickly," she said. "It is not safe with a dragon loose." She turned away.

"What about the Volunteers?" Guin asked.

Hekaterine stopped and regarded Guin, and Cee wished her friend had kept her mouth shut. "What of them?" Hekaterine asked.

"Are they in danger? From the dragon?"

"They are safer together than apart," said Hekaterine. "This is true of all things, is it not?" She glanced up at her glowing companions.

"How do you know the dragon is even still in the forest?" Cee asked. "It can fly, right?"

Hekaterine tilted her head and looked at Cee for a long time. "I know a dragon when I see one," she said.

Cee's breath froze in her lungs, her heart halted in her chest.

Then in a whirl Hekaterine turned away again, her hair and gown spinning after her. "Besides, we fly too," she said and then she was gone, just another bobbing light on the still evening air. The fireflies eddied upward and disappeared.

Cee didn't take another breath until her lungs screamed, and then she gulped the air, shuddering. "She knows."

"If she knew she would have taken you into custody," said Beverly, but her sharp tone undercut her certainty.

"I think Cee's right," Valentian said grimly. He stared in the direction the fireflies had gone. "I don't know why she didn't insist on taking you, but I think she at least suspects what you are."

"The fireflies were here while we were talking about it," said Guin, "about how Cee smells different. They must know."

A fresh fear leapt through Cee. "And about Marcus. What if they've gone to warn the Magi?"

Valentian's face pinched in on itself at the idea, and Beverly said to him, "We have to get them out. Now. Friends or no friends."

"*We* have to get out," said Valentian, "if Hekaterine has gone to tattle to Sabine. It wouldn't take the Guard long to get here."

"And it'll take Hekaterine less time to fly there," Beverly pointed out. "The Guard could be on its way already."

Cee didn't require an explanation of who or what the Guard might be. Even so, she couldn't leave without seeing Marcus. She looked at Valentian, and suddenly he appeared young and vulnerable to her. What were his choices? To be caught and punished, or to exile himself and live in fear and hiding? "Let them take us," she said.

Both Valentian and Beverly looked at her as though she'd gone mad. Guin however, Cee noted, set her jaw in a stubborn way.

"Or me anyway," Cee said. "If they take me to the camp, I'll see Marcus."

"Oh, by the First Case Study!" exclaimed Valentian, and Cee wondered what that was supposed to mean, "Let him go already!"

Cee's mouth fell open. She guppied for words.

Beverly stepped in. "If they take you to the camp, you still aren't likely to see him," she said.

"I'll worry about that when I get there," said Cee. And when they all continued to stare, she added, "He'd do the same for me."

"No he wouldn't." Guin's voice was so quiet Cee almost didn't catch her words. Almost.

Cee whirled on her. "Yes. He would. He would want to be sure I was okay and happy. He *would*." Tears prickled behind her eyelids and she had the childish urge to stomp her foot, only just stopped herself from doing it, settling for balling her hands into fists. She turned a pleading gaze on Valentian. "Just point me in the right direction. Then I don't care what you do."

At first Cee thought he would simply refuse. Then she thought he might be devising a way to grab her and haul her out of the forest against her will. Then, incredibly, Valentian said with a resigned sigh, "You can't go alone."

"You have got to be kidding me!" said Beverly. She threw up her hands. "I'm out."

Guin frowned at her. "I thought this is what Vulpes do."

"What? Sneak into places? Sure," said Beverly. "Steal a few sandwiches? No problem. Walk right into the farmhouse so the farmer can skin me and hang me on her wall?" She shook her head. "I'm not that stupid."

Valentian nodded. "That's fair. Thank you for your help thus far."

Beverly stared at him.

"What?" Valentian asked.

"If I go back to—" She looked at Cee and Guin and stopped whatever words were about to come out of her mouth. "And tell them you just decided to..." She shook her head again. "Quick and easy, they said. Take the Magus, he's logical, reasonable, he'll make sound decisions."

"They assigned me to you because they knew you would need me," said Valentian.

Cee caught Guin's eye. There was clearly much more to this. Hadn't Valentian said there were more of them? How many, Cee wondered. And what was their purpose?

"Well, I don't need this," said Beverly, gesturing broadly at Cee and Guin. "But I'm willing to bet you're going to need me." She lifted her gaze to the now completely dark sky. "Might as well do it now, get it over with." She adjusted her knapsack on her shoulder and looked at the rest of them expectantly.

Valentian nodded. "Right. Okay. Let's, um..." He turned right and left as if searching for something, and Cee realized he was completely out of his element. His mission to send them out of the Far Eastern Wilderness was one thing. Walking them right into the Magi camp was something else entirely.

Cee's heart sank. *We're all going to die.* For the first time, it felt like a real possibility.

If so, Livian answered, *I'm swallowing a few people on the way.*

BEVERLY LED, and Cee was amazed at how quietly she moved, even in human form. The Vulpes slipped between trees seemingly without touching them. Cee tried to follow suit but felt clumsy by comparison, very aware of every rustle she made as they walked. But if it was a problem,

Beverly didn't mention it. Either Cee was quiet enough or, Cee supposed, Beverly might just be resigned to them being caught and... whatever came after.

Cee could sense Guin's growing reluctance with every step they took. It wasn't that Guin was scared, Cee knew, more that Guin would rather have stayed and waited for Rand. The farther they went, the further the tension in Guin stretched, until Cee felt it like an elastic that had been pulled taut to the point of snapping. She kept glancing back to make sure Guin still followed, earning frowns from Valentian as he brought up the rear.

After some time, Beverly's steps grew slower. Cee nearly ran into her before changing her own pace to match, though what she really wanted was to sprint ahead, get there as soon as possible. Her impatience directly opposed their need to be careful.

The trees began to grow farther apart, and even Cee understood this reduced their cover, made them more easily spotted. Beverly half crouched as she walked, so Cee stooped too, though it hurt her back and made Livian complain she was crowding him.

Finally, Beverly came to a stop behind the scant protection of one of the trees. "There it is."

Cee peered around the tree trunk and saw vast clearing crowded with tents and dotted with campfires. Indistinguishable figures moved in and out of the shadows and light. "Where's Marcus?" she asked as Guin and Valentian moved to join them where they stood.

Beverly looked at Cee as if she'd lost her mind. "You thought he'd just be sitting out there on display?"

Cee didn't know what she thought, before or at that moment. She shrugged and turned to Valentian. "Which tent?"

Valentian grimaced. "It's around toward the back of the camp. A big, green tent. He'll be guarded," Valentian added.

"And good luck crossing the field without being noticed," Beverly said, gesturing toward the camp with her chin.

Cee conceded she had a point; the nearest tent was roughly twenty yards away. They—she, at least—would have to cross the clearing first, then hope to be able to move from tent to tent along the periphery without being seen.

"You're going to have to dampen your thoughts," Valentian said. "If you start broadcasting your intentions, they'll find you no matter how well you hide, and they'll tighten security around your friend, too."

This was getting harder by the second, and for a fleeting moment Cee wondered whether the others were right and they should just leave while they still could. Maybe it was better to live with fond memories of Marcus than discover he was already gone and she'd come too late. But deep down Cee knew if she didn't try she would carry the weight of her regret the rest of her life. However short that life happened to be. It seemed to be getting shorter by the minute.

Cee stood up straight and squared her shoulders. *Livian? You said you could shield my thoughts?*

The dragon heaved a sigh that Cee suspected was relief. *I'll do anything if you promise not to hunch over like that all the time. It's tight enough in here as it is. Can't you make yourself taller?*

Cee was momentarily thrown by Livian's suggestion. *No! Focus. Thoughts.*

The three others were watching her, and Cee wondered how much they could hear of the conversation. She tried to stand taller. *I'm not really short...*

Suddenly her thoughts became muffled. Cee felt as though someone had dropped a heavy velvet cloth over her brain. As ridiculous as it sounded, Cee's immediate thought was, *My mind can't breathe!* It was as if a cloud had gathered in her skull, and sweat broke out across her brow like rain.

I warned you wouldn't like it. But look at them.

Valentian, Guin, and Beverly had all drawn back slightly. They each stared at Cee with suspicion.

"How did you do that?" Valentian asked.

"Livian," Cee said. It took all her breath to say the one word. The weight of the mental veil made it impossible to talk. How would she communicate with Marcus?

"Nice trick," said Beverly. "We should keep to the trees as long as possible, circle around to the back of the camp, since that's where they're keeping your friend." She looked to Valentian for confirmation. He gave a curt nod, and without further discussion Beverly started off along the tree line, crouching again, moving swift, silent, and sure and leaving the rest of them to keep up.

With a silent apology to Livian, Cee hunched and followed. Minutes later Beverly halted again, and Cee did too, leaning to survey the tents from the new vantage. It took her a moment to identify the green one, as in the darkness it appeared almost black. On the plus side, there was not as much activity at the back of the camp.

"A patrol comes around every four minutes," Valentian whispered. At first Cee worried he had read her mind despite Livian's efforts, but a glance at his sharp and serious profile told her he was only relaying facts.

"Can we get around to the front of the tent without being seen?" Guin asked. "Won't there be guards there, too?"

"We'll go in under the back," said Beverly.

Apprehension flooded Cee, and something else, too. She hadn't considered all of them going into the tent. Confronted with the notion, Cee realized she wanted to see Marcus alone. Just them, like the days they spent sitting among the trees after school. Her last memory of him would not be framed by these others.

"Just me," she said.

Valentian inhaled sharply, ready to protest, and Guin's eyes got wider than Cee thought possible even for her, but Beverly said, "Fine." She pointed at the tent. "You see how it's tethered every six inches or so? You'll need to pull up a couple stakes in order to wriggle under. Be quick but don't make a mess or the patrol will notice. Len, give her your cloak."

Len? Cee was sure Livian was snickering.

Valentian unfastened the cloak but didn't look happy about it. Cee swung it around her shoulders and found herself engulfed in Valentian's remaindered body heat, the woodsy smell of him. It felt too intimate, and she almost threw the garment off. But she knew she needed it. If she were noticed, the cloak would buy her time as the Magi might at first think she belonged there.

Cee readied to cross to the tent, but Beverly put a hand on her arm. "Wait until the next patrol passes."

It felt like ages, but at last the two cloaked and hooded figures strolled around the corner of the tents. Their heads were bent toward one another as if in conversation. The hoods hid their faces. Each carried a staff, roughly a foot longer than either was tall, and made out of what appeared to be pewter.

Cee held her breath as they passed Marcus's tent and moved on. It was another two minutes at least before they reached the far corner of the camp and disappeared again.

"Okay, go. Go!" Beverly hissed, giving Cee a shove out into the open.

Cee stumbled, and for a moment only stood there, dumbly, as a confused animal might. Then, collecting herself, she ducked and half ran toward the green tent. Toward Marcus.

TWENTY-FOUR

*E*very Clan has a right to its own political process within
said Clan, including and up to exercising elections for
or making appointments to the Council of Clans. The
Council of Clans will be responsible for all laws governing inter-
and intra-Clan relations.

—Code of Clans

IT WAS Diodoric who greeted her.

Cee made it across the clearing and fought the tent
stakes, half in a panic that the patrol would return before
she could get them out of the ground. They were in deep.
But she finally succeeded, with some broken fingernails and
a minimum of mess, and slithered in under the heavy drape
of the cloth, silently hoping she wasn't appearing right
between the feet of a guard.

I'd have warned you if you were, said Livian.

Thanks. Cee remained flat on her stomach in what was

left of the grass—the clearing had probably been lovely, freshly green for spring, before the Magi came and trampled it—and listened for breathing, movement, anything that might tell her who occupied the tent.

"It's safe."

At first Cee thought Livian had somehow spoken aloud. Then the forest green hem of another cloak swung into view. Cee lifted her chin and her gaze traveled upward to Marcus's austere features, his straight nose and angular cheekbones. His generous mouth. And hair gone wild.

Except it wasn't him.

It wasn't just the eyes being the wrong color. It was the way he looked at her. Marcus *never* looked at her like that. Despite Cee dreaming that he would.

Diodoric's eyes twinkled in a way Marcus's did not. Oh, Marcus had a sense of humor, a dry wit, though it had been largely absent in recent days. Remembering it pushed a sweet pain through Cee, an acute yearning for things to be the way they were before... everything.

Diodoric knelt to regard her, head tilted speculatively. "You're hiding your thoughts."

A sob worked its way up Cee's throat. "Is he...?" She couldn't bring herself to say "gone" for fear of making it true.

Diodoric appeared perplexed for a moment as he worked out what had upset her. "Oh," he finally said, "no. He's here."

Cee blinked away the tears that had threatened and pushed into a sitting position. She stared expectantly at Diodoric, and he stared back until she said, "Can I speak to him?" She felt ridiculous, like knocking at Mrs. Doyle's door and asking if Marcus could come out to play.

Diodoric stared a while longer, his gaze hot, eyes like

227

molten gold. Cee became fidgety under his scrutiny; her skin began to crawl and itch, but she made herself remain still. No sense letting him know how uncomfortable he made her.

"He can't right now," Diodoric said at length. He stood and offered her a hand to help her up. Did all the Magi learn these manners, Cee wondered? But no, the parents didn't know they were Magi... Did they? Was there something encoded in them that made them gallant?

Cee ignored the hand and wobbled to her feet. The inside of the tent was remarkably large and made stiflingly warm by a large brazier in the center. Its flames gave everything a cozy orange glow. A narrow but ornately carved bed stood in one corner, piled with blankets. Next to it was a similarly carved table on which sat a cup, bowl, towel, soap and ewer. There was a trunk, too, at the foot of the bed, and who knew what it held. Cee idly wondered how the Magi managed to travel with so much stuff.

"We don't have a lot of time," said Diodoric, thus drawing Cee's attention away from her wandering thoughts. "They will be in to check on me soon."

"Check on you? Why?" Cee's eyes swept Diodoric's figure for a proper look. Fresh clothes along with the cloak.

"They're eager for me to finish. Resolving." Cee's horror must have shown on her face because Diodoric lifted his hands. "It cannot be rushed. Though," he added with a sigh and a grimace, "I'm discovering it *can* be slowed down by a stubborn host."

Elation lifted Cee's heart. Marcus was fighting!

Diodoric ran a hand through his hair, mussing it further, and looked aslant at Cee. "We need your help," he said.

Cee's eyebrows went up, and something hard and cold as stone settled into her center. "We?"

Her attitude did not deter him as she hoped. Diodoric took Cee's hands in his own, and the warmth of them startled her; next to his, her skin felt all but dead. *Aren't you supposed to keep me warm?* she asked Livian.

He seems to be doing well enough, the dragon sniffed. Cee felt his displeasure like heartburn, but it did nothing to warm her hands.

"He's only staying for you, Cee," Diodoric told her. "If you talk to him, convince him that it's all right and you'll be okay..."

Cee's hands were beginning to tingle. She started to pull them free, but Diodoric held firm. "You want me to lie?"

Diodoric appeared mystified by her question. "It's not a lie. I'll take care of you."

The numbness crawled up Cee's arms. *You're too receptive to him*, Livian admonished.

"I'm not your enemy," Diodoric continued. He tugged Cee over to the bed and guided her to sit.

Cee thought of Marcus on her bed, stretched out and completely at home. His easy grin. She thought of how many times she'd wished he would hold her hand and look at her with that burning in his eyes, even though she knew it was impossible. Except now it was happening. Sort of. Not exactly. This was as close as she would ever come to a dream come true.

Don't, Livian hissed.

Cee's elbows were made of water, her arms limp. If not for Diodoric continuing to hold on to her, she might have fallen over entirely, collapsed onto the inviting heap of blankets.

"You said..." The numbness had reached her brain; she could feel it crawling under the weight of Livian's protective shield like bugs under a carpet. "They... soon..." She wanted to look toward the tent's main flap to be sure the guards weren't already there but she couldn't tear her eyes from Diodoric's.

He nodded. "They will be here soon, yes." He squeezed her hands. "But don't worry. I'll tell them you've come for help. Mother won't be angry."

Cee swayed where she sat. Then she yanked her hands free of Diodoric's grasp.

The effect was immediate, like having cold air blown into her face. The tingling subsided, and Cee's mind felt clear—or as clear as possible with Livian muffling it.

"I'm not here for your help," she said. "Or to help you. I came here to talk to Marcus, to—to make sure he... we..." Cee's throat closed over the words and the tears returned.

Diodoric reached for her again, and Cee bounced backward on the mattress to evade him. "You want to keep that... thing in you?" he asked, and Cee opened her mouth to rebuke him, but saw honest bewilderment in the Magus's eyes. She realized he could not understand her situation. So in order to understand his perspective, she asked, "Why shouldn't I?"

He answered without hesitation. "It's dangerous."

"To whom?"

"Everyone!" His amber eyes blazed with genuine concern. "You most of all. Cee, it can't be controlled. Once it gets strong enough—"

"Not an it," Cee corrected. "He. Livian."

Diodoric's face twitched in a minor spasm. "You saw the destruction."

"That wasn't me. Or Livian," Cee pointed out. "Just

because one Dracona does something terrible doesn't mean we're all evil."

"The resources required to sustain such a creature..."

"Not if I stay in human form." *Right?* she added silently. Livian didn't answer.

Diodoric sighed and played his trump card. "But Cee," he said, "if you don't agree to let them remove him, they'll kill you."

Cee studied his face, so familiar and foreign at the same time. All those lines—she could draw them in her sleep. But though Marcus often looked at her with pity, and some friendly affection, and even on occasion worry, the combination in Diodoric's expression was unique. New.

Don't trust him, said Livian.

But Cee did. She reached over and took his hand, opened herself, and sought the truth in him by first adopting his abilities. Within seconds her body was on fire, even as Livian thrashed in protest. Cee itched all over but resisted the urge to let go of Diodoric and scratch. She concentrated. Diodoric was a Magus, and almost certainly telepathic. If she could tap his power, she would then be able to read his mind. Know if he truly had her wellbeing at heart.

The veil Livian had draped over Cee's own thoughts slipped off.

Cee experienced the sensation of waves on a shore, rolling in and out over the sand. She simultaneously drew Diodoric into herself while extending herself into him. It left Cee lightheaded, breathless, as though she were bobbing on an ocean current with no control over her direction or destination.

Then she felt him, gently guiding her in. It came as a

burst of golden light behind Cee's eyelids, a flood of warmth. He *did* care. He *loved* her.

Cee was so startled she nearly broke off contact, but Diodoric held on to her. Livian snarled and gnashed his teeth. *Get him out!*

Another voice countered the dragon: *We must go carefully. If you or I rush out, we could do damage.*

Cee nodded her understanding. It was like extracting a raindrop that had fallen into a river—one could remove a drop, but perhaps never that exact drop. The drop—the one that had fallen and been absorbed by the greater water—was forever altered, part of the river just as the river would be part of any drop removed. *We are...* But Cee couldn't think of a word for it.

United, Diodoric supplied.

Tainted, Livian hissed.

Diodoric receded. Cee flowed back into her own body, no longer itchy or uncomfortable but satisfied. Fulfilled. "How?" she asked, and when Diodoric's brow puckered, "How can you love me? You don't even know me!"

"No one knows you better than he does," said Diodoric. "So I know you, too." He eased closer to her, and this time Cee did not move away. "I know I'm a stranger to you, but—"

His words halted abruptly, and his attention swerved to the tent flap. "Get under the bed."

Cee sat frozen, her eyes also riveted to what served as the tent's entrance.

"Now!" Diodoric's voice was low but urgent. He all but pushed Cee from the mattress. Her stasis broken, she scrambled to hide, a blanket falling over the side of the bed just as she managed to completely conceal herself from view.

Then an edge of the blanket was lifted, and some upside-down curls appeared. "And get that serpent of yours to shield your thoughts again!" Diodoric hissed. Then he was gone.

Livian...

The dragon turned circles in her stomach. *You cannot possibly consider him an ally.*

Livian, you must shield us!

Or worse, Livian continued, *fall in love with him.*

Cee's heart stuttered, but she couldn't tell whether it was from fear of discovery or fear that Livian was right. *Of course not*, she thought. *I don't even know him. And he's trying to take Marcus away from me.*

That's right, Livian encouraged. *He's the enemy. All of them are.*

"Marcus isn't," Cee whispered. She wondered if Diodoric had been lying about Marcus still existing. She hadn't sensed Marcus inside Diodoric, but then again, she hadn't sensed any falsehood in him either.

Magi are good at making their lies seem like truth, Livian cautioned.

So maybe Diodoric didn't love her? Maybe he was simply faking it? To get her to help him obliterate Marcus?

Cee was so startled by these ideas, she nearly sat up and banged her head on the underside of the bed. What was she thinking? Of course she didn't want Diodoric to replace Marcus!

Let them hold your hand for a minute, and you'll do anything, derided Livian.

Cee's whirl of thoughts ended abruptly as the weight of the unseen veil shrouded them. Just in time. The tent flap thwapped open and Diodoric said, "Mother." From the sound of his voice, he was no longer on the bed but some feet away. Cee tried to read into his tone—was he happy to see his mother? apprehensive?—but it was too flat and colorless to tell.

A woman answered, rich and throaty. "Still not entirely Resolved?" She sounded more concerned than angry. "He's a fighter, is he? It's just as well; you'll need the strength.

"Are you hungry?" she went on. "Or maybe you should try to sleep."

"No," Diodoric answered. "I want to be awake when it happens."

Fire surged through Cee; it took all her self-control not to fly out from under the bed and strangle Diodoric, consequences be damned. But hurting Diodoric meant hurting Marcus, too... assuming there was still a Marcus to hurt.

A piercing cry ripped Cee's thoughts apart. Another shriek, and another. Cee clapped her hands to her ears, though it did no good. Was it an alarm? Had she or her friends been discovered? She curled into a ball and waited for hands to pull her from her hiding place, but then she heard the woman say, "Stay here."

The edge of the blanket lifted, and Diodoric crouched in front of her. "It's the Kornyx."

Rand! This time Cee did sit up so fast she hit her head.

"Careful," said Diodoric. He guided her out. "Are you okay?"

"What did you mean you want to be awake when it happens?" Cee spat.

"I do. I don't want him to be alone."

Something in Cee's chest crumpled—she suspected it was her heart. "Die alone, you mean."

"It's not death really."

"Yeah, it kind of is," said Cee. "He stops existing."

"But I have his memories. So he lives on in a way."

"So if I quit existing, but Livian still had all my memories, you wouldn't say I died?" Cee asked.

Diodoric frowned. "That's different. He's a dragon."

"If he were a person?" Cee pressed.

Diodoric shook his head. "But he's not. Your scenario, it doesn't make any sense."

Cee sighed. He clearly didn't understand. Or she didn't.

Another caw split the air, and reflexively they both looked to the ceiling. "Will they hurt him?" Cee asked.

"Depends on what he does to them," said Diodoric. "But if you don't plan to have my mother help you, now would be the time to leave."

"Not until I've spoken to Marcus," said Cee.

Diodoric looked pained. "He's not strong enough, Cee, I'm sorry."

"Then you'll have to come with me. Because he can't go without saying goodbye."

"Don't be absurd. I'm not going anywhere."

"Then you really don't love me." Cee said it not to be cruel but as a realization. "You were lying. Are lying. Is Marcus even really still in there?"

Shouts and cries were rising outside the tent.

"If you stay much longer..." Diodoric warned.

"Is he in there?" she shouted. "Tell me the truth!"

"If I go with you, it'll be worse! You think my mother is just going to let me disappear?"

Cee remembered the care in the woman's voice. Devotion. She was not only Diodoric's mother—Marcus's, too, Cee realized—but head of the Magi. And her hopes, her legacy, were invested in her son.

No, she would not let him go.

And, Cee further realized, her heart crumpling into a

still tighter wad, she herself would never know that kind of love.

Her mother was ostensibly in the camp, a Magus herself. Yet instead of welcoming Cee as a blessed daughter, she would, what? Condemn her? Sentence her to die? Or at the very least insist a part of Cee be cut out of her in order for her to be accepted?

Cee didn't know she was crying until Diodoric reached up and gently swiped the tears away. "Don't. Please don't. I'll—I'll come if you want. I just... I don't want you to be hurt. And they'll hurt you, Cee. If you don't accept their help, their terms, they'll hurt you. And I won't be able to stop them."

Cee leaned her cheek into Diodoric's palm. It was warm, soft. Her face began to tingle.

Oh, by all the ancients, grumbled Livian.

Another shriek from Taranis, this time accompanied by the sound of rending fabric. The shouts and screams grew louder, and Cee jerked herself upright and back into alertness. "He can't fight them all, not alone," she said. She turned for the tent flap.

Diodoric grabbed her arm. "We can't fight them either. And if we go out there, it will only get you or him harmed, or worse."

"Well what then?" Cee demanded.

"Where is Guin?" he asked.

Cee pointed toward the back of the tent just as it disappeared. It took Cee a moment to understand what had happened. All at once, cold night air assailed her on every side, and the huge fire in the brazier guttered and tossed its fiery mane of flames.

The tent was gone.

She looked up just in time to see Taranis drop the huge

and heavy cloth over an organized band of Magi marching in their direction. Then the oversized blackbird returned to circle above them, screeching, his form only made visible where the firelight touched it. Otherwise he was all but invisible.

But there was no time to admire the Kornyx's beauty or talent. Above the sounds of chaos, a strong voice rose—Diodoric's mother. The Magi were marshaling.

Cee looked to Diodoric. His jaw clenched with determination, but his golden eyes glowed with fear. He squeezed her hand and gave a tiny nod.

They turned toward the trees and ran.

CHAPTER
TWENTY-FIVE

I **vy:** *To every end, a new beginning.*
     Starlight: *For every beginning is an end.*

—"The Fey Wager"

CEE RAN SO HARD the sound of her own gasping breath drowned out the cries of the Kornyx above them. Her vision narrowed to a dark tunnel so that she ran without seeing where, only trusting her instincts to know the way. She was aware of Diodoric somewhere to her right, had a vague sense of the gargantuan bird overhead—nothing but that and the need to get away.

When they hit the tree line, Cee stumbled and slowed, gulping quantities of air. She had no time to orient herself, however; Diodoric had her by the arm again and was yelling, "Keep going!" Cee tried to look around for the others, but she didn't see them; everything was a blur. From behind them she could hear the shouts of the Magi and knew Diodoric was right, they had to get deeper into the woods, find cover.

Running through trees proved far more difficult than crossing a clearing. They were forced to go slow to avoid hitting or tripping over anything. They dodged and waded more than ran, trying to keep one another in sight while still moving quickly. The thicker the trees became, the slower they moved. Cee began to regain her breath.

Finally, Diodoric stopped, so Cee did too. He leaned against a tree trunk and peered up. "The Kornyx..."

Cee strained her ears but didn't hear anything. No flap of wings, no sharp caw. "I hope he's not lost again." The words came out in panting bursts.

"We're more likely to be lost than he is. Kornyx have sharp eyesight and a natural sense of direction." He stopped and listened. "I don't hear anyone coming in after us, either."

"Would we hear them?" Cee asked. She had no idea what the Magi were capable of. Diodoric had been able to float, after all. Maybe others of them flew.

"Good point," said Diodoric. "Though, given the coverage, I think we'd hear *something*."

Cee looked left and right, wondering where Guin, Beverly, and Valentian were. They'd run so blindly she didn't know how far off they might have gone from where she'd left them. With the Magi marching right for them, Cee was sure they had also gone deeper into the woods. She hoped. Better that than them being captured.

Something crashed through the canopy off to Cee's left, and her body tensed like a tight spring. She threw a wild look at Diodoric only to find him crumpled at the base of the tree against which he'd been leaning. Cee froze, terrified to move lest she make noise and give away their location.

But after holding her breath for what felt like an eternity and hearing nothing else, she dived for where Diodoric lay.

His eyes were open but sightless; they stared vacantly at the ground that stretched in front of him. He looked to Cee like an oversized doll, or worse, a corpse. Her brain touched on the word then bounced away from it in horror. He was not dead! He could not be! No one fell dead like that except in fairy tales.

Cee's heart seized up at the memory of those tales, the very ones in which people did fall dead like puppets with cut strings—tales of enormous blackbirds that came to mete out punishment to evildoers.

Marcus was not evil. And Cee was beginning to believe Diodoric was not evil either.

You can't believe it because you think he loves you.

Shut up, Livian, Cee thought with as much fury as she could put behind unspoken words. *Help me!*

How can I help you if I shut up?

Cee tapped at Diodoric's cheeks, unwilling to fully slap him. His skin was cool to the touch.

From somewhere in the woods came a rustling. Movement.

Livian! Cee cried silently.

Fine. If the dragon could sigh, Cee was sure he did at that moment. *Put your hands on his cheeks.*

Cee did, marveling at the smooth perfection of the skin beneath her palms. Like a statue.

Stop it. Or I won't help.

Cee concentrated on listening for more sounds in the woods, any potential threat. She focused so hard she was unaware of the heat flooding her palms. It was only when Diodoric inhaled sharply that Cee looked down and saw the bright red marks on his face where her hands rested.

He blinked up at her. "What's happening?" And when Cee only stared, "Why are your hands on my face?"

"You..." Cee released him and shook her head to show she didn't have any more answer than that.

Diodoric sat up. "Where is everyone?"

Cee frowned. Something was wrong. "The Magi, remember?" she asked. "We're hiding, and something..." She peered at Diodoric; he looked blank, confused. And then realized. His eyes were green.

"Marcus," she breathed. She threw her arms around his neck, nearly knocking him down again. "You really are still here."

Marcus endured the embrace for longer than Cee would have expected given the blatant disregard for the Code of Conduct before gently pushing her off him. "Yes, I ..." The sight of his new clothes distracted him. "I'm wearing a cloak."

Cee bit her lip. "It's not that I'm not happy to see you, and there's a lot we need to talk about, but you picked the worst possible moment to come back."

"*You're* wearing a cloak," said Marcus.

Brilliant, sighed Livian, which startled Cee; she hadn't even noticed his return. *But there's something coming.*

More rustling from off to the left. Louder this time. Closer.

Cee looked deep into Marcus's eyes, desperate for any little bit of gold. There was nothing but green. No one but Marcus. And he was frowning.

"What?" he asked then answered his own question. "You're looking for *him*, aren't you?"

"He may be the only one who can save us," Cee said.

What about me? Livian huffed.

"Unless you eat someone, that is," said Marcus. He pushed himself to his feet.

Cee remained on the ground, looking up at him. "You want me to eat your mother?"

Marcus appeared nonplussed. "What?"

"Were you not aware of what was going on while Diodoric—?" The sounds were very close now, though whoever or whatever was coming was being careful. Cee jumped up, primed to run, transform, whatever it took.

"You can't eat all of them," Marcus murmured.

We could try, Livian offered.

A scrawny red fox stepped from between two trees, and Cee let out a great sigh of relief. "Beverly!" She leaned toward the fox, though it was a yard away. "It is, right?"

The fox turned and went back the way it had come. Cee started after it, but Marcus asked, "Where are you going?"

"The fox is a friend. I'll explain it later, but right now we need to go." Cee reached back and took Marcus's hand, something she would not have dared even hours before, but he looked so lost and confused she felt moved to help him, to connect with him physically. She squeezed his hand and towed him behind her as she followed the fox, trying to keep her eyes on the quick, quiet creature as it flashed in and out of patchy moonlight. To Cee's surprise Marcus did not protest, did not pull away.

"A Vulpes?" Marcus asked. "You said they were untrustworthy."

"This one proved me wrong," said Cee. "Why did you leave, anyway?"

"Leave?"

"Walk off like that," Cee said. "I... I was worried you were angry with me. Because I don't want the Magi to cut Livian out of me. Or whatever they do."

They weaved their way through the trees, Cee swinging Marcus around the slender, sturdy trunks. It would have been easier to let him go, but she'd only just found him again. She wasn't ready to let go, didn't trust what felt like so tenuous a connection. When had it frayed away to almost nothing? Their bond used to be so strong.

Cee was certain Marcus tightened his grip. She took comfort in the idea he wasn't ready to let go either.

"I don't remember leaving," said Marcus.

"Well, what do you remember?" Cee asked.

"Walking. Talking with you. And then I saw Arlon and Ernesta."

Cee almost stopped walking. "Arlon and Ernesta? When? Where?"

"In a tree. Two eagles, anyway," he said. "I assumed it was them, but come to think of it, I don't... I went to say something to them, and that's the last thing I remember."

The vision flashed behind Cee's eyes: two eagles perched on charred bones. And didn't the burned trees look just like bones?

"You don't know if it was Arlon?" Cee pressed. "If not him, then who else could it have been?"

"I don't know, Cee. Why don't you tell me why we're following a fox?"

Cee gave Marcus a condensed version of events since he'd disappeared, stopping at her sneaking into Diodoric's tent. For reasons she could not identify, she wasn't ready to tell Marcus what had passed between her and his alter ego.

To Cee's relief, Marcus didn't ask. Instead he said, "My mother? My mother is leader of the Magi?"

Cee's heart crumpled a little. She knew Marcus didn't mean anything by it, but to hear him speak of his mother, and to think of the love and care in her voice when she'd been talking to Diodoric, acutely reminded Cee that she had no one. Not even Marcus, at least not for much longer.

Maybe Diodoric... Cee thought waywardly.

No! hissed Livian.

The fox halted and Cee, lost in thought, only just stopped herself from stepping on it. "Sorry," Cee mumbled when the fox glared up at her.

The fox sat down.

"Now what?" Marcus asked, finally removing his hand from Cee's.

Cee looked at the fox expectantly. It just sat there. Its attention was directed ahead of them at a patch of dirt that Cee supposed counted as a clearing, though it couldn't have held more than a dozen people. On the other side of this dirt circle was an oddly regular stand of trees—they stood in a horizontal line, evenly spaced, as if planted that way. A natural fence.

"Well?" Marcus asked, impatience leaking into his tone. The fox glanced back at him then went back to watching the trees.

Cee watched, too, and this time noticed the winking of lights in the darkness between the tree trunks. A spike of fear rose through her. The fireflies? Had the fox betrayed them to the enemy?

But then she realized the lights were all in pairs and low to the ground. Eyes. Fox eyes.

"Your Clan?" Cee asked quietly.

The fox ignored her and stepped out into the clearing. Cee waited, unsure whether she was meant to follow. From the trees, a larger fox materialized. It gave the small fox a nuzzle behind its ear. Cee couldn't help but say, "Aww."

She could practically hear both Marcus and Livian roll their eyes.

Both foxes looked at her. Then the larger one began to transform.

"Beverly!" Cee cried. "But then who...?"

"My little sister Anthea," said Beverly. To the fox she said, "Go on, Anthy." The little fox vanished into the trees without looking back.

"Not like you to go trusting strange foxes," muttered Marcus.

Cee started to say they all looked alike then thought better of it. Instead, she asked Beverly, "Where are Guin and Valentian?"

Beverly glanced back at the trees, the watchful and curious eyes. "Your friend, the Kornyx..." She grimaced.

"Rand?" Cee asked.

"We're doing what we can," Beverly said. She squinted at where Cee and Marcus still stood in the shadows. "What's *he* doing here?"

Cee opened her mouth but had no answer. Marcus stepped around her and into the clearing to face the Vulpes, his tall frame towering over her petite one. "I don't want to be a Magus."

Cee's breath stopped in her chest. Her feet were rooted, unable to move.

Beverly peered up at Marcus. "I don't think you have a choice," she said. "And coming here puts us all in more danger. You should go back."

Marcus and Beverly locked gazes, and Cee felt their silent contest of wills. Why didn't Marcus want to be a Magus? Was it only because he did not want to Resolve himself into a new persona? Was he really willing to give up everything being a Magus offered—the power, belonging to a family—simply because of that? It made no sense to Cee. Yes, she wanted Marcus to stay... Or she *had* wanted Marcus to stay, but... She put her fingertips to her temples, a headache threatening like thunder behind her whirling thoughts.

"At least let me say goodbye to them," Marcus finally said.

Beverly's eyes narrowed with suspicion. "You didn't seem to care much about that when you disappeared earlier."

Cee's feet came loose and she stepped into the clearing to join them. "That wasn't his fault."

Beverly spared her a glance then shrugged. "Fine. Come on." She turned toward the trees from which she'd earlier emerged then stopped and pegged Marcus with a look. "In and out. No lingering. The longer you're here the more dangerous it gets." When Marcus only continued to stare, Beverly sighed and slipped back into the tree cover, leaving him and Cee to follow.

"You live here?" Marcus asked.

"Yes," answered Beverly.

"The Far Eastern Wilderness isn't meant to have any Clans," remarked Marcus.

Beverly did not respond.

Then the settlement was in even more danger than Cee had thought. And besides the possibility of discovery...

"The fire..." Cee began but didn't know what else to say. A Dracona had destroyed a huge portion of the Vulpes' home. Yet they were helping her. And she had nothing to offer them in return. Cee's heart shriveled even more and plummeted into her toes. She'd thought Vulpes would be the worst Clan to end up in. Turned out Dracona won that title.

"It was bad," Beverly acknowledged but seemed disinclined to say more. They continued on in silence, the trees tightening around them so that Cee found it increasingly difficult to navigate through them. Then, gradually, they began to unknot again. Cee imagined she'd been clutched then released by huge, barky hands. She thought again of the vision of the Aerie atop the dragon's claw then wondered belatedly where the foxes watching them had gone only to be startled as one darted past her through the underbrush.

Though the way had become easier, Beverly slowed her steps, and Cee soon saw why. Ahead was another clearing, larger than the last but only a quarter the size of the Magi camp. It was filled with what Cee could only call huts, though someone less generous might have used "shacks" instead. They were wooden, in any case, and worn, small, but seemingly well made. One low-burning campfire glowed orange-red in the center of them. Children—not given up for fostering, Cee realized—ran around the warm embers and in and out of houses, messy but cheerful, and adults stood conversing outside open doorways. At a glance the adults appeared not to be minding the children, but now and then Cee caught one or another of them tracking the young ones with his or her eyes; the disinterest was merely a guise. This was an alert population. Cee could feel it as a thin thread of tension in the air.

She felt something else, too, but she couldn't name it. Warmth, not in physical temperature, but...

"Love," Marcus murmured from beside her. Cee looked at him, startled. "Your veil slipped," he said.

Oily dread oozed in Cee. How much could he read? Her voice came out high and reedy as she asked, "Have you always been telepathic?"

"It wouldn't take telepathy to read you, Cee," said

Marcus. "Everything you think and feel shows in your eyes."

The dread pooled into a confusing mixture of uncertainty. Had that been a compliment or a condemnation? Or a mere observation? With Marcus she could never tell.

"But no," he went on, answering her question. "This is something of *his*, I think."

"Diodoric," said Cee. Her stomach flipped at the taste of his name in her mouth. Cee bit back on the strangely sweet nausea and risked a glance at Marcus. How much was she giving away?

"Love," Marcus said again, and this time the word was bitter.

Beverly, Cee suddenly realized, had turned to rest her back against a tree. Her arms were crossed over her chest, and she was listening to them without bothering to hide it. "Are we done?" she asked when she noticed Cee looking agape at her. Neither Cee nor Marcus answered, so Beverly turned and pointed. "They're in the second den on the right. I'm going to lead you in. Don't make eye contact; it's a sign of aggression. In fact, the lower you can hunch, the better."

Cee did her best to look small as she followed Beverly into the village. Her short stature helped. Marcus, however, walked as tall as ever, though Cee observed he kept his eyes focused on the den ahead of them.

A blur of movement on Cee's left caused her to turn and look as they walked. A child of about age two ran toward them, a brilliant smile on his plump face, golden curls bouncing. Cee naturally smiled back, but an adult standing near the fire barked something while another grabbed the child by the arm before he could reach them. The boy's brown eyes widened with surprise as he was whisked backward and away.

They reached the den and followed Beverly inside. Candles, some in protective glass chimneys, lit the cozy space. Everything crowded the one room: a rocking chair, a small rug, a wooden table with chairs, a wood-burning stove with dented pans on the cooktop. Yet the longer Cee looked, the less rustic things appeared. A wooden wall cabinet displayed chipped dishes but also brightly colored plastic water bottles. Another shelf similarly held many much-thumbed crossword books, jigsaw puzzles, and decks of cards. Atop this rested a shiny, relatively new-looking radio and com unit, its antenna stretched to the maximum.

The woman who greeted them wore jeans and a tunic sweater. Her reddish-gold hair was pinned up and turquoise earrings swung from her lobes. She walked toward them from the back of the cottage, and it was then Cee noticed the beds along the back wall, one large and four bunk beds. In the large bed rested a dark figure covered by colorfully knitted blankets.

"Rand!" Cee gasped.

Two figures beside the bed turned their way. Valentian was standing, Guin sitting in a chair pulled as close to the bedside as possible.

"I think he'll be all right," the woman said.

"What happened?" Cee asked.

"Mari, this is—" Beverly began but was cut short when Valentian strode over, thrust a finger at Marcus and demanded, "What's *he* doing here?"

Though it was difficult to tell in the candlelight, Cee thought Marcus went even paler than usual. Bright red spots burned along his cheekbones as his green eyes met Valentian's ale-colored ones. Their gazes locked, and then suddenly as if by unspoken agreement each of them looked away. Cee noticed the back of Valentian's neck turning red, the color climbing around the outsides of his ears.

"He doesn't want to be a Magus," Cee said. She didn't know if, as a Magus himself, Valentian would be offended, but she felt compelled to say something to explain Marcus's presence.

Valentian's brow furrowed and he turned toward Marcus, but this time Marcus did not meet his gaze. "What happened to Rand?" Marcus asked, his tone flat. If Cee hadn't known better, she'd have thought Marcus didn't really care. That he'd only been changing the subject.

Beverly cleared her throat. "Mari," she said again, gesturing to the woman beside her, "this is Cee and Marcus."

Mari nodded. "Your friend was struck by a Magus quarterstaff. They can do quite a bit of damage, but I believe his Kornyx took the brunt of it. I have no way of knowing how the bird is doing, but your friend, well, it could have been a lot worse."

"Marigold is a nurse," Beverly explained.

Cee looked to where Guin hunched over the bed clasping Rand's hand.

"Go ahead," Mari said.

With a glance at Marcus and Valentian, neither of whom seemed inclined to move, Cee tiptoed over to stand behind Guin. "How is he?" she whispered. Despite Mari's optimistic prognosis, Cee needed to hear it from Guin.

Guin lifted red, tear-filled eyes to Cee. "He's in pain, Cee. I can feel it."

Cee didn't know what to say. Had Guin's psychic ability increased? Or was it simply her strong bond with Rand that made her able to feel what he felt?

Impulsively, Cee reached over and placed a hand on Rand's arm where it lay outside the blanket. A rush of heat traveled down her own arm to her palm similar to what had happened when she'd touched Marcus's cheeks in the woods. Cee sensed Livian there, but he stopped at her palm, creating a concentration of heat that built until she thought her skin might melt off.

I can't, he said.

Can't?

Can't go in. It only works with Magi and other Dracona.

Cee's palm was prickling now. "But you picked up Guin's abilities," she said, not realizing she'd spoken aloud until Guin looked up at her again.

She is open. He is closed.

Cee pulled her hand away and shook it to cool it. She answered Guin's questioning look. "I wanted to see if I could help. But Livian can't get in. Where is he hurt?"

Guin pulled the blanket down to Rand's waist and lifted the shirt to expose a squishy bandage.

"It's a poultice." Cee jumped as Mari's voice sounded from right behind her. "A bandage with medicine in it to help him heal."

It smelled strange, and from around the edges Cee could see stuff oozing. She hoped it was from the poultice and not Rand.

"It's deep," Mari went on. "Quarterstaffs are concentrated weapons. He was lucky it didn't seem to strike anything vital. To him, at least. I can't speak for the bird."

"What happens if Taranis dies?" Cee wondered as Guin carefully tucked Rand back in.

"Is that its name?" Mari asked. "I honestly don't know. I've never met a Kornyx before. Thought they were a myth used to scare children into behaving."

"I'm going," Valentian declared from the front of the den. Cee looked over and tried to make sense of what she saw. Beverly, Valentian, and Marcus stood in a loose semi-circle, each pointedly avoid the others' eyes, and all of them looking angry.

"I've been gone too long already," Valentian continued. "Hopefully in all the chaos it wasn't noticed." He risked a glance at Marcus. "You should come back with me."

"I don't want to go back," said Marcus.

"Staying here puts everyone at risk," said Beverly. "You're Sabine's son! You don't think she won't send out a hunt? She's not going to just let you go."

Marcus shrugged. "Then I'll leave. But," he added with a look at Valentian, "I won't go back there."

Fear crawled up Cee's throat. Marcus out there alone? "Leave to go where?" she asked, despising the way her voice quavered.

Marcus shrugged again. "Where were you going to go?"

Cee hated to admit she hadn't gotten that far in her thinking, and she didn't have to as Beverly countered, "And what will you do when your other one..." She waved a hand over him. "Does whatever it is he does?"

"Resolves," Valentian supplied. "When your persona Resolves."

Marcus's jaw went tight. "I won't let him."

Beverly yelped a laugh, but Valentian asked, "What makes you think you can stop him?"

Cee looked hard at Valentian. As a Magus himself, surely he knew whether it was possible to keep one's original persona? But from the expression on Valentian's face, the question was an honest one.

Marcus grimaced. "I don't. But I'll fight him. Whatever it takes."

Cee studied Marcus, tall and thin, the green in his cloak making his eyes seem even greener in the flickering light of the den. She realized with a sharp intake of breath that the glow she normally saw around Marcus was gone. He no longer drew all the light in the room to him. He only looked proud and severe... and determined.

When had he lost his halo?

An image of Diodoric in the tent flashed unbidden through Cee's mind. The warmth in his eyes... Had *he* been glowing?

Cee shook her head, tossing the thought aside. Of course she wanted Marcus to stay! And to stay with her, too. They were best friends. This was what she'd always wanted, for them to be together.

Be careful what you wish for, whispered Livian.

"Cee," Valentian said, snapping her from her internal whirl, "my cloak?"

"Oh. Right." Cee slipped it off and brought it over to him. It felt strangely final, like a formal parting. "Thanks," she said. "For everything."

He nodded as he clasped the garment. "Good luck to you." Then with a glance at Marcus, "All of you." He gave Beverly a quick hug, waved to Mari, and disappeared into the gradual dawn.

"Will he get in trouble?" Cee asked.

"I hope not," said Beverly grimly. She eyed Marcus. "But we will if you stay."

Cee turned to where Guin hunched over Rand, and Mari said, "He won't be going anywhere for a while." Cee knew that meant Guin wouldn't be going anywhere either.

"We can keep them safe," Beverly said. "Maybe even you, but not him." Another nod at Marcus. "Sabine will be more concerned with finding him than any dragon."

Cee and Marcus looked at each other, and Cee's heart leapt when she saw a tiny streak of gold cross his iris. Then crashed with guilt. What kind of friend was she? Whose side was she on?

Inside her, Livian snarled. *Eat them both. Problem solved.*

Cee ignored him. "Where will we go?" she asked softly.

Marcus's eyebrows went up an inch. "We? You're coming with me?"

"Only if you want me to."

He smiled—a real, true smile—and for a moment the light sparked around him again. "Of course I want you to."

"I'll pack you a few things to take with you," said Mari.

Cee went to where Guin sat and leaned over. "Guin, Marcus and I are—"

"I know." Guin's voice was ragged, though Cee couldn't tell whether it was anger or grief that made it so. Perhaps both.

Then Guin threw her thin frame at Cee and captured Cee in a surprisingly strong hug. "Be careful. Rand and I, maybe we'll try to find you? Where are you going?"

"To the Aerie," said Marcus, and when Cee's mouth fell open in astonishment, "It's the only place I have."

Cee exchanged a glance with Guin, and she knew Guin was also seeing the two birds perched on the charred remains of the dragon. Cee squeezed Guin's hand. "It'll be fine."

"Their territory is in the north," Mari said as she handed Cee a knapsack similar to Beverly's. It was unexpectedly heavy. "Stay in the cover of the Wilds, and when you get to the northern edge go west. You'll come to a large lake and see mountains in the distance. The Aerie have territory there."

"It's at least a three-day walk," Beverly put in.

"I've packed as much as I think you can carry," Mari added.

Cee rather thought it was more than she wanted to carry, but she thanked the Vulpes anyway. From their lifestyle, it seemed they didn't have much to spare. Yet here they were, helping a stranger. A Dracona, the likes of which may have ruined part of their homeland.

"No dragon did that," said Beverly, and Cee mentally kicked Livian for leaving her open. Then Beverly's words sunk in.

"A dragon *didn't* start the fire?"

"Beverly," Mari warned, "we've talked about this." Turning to Cee, she said, "We don't know for sure what started the fire. Could even have been careless campers."

"But that's not what *you* think," Marcus said to Beverly.

Beverly pressed her lips together in a show of not saying anything.

Cee didn't know whether she felt relieved or disappointed. Relieved because maybe a Dracona wasn't responsible for the damage after all, meaning she had no reason to feel guilty on behalf of her kind. Disappointed because it might also mean there were no other dragons. She might really be alone in the world.

But she wasn't alone, she reminded herself. She had Marcus. And he was moving toward the door.

Cee threw her arms around Guin one last time and gave Rand's hand a final squeeze. She thanked Mari, who rewarded her with another hug. Beverly settled for a handshake. "North is that way," Beverly said, pointing right as she walked them to the door.

Cee shouldered the knapsack. Marcus surprised her by taking her hand. When she looked up at him, two more golden stars rocketed across his left eye.

These might be our last days together, our last hours, Cee thought. She felt as if she were with a terminally ill patient, waiting out the inevitable. Her father always said death was just the start of a new phase, a new adventure, nothing to be sad about. "It's like the end of a birth," he'd said once. Cee hadn't really understood what he meant until now.

"You're sure?" Marcus asked.

Cee nodded. He needed her, and she owed him that much—to see him through whatever end, or beginning, was coming.

Together, she and Marcus stepped into the gilded light of sunrise.

EPILOGUE

Annice Bradshaw shifted against the sticky leather of the couch. They'd been in the Brigade Office holding apartment for almost a week, and she still didn't know why. At first, every time she asked her parents why, or when they would be allowed to leave, they gave her empty assurances. Now, however, they no longer bothered to answer at all. Her mother's face had become a blank, staring horror. Her father had taken to hanging his head like a sad dog.

The apartment was painted a pale sort of blue and filled with black leather furniture that looked better than it felt. There were two separate bedrooms, and a bathroom with a shower. Mr. Dougherty had been with them the first couple days, but then they'd taken him away. Annice thought it would be fun to be out of school for a few days, but now she was bored. The Brigade officers brought books, but Annice didn't like to read. She missed being outside, playing soccer with her friends, tending the animals on their farm. She hoped Mrs. Montague was taking good care of them.

The officers brought meals. Every now and then they

asked Annice's mother or father to go downstairs to answer some questions. The only time they'd interrogated her occurred when they'd first been brought to the office. An officer had sat Annice in a room with a table and two chairs and asked whether she'd been at home when Mr. Dougherty arrived. Annice told the officer she'd been on her way to school. "I saw him," Annice said, "but only from a distance since I'd already started walking."

"You didn't hear Mr. Dougherty say why he came back from the Far Eastern Wilderness?" the officer asked. She was pretty with shiny blue-black hair. Her name badge said Wu.

"No," said Annice. They'd never questioned her again.

Now her parents sat in the leather-and-chrome chairs positioned between two potted palm trees. Her mother was desultorily flipping through an old magazine—one she'd thumbed through many times already—and her father was stirring but not eating the cup of soup the Brigade had brought. Annice thought, not for the first time, their forced stay at the apartment was like being trapped in a waiting room. But what were they waiting for? And how long were they expected to remain?

She was wondering whether the Brigade officer might be persuaded to bring her a jump rope when she heard the tapping. Annice looked first to her parents to see who or what was making the noise. Then she realized it originated on her left. At the window.

There was one window, and it was in the main room of the apartment. It looked down onto the common. Annice had watched Community Day from that window a few evenings before. But it was surely too high up for anyone to be tapping on it.

"Do you hear that?" she asked her parents.

They didn't even look up.

Annice stood and stepped toward the window. It was covered in lace panels that let in light but obscured the view. She half tiptoed, expecting someone to shout to stop her or drag her away from the glass. But she got all the way to the window without her parents saying or doing anything, and no pounding footsteps echoed up from the stairwell outside the door.

Tap, tap, tap.

Annice extended an index finger and parted the lace curtains.

The tapping ceased.

Movement—the quick cocking of a head, the blink of a round, golden eye.

Perched on the outer windowsill of the Brigade Office holding apartment was an extremely large eagle.

SPECIAL PREVIEW:

CHANGERS #2 - THE GREAT DIVIDE

ANNICE TOOK AN INVOLUNTARY STEP back from the window.

The eagle cocked a bright eye at her and tapped again at the glass.

"Mom..." Annice's voice quavered. She looked over her shoulder in search of parental support, but neither her mom nor dad seemed to have heard. They continued to sit lost in their separate thoughts.

The eagle paused, watched, tapped again. It clearly wanted something. And eagles weren't dangerous, were they? Only to mice maybe?

She wasn't a mouse.

Annice stepped to the window and lifted the sash.

CEE STARED up at the river of stars coursing its way between the treetops. She wished they could stay that way forever, her and Marcus, shoulder to shoulder and wrapped in shared warmth from a borrowed blanket.

Even if the blanket did smell a little musky. And itched a bit.

Beside her, Marcus shifted slightly. They hadn't spoken in hours, but Cee borrowed Livian's keen sight to check Marcus's eye color despite the darkness. She found herself holding her breath every time, though why she didn't know. Was she afraid Diodoric would surface... Or was she hoping he would?

For two people, they were abnormally complicated. She had a dragon living inside her, and Marcus had an entirely different personality threatening to take over and abolish him.

Cee couldn't let that happen.

She'd known Marcus for twelve years, since they were four, and she'd loved him... She didn't even know how long, couldn't pinpoint the moment the bud of friendship had bloomed into something big and sweet and beautiful inside her. Even if he didn't love her back—couldn't, because he wasn't made that way, to love girls—she couldn't stand the thought of losing him. Of there being no more Marcus in the world.

The memory of Diodoric's molten gaze intruded on Cee's thoughts. Marcus's alter ego, the person Marcus would eventually become if they didn't find a way to stop the transformation. The dissonance of Marcus looking like Marcus (except for the eyes, of course, Marcus's being green and Diodoric's gold) yet behaving so *un*like him rattled Cee. Yet Diodoric had called Cee "pretty" and clearly liked girls, Cee in particular. Maybe...

No. She could not have them both, and if forced to choose, it was Marcus. Always. He needed her.

Cee turned to look at the sharp, pale profile and resisted the urge to reach over and run her fingers through the mess of Marcus's dark hair. He sensed her gaze and tilted—only slightly—in her direction.

His eyes were still green.

Cee exhaled. "You're looking for them," she said.

Marcus's gaze drifted skyward once more, roving. Cee watched the tiny tics of movement at the corner of his eye. He let out air, slowly, like a dying balloon, before saying, "I'm only worried."

"They're probably looking for us," Cee assured. "And if they don't find us first, we'll see them when we reach the Aerie." Assuming they reached the Aerie, she thought but didn't say. They had only the vaguest notion of where the Clan of eagles lived and how to get there. And even if they managed *that*, Cee didn't know what the Aerie could do for them. But they had no other options. The Safety Brigade was searching for them, so they couldn't go home to Morrowville, and the ruling Clan of Magi weren't terribly happy with them either. Their only hope was that Marcus's brother Arlon, who was an Aerie, would shelter or at least advise them.

Arlon and his mate Ernesta had been helping Cee, Marcus, and their friends Rand and Guin but had since disappeared. Rand and Guin had stayed with the Vulpes Clan after Rand had been injured fighting the Magi. It came down to just them now. It occurred to Cee she once would have counted this a dream come true, being alone with Marcus, sharing a blanket and talking late into the night. Then again, "alone" was relative when one had a split personality and the other was inhabited by a dragon.

As if intuiting her thoughts, Marcus turned his attention back to Cee and asked, "Have you eaten enough?"

His concern knotted Cee's heart. Livian required a lot of fuel, and though he and Marcus (and Diodoric) were born enemies, the idea Marcus cared enough to look past that testified to their bond. Their friendship was rooted much more deeply than any of these superficial hatreds. It had to be.

"I'm fine," said Cee. "He's sleeping." Even as she spoke, Livian snorted and stirred inside her like a restless dog. A large, fire-breathing dog.

I don't breathe fire, Livian told her. *Yet.*

"Yet?" Cee asked aloud, and Marcus quirked an eyebrow.

I'm not big enough for that.

Probably for the best, Cee supposed. She opened her mouth to answer Marcus's unspoken question then snapped it shut again as a light amid the trees drew her attention. Small and nimble, it danced like a star on a breeze... Except the night was utterly calm.

Marcus's frown deepened and he followed her gaze. Just the one tiny light, bobbing.

Cee sat up as it began to transform into a tall, beautiful woman gowned in yellow-green and black. Marcus sat up, too, albeit more slowly, the maroon and gray blanket they'd been under tumbling to their waists. Cee became vaguely aware of the cool spring air moving in to replace where it had covered her. At the same time, she silently shushed Livian, though she sensed it was unnecessary. He'd gone cold and quiet inside her like a dying fire.

Hekaterine, Queen of the Insecta, turned her semi-luminescent eyes in their direction. "You were meant to leave these woods," she said in clipped and stilted tones, and Cee again wondered where she came from. Clearly English was not her first language.

"We are," Marcus said before Cee could respond. "But it will take some time. The forest is large."

"Not you," Hekaterine told him. "You are wanted by your mother."

Cee scanned the silhouetted trees, then the open sky, for signs of other fireflies, Hekaterine's henchmen or army or whatever she had. But aside from the Insecta queen's faint glow and the distant spray of starlight, all was dark. Not even a moon.

Motion beside Cee drew her attention; Marcus pushed off the blanket and stood up. His jaw was set, but his tone was unfailingly polite, the same as when he spoke to teachers at school. "Who are you?"

Hekaterine cocked her head slightly, her long, caramel-colored hair swinging with the motion. Her skin was so pale Cee could almost see through it to where the blue veins ran like rivers beneath. "You do not know? No, perhaps not, but your other self, your true self knows me."

"I am my true self," said Marcus.

Hekaterine moved both swiftly and fluidly, crossing the space between them so fast Cee couldn't stand up before the Insecta queen had her spindly hands on either side of Marcus's face. Marcus was tall, but Hekaterine bested him by a couple inches. She peered into his green eyes. "He is there. He must be."

Marcus did not move or speak. Cee felt paralyzed, wanting to run, or push Hekaterine away from her friend, or even just shout at her to leave him alone, the jumble of impulses leaving her unable to do anything. Inside her, Livian trembled, though with fear or outrage or just the chill of the night she wasn't sure.

Meanwhile, Marcus continued to stare placidly back into Hekaterine's eyes. "I don't want to go back," he finally told her, making it sound completely reasonable.

Hekaterine dropped her hands, and Cee began again to

search the skies for the swarm of fireflies that was surely coming to take them into custody. But the air remained dark.

The Insecta queen turned her head in Cee's direction, just a fraction. "I told you before," she said, "I know a dragon when I see one."

Livian blazed. Cee felt him as a fire lit within her abdomen, her skin growing warm and turning pink with the flush of his heat.

"My men, however," Hekaterine continued, "do not."

Livian curled into a question mark in Cee's chest.

Hekaterine looked again to Marcus. "She will do anything to have you. Tear this world apart if necessary. This is the power of being a mother."

Marcus appeared momentarily perplexed, his brow furrowing. "I am not the son she wants. Nor do I wish to be."

"You cannot change who and what you are," Hekaterine said.

"I don't understand," Cee interjected. "Are you helping us? Why?"

"I am not helping," said Hekaterine flatly. With her agitation her odd speaking habits increased. "I am warning. Wherever you go, you will bring trouble, unless you go where you are meant to go. This is simple, yes?"

"No," said Marcus.

At the same time, Cee blurted, "I have nowhere to go!"

Marcus turned to her, startled, and Hekaterine looked at her with derision. "You are a dragon," the queen said. "You go where dragons go."

"But there are no other dragons," said Cee.

Hekaterine waved a dismissive hand. "Who burned the forest? You?"

"No!"

"Then there is another dragon," Hekaterine said. She made it sound as simple as two plus two equaling four, something hardly worth her time, something she should not have to explain. She turned back to Marcus. "And you I must take to Sabine."

"No," Marcus said again. Not defiant, but with the same certainty he'd had in school when giving the correct answer.

But Cee still could not wrap her thoughts around Hekaterine's implication. "Another dragon? There can't be. According to Valentian I'm just a—a mutant. A Magus gone wrong." She looked to Marcus for confirmation.

Hekaterine turned her head and appeared surprised to find Cee still standing there. Then she frowned as though confused. "You want to go back to the Magi?"

"No," said Cee. "Neither of us do."

"This one," Hekaterine insisted, pointing at Marcus, "must. You—" Again she waved a hand, though whether she was being dismissive or meant for Cee to fly away, Cee wasn't sure. Maybe the two amounted to the same thing.

Marcus continued to stare at the Insecta queen, his sea green eyes narrowed in thought. "Why are you alone?" he asked.

Again Cee reflexively looked to the sky.

Hekaterine spread her hands. "I hoped to make it simple."

"Make what simple?" Cee asked.

"He must come back. If he does not, she will start—" The hands flapped like incandescent butterflies. "We do not want another war," she finished. She looked at Marcus. "You," she said. "You do not want to be the start of another war." Her gaze slid off him, toward the black on black of the trees against the night sky. "All the death," she murmured, eyes glazed as if envisioning it. "All the hate."

"If you want peace, just let us go," said Marcus.

Hekaterine blinked at him. "That is not possible. That would be the very opposite of peace!" She placed her hands on Marcus's chest. "You. You are one person. If you go, you will cause the loss of hundreds, maybe thousands!"

Marcus turned worried eyes to Cee, his face paler even than usual, his expression stricken. "You met her. My mother. Would she really start a war?"

"I didn't meet her," Cee corrected, "just... overheard her." She didn't elaborate, didn't volunteer the fact Sabine's love for Diodoric had been obvious even to someone hiding under a bed at the time.

Marcus knew anyway. Because Diodoric knew, and from the way Marcus tilted his head to one side as if he were listening to something, Cee could tell the Magus personality was communicating with him. Probably encouraging him to go back and embrace his transformation. Cee wanted to reach out and shake Marcus, tell him not to listen, but she waited. Hekaterine also watched expectantly.

A golden comet traced an arc across Marcus's right pupil.

He blinked rapidly as though there were something in his eye and then they were green again, clear as the sunlit sea.

"What about you?" he asked Cee.

"She will go. Fly," Hekaterine said, throwing Cee a look that brooked no protest.

Cee protested anyway. "I went all the way back for you!" she told Marcus. "For nothing? I thought you didn't want to be a Magus!"

"I don't want to incite a war either!" said Marcus.

Cee spared a glance for Hekaterine. "I'm sure Her Majesty is exaggerating." Despite the fact that it seemed unlikely Hekaterine possessed the kind of imagination required to hyperbolize.

"Don't listen to him," Cee pleaded as Marcus wavered.

Marcus looked at her strangely. "Don't listen to who?"

"Diodoric."

"Why not?"

"He's the one telling you to go back, isn't he?" Cee asked.

Marcus shook his head. "No, he..." He looked at Hekaterine's avid expression and grimaced but plunged on with his words. "He wants to stay with you."

Cee felt as though an arrow had struck through her. "*He* wants to stay with me? And you don't?"

"You know I care for you, Cee. I mean, not—" He looked away. "Not like that, but... I can't let her hurt people on my account."

"Then we'll have to stop her," said Cee.

"How?" Marcus asked.

They both turned to Hekaterine, whose cat-colored eyes were wide as she absorbed their conversation. "What?" the Insecta queen asked. "Why do you look at me like this?"

"You know her," Cee said.

"You work for her," Marcus added.

Hekaterine's eyes darted between them as she worked to comprehend their meaning. Then she gasped. "No," she said flatly. "You must come back to the Magi camp," she told Marcus. "That is the end of it."

"You don't want her to start a war any more than we do," reasoned Marcus. "And it can't possibly matter to you whether I become a Magus. In fact, it would be better for you if I didn't. With no heir, the Clan will turn to infighting and not have the time or energy to do anything to anyone else."

Hekaterine gave her head a vehement shake, hair rippling behind her. "No. Without the Magi, the Clans too will fight for more power. It will be catastrophe! We must keep the peace, the line of succession. You will marry your betrothed—"

"Betrothed!" Something squirmed in Cee that wasn't Livian.

Hekaterine looked at Cee as if she were an unfathomable idiot. "Of course. These things cannot wait, must be planned."

Cee was aware her mouth was hanging open but couldn't seem to find the muscles required to close it. She turned to Marcus, whose eyes had gone unfocused.

Suddenly, he shook his head as though to clear it and smiled at Cee in a way that made her stomach knot. *Not* a Marcus smile. "That's it," he said. "That's the answer."

Cee searched his face, bit her tongue as she noticed the starbursts of gold forming around his pupils. "What is?" she half whispered.

"You and me, Cee," said Diodoric. "We have to start a new dynasty."

CHANGERS #2 - THE GREAT DIVIDE

COMING JULY 2026

PREORDER NOW

ABOUT THE AUTHOR

Amanda Innes has worn many creative hats—film production assistant, community theater crew, Shakespearean performer, summer camp instructor, and publishing industry professional. After years spent supporting other stories, she turned her focus to her own. Originally from Texas, she earned her graduate degree in Massachusetts and now lives and writes in Northern California.

ALSO BY AMANDA INNES

The Ghosts of Marshley Park

The Switchgrass Crown

Drew & Rayze

One Night in Wildcat Woods

One Day at Middleview Mall

One Night in Wyland High

One Day of Sun & Sugar

Changers

Manifesting Destiny

The Great Divide (COMING JULY 2026)